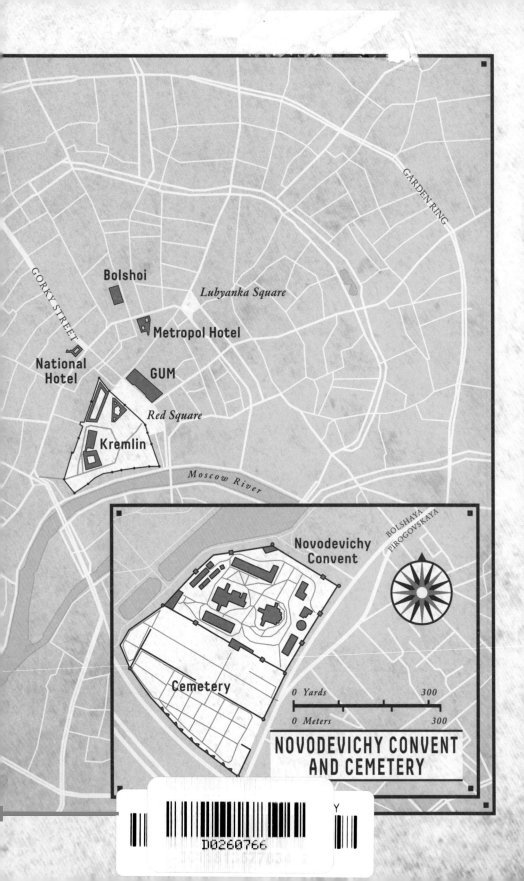

Bolshoi

Lubyanka Square

GORKY STREET

Metropol Hotel

National
Hotel

GUM

Red Square

Kremlin

Moscow River

GARDEN RING

Novodevichy
Convent

BOLSHAYA
PIROGOVSKAYA

Cemetery

0 Yards   300

0 Meters   300

**NOVODEVICHY CONVENT
AND CEMETERY**

DEFECTORS

ALSO BY JOSEPH KANON

DEFECTORS

JOSEPH KANON

**SIMON &
SCHUSTER**

London · New York · Sydney · Toronto · New Delhi

A CBS COMPANY

First published in Great Britain by Simon & Schuster UK Ltd, 2017
A CBS COMPANY

1 3 5 7 9 10 8 6 4 2

Simon & Schuster UK Ltd
1st Floor
222 Gray's Inn Road
London WC1X 8HB

Simon & Schuster Australia, Sydney
Simon & Schuster India, New Delhi

www.simonandschuster.co.uk
www.simonandschuster.com.au
www.simonandschuster.co.in

A CIP catalogue record for this book
is available from the British Library

Hardback ISBN: 978-1-4711-6261-9
Trade Paperback ISBN: 978-1-4711-6262-6
eBook ISBN: 978-1-4711-6263-3
Audio ISBN: 978-1-4711-6606-8

Printed and bound by CPI Group (UK) Ltd, Croydon, CR0 4YY

Simon & Schuster UK Ltd are committed to sourcing paper
that is made from wood grown in sustainable forests and support the Forest
Stewardship Council, the leading international forest certification organisation.
Our books displaying the FSC logo are printed on FSC certified paper.

For Marietta von Bernuth and David Esterly

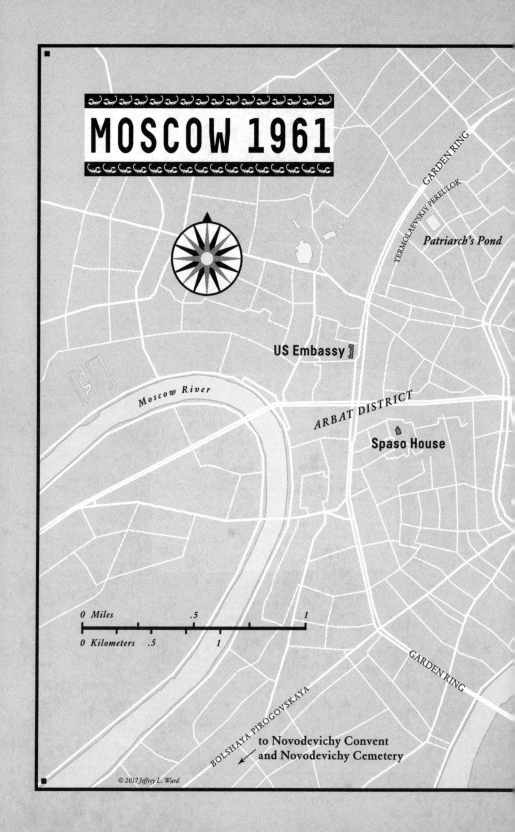

MOSCOW 1961

GARDEN RING

YERMOLAEVSKIY PEREULOK

Patriarch's Pond

US Embassy

Moscow River

ARBAT DISTRICT

Spaso House

0 Miles .5 1

0 Kilometers .5 1

GARDEN RING

BOLSHAYA PIROGOVSKAYA

to Novodevichy Convent
and Novodevichy Cemetery

© 2017 Jeffrey L. Ward

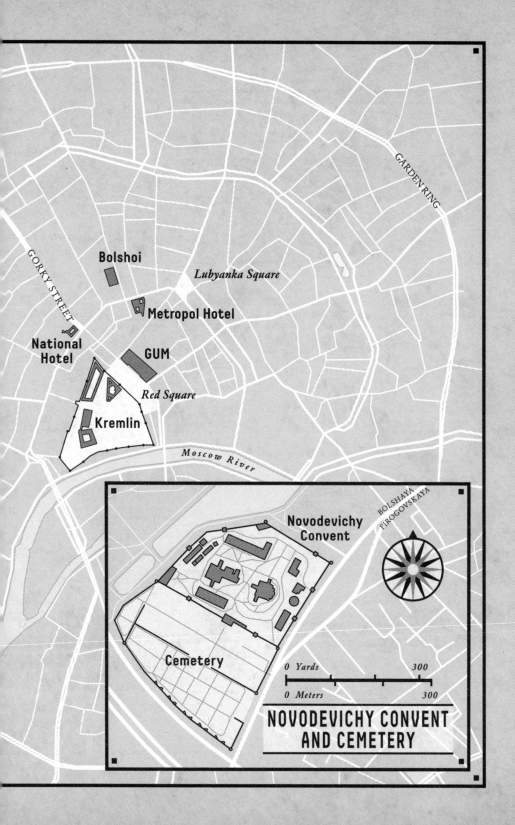

Bolshoi

Lubyanka Square

GORKY STREET

Metropol Hotel

National
Hotel

GUM

Red Square

Kremlin

Moscow River

GARDEN RING

Novodevichy
Convent

BOLSHAYA
PIROGOVSKAYA

Cemetery

0 Yards   300

0 Meters   300

NOVODEVICHY CONVENT
AND CEMETERY

1

IT WAS STILL LIGHT when they landed at Vnukovo, the late northern light that in another month would last until midnight. There had been clouds over Poland but then just patches so you could see the endless flat country below, where the German tanks had rolled in, all the way to the outskirts of Moscow, nothing to stop them, the old fear come true, the landscape of paranoia. Even from the air it looked scrubby and neglected, dirt tracks and poor farmhouses, then factories belching brown lignite smoke. But what had he expected? White birch forests, troika races over the snow? It was the wrong season, the wrong century.

There was no seat belt sign. Simon felt the descent, then the bump and skid of wheels on the runway, and looked out the window. Any airport—a terminal and a tower, some outlying buildings, no signs.

"Sheremetyevo?" he asked his—what? handler? A human visa, someone the Russians had sent to Frankfurt to travel with him.

"No, Vnukovo. VIP airport," he said, evidently meaning to impress.

But in the fading light it seemed dreary, empty runways with clumps of grass running along the edges, a lone signalman in overalls waving them away from the main terminal. They taxied to one of the other buildings.

"No customs," his handler said, part of the VIP service.

Simon peered out, his face pressed against the plastic window. What would he look like now? Twelve years. In the one picture Simon had seen, the one the wire services had picked up and sent around the world, he'd been wearing a Russian fur hat, flaps up, and a double-breasted coat, the onion domes of St. Basil's just over his shoulder, the kind of picture authors used on book jackets. But now it was spring, no heavy clothes to hide behind. He'd be Frank. If he was there. So far nobody, just the empty tarmac, away from the bother of customs. It occurred to Simon then that they didn't want anyone to know he'd come, shuttling him off to an out building, whisking him away in some dark car like an exchanged prisoner, as if he'd been the spy, not Frank. Maybe they'd anticipated reporters and flashbulbs, the foreign press still fascinated by Frank. The man who betrayed a generation. Twelve years, a lifetime, ago. But nobody had told them. This end of the runway was empty, just two airport workers wheeling a staircase up to the plane. Someone was coming out of the building now, heading toward them, a soldier's rigid shoulders. Not Frank.

Simon put on his coat and headed for the door, his handler following with the luggage. How could Frank not come to the airport? His brother. And now his publisher, the one Frank had asked for, arranging the visa to come work on the memoirs, an excuse to see him, maybe even explain things, all these years later. Things you couldn't say in a book, not one that would have to pass his bosses' vetting. Line by line in some office at the Lubyanka. Well, but hadn't we done the same thing? Pete DiAngelis in the small conference room, making notes.

"We have to be sure our people aren't compromised," DiAngelis had said. "You understand." His tone suggesting that Simon didn't, that he was some kind of traitor himself, aiding and abetting. An opportunist too greedy to realize what was at stake.

"He doesn't mention any agents by name. Not active ones. He's not trying to give anyone away."

"No? That didn't stop him before. He write about that? The people he set up? The ones who didn't come back?"

"See for yourself," he said, gesturing to the manuscript. "It's about him. Why he did it."

"Why did he?" DiAngelis said, goading.

Simon shrugged. "He believed in it. Communism."

"Believed in it. And now he's going to say he's sorry? Except he's not. *My Secret Life*. Here's my side. And screw you. For two cents I'd shut the whole thing down. Who gives a fuck what he believes?"

"People. Let's hope so anyway."

"Or you're out some cash, huh?" He looked straight at Simon. "Paying him. Making him rich. For fucking us over. Freedom of the press."

Simon nodded at him, a silent "as you say."

"Don't think anybody's happy about this. He wants to make the Agency look bad, all right. Who the fuck would believe him anyway? But if he names any of our guys, even hints—"

"We take it out. You think I'd want to endanger anyone in the field?"

"I don't know what you'd want."

"There's nothing like that in there. Read it. The other side already has, don't you think? So now it's your turn. Just leave something for the rest of us, okay?"

Another look. "One thing. Satisfy my curiosity. How'd you twist the Agency's arm? Get them to go along with this?"

"Are they going along? I thought that's what you were here for. Throw red flags all over the field."

In fact, it was *Look* whose involvement had given the Agency the needed push, the promise of publicity, even a court fight, if they tried to stop publication. The *Digest*, the *Post*, wouldn't even look at an excerpt, and though Luce was tempted, sensing a story big enough for a special issue, he finally fell back on principle too ("we don't publish Communist spies"), which left *Look* and the serial sale that made the deal happen. Without that, Simon never could have raised the money the Russians were asking. More than M. Keating & Sons had paid for anything, a pile of chips all shoved now on red, for what had to be a best seller. Diana's father, a Keating son, had reservations, but in the end went along with Simon. What choice did he have? After Frank's defection, Simon had had to resign from the State Department, and it was Keating who'd come to the rescue, offering him a career in publishing. Now Simon was running the company, Keating just a genial presence at the Christmas party. Too late now to change succession plans.

"You realize this is a first draft?" Simon said to DiAngelis. "You're just going to have to go through it again when I get back. So leave something."

"There's more? You want him to put stuff in?"

"I want to know what he did. Actually did. Besides defect. That's all anybody knows really. That he—"

"Ran," DiAngelis finished. He looked at Simon. "You want him to be innocent. He wasn't."

"No," Simon said. "He wasn't."

But he had been once. You could see it in the old home movies, the boys like colts trying to stand on wobbly legs, making faces at the camera. In the end Simon became the taller, but when they were boys it was Frank who had the crucial extra inch, just as he had the extra year. The films, jerky and grainy, showed them opening

Christmas presents, dodging waves at the beach, waving down from the tree at their grandmother's house, and in all of them Simon was trailing after Frank, a kind of shadow, his partner in crime. Frank knew things. Where to find clams in the mud flats. How to get extra hot fudge sauce at Bailey's. How to skim their father's pocket change without his knowing or missing it. Years of this, in the old house on Mt. Vernon Street, bedrooms separated by a narrow hall, the model train running between, so that it really seemed like one room.

It was their mother who decided to separate them. Frank was sent to St. Mark's, a Weeks tradition, but the following year, Simon's turn, his mother decided on Milton instead.

"It'll be good for you, to be on your own. Think for yourself. Instead of listening to your brother all the time."

"I don't listen to him all the time."

"A lot of the time then."

Frank tried to be reassuring. "You're the smart one. She wants you to concentrate on your studies."

"You're smart."

"Not the way you are. Anyway, the headmaster's a friend of Aunt Ruth, that's how they know about the school, so he'll be nice. Always good to have the top guy on your side."

"Maybe she'll change her mind."

But Emily Weeks wasn't in the habit of changing her mind, and the separation was permanent. She had been right—Simon thrived on his own—but years later he still felt the loss, like some finger that had been snipped off in an accident and never replaced. During the holidays it seemed almost the same, talking late into the night up on the third floor, the Weeks boys again. But inevitably they grew apart. They had never resembled each other—except for the Weeks jaw—but now, unexpectedly, even their voices began to differ, Frank's a rich baritone with a boarding school drawl, Simon still Mt. Vernon Street.

Then they were together again at college. School was one thing, but Weekses went to Harvard.

"All this Weeks business," Frank said. "Weekses do this, Weekses do that."

"Well, Pa's like that."

"And getting worse. I thought, when he went to Washington—but no, now he's back, it just gets smaller and smaller."

"What does?"

"His world. You realize he can walk everywhere he goes? That's how small it is. The office on State Street, the Athenaeum, the Somerset Club. He never has to drive. His whole world is in walking distance. Like a native or something."

"There's the Symphony," Simon said.

"And he walks there. My point."

Once a week on matinee day, as he had for years, up Commonwealth and back on Marlborough, a full-length wool cape against the cold, a walk so fixed it had become a Boston sight, like the swan boats.

For a while it seemed they were closer than ever. Frank enjoyed showing him the ropes—which lecture course to avoid, which seminar virtually guaranteed you an A, where to get your hair cut. And Simon absorbed it all—the right book, the right portion of gin, everything but Frank's effortless ease. There were parties in Frank's large suite in Eliot House, facing the boathouse, everything Simon had always imagined Cambridge would be. But that was the year things turned political, Frank loitering around the edges, then taking his first steps. At first just small statements of class rebellion—a refusal to join the Porcellian after they'd punched him, a disdain, usually comic, for the parties his roommates still gave, and almost inevitably, the prickly dinner arguments with his father. Francis Weeks had served in the Treasury, a reluctant New Dealer, and he was concerned about the fascist threat overseas and social justice at home, but it simply wasn't in him to walk a picket line or demonstrate in rallies, both of which Frank now did, provoking more arguments. Simon watched from the sidelines, ready to take Frank's side but dismayed to see his father looking suddenly older, wounded and puzzled, his safe, small world upended. It'll pass, his mother said.

And then, in the summer before his last year, Frank volunteered for Spain, surprising everyone and making Simon feel left behind, conventional and cautious while Frank went out to slay dragons.

"How can he not finish his degree?" his father said. "Thank God you have more sense."

"He's right, though. To go. The fascists—"

"Oh, right. Watch he doesn't get himself killed. You can't get righter than that."

"Francis," Emily said.

"I know, I know. But it's not a game. What's Spain to him anyway?"

"It's not just Spain. They're using it as an exercise. A warm-up. If we don't stop them there—"

"We're not going to stop them there. Whatever Frank thinks. He'll get himself killed for nothing." No longer blustering, his voice suddenly breaking.

But he didn't get killed. Instead he took a bullet in the shoulder and managed to survive sepsis in the field hospital, which took him out of the war and out of politics, cynical now about both sides, embarrassed to have ever been naïve enough to think that Communists, anybody, could claim the moral high ground. He became, predictably, his parents, but not quite—Spain had left some itch for adventure. He finished his degree, played at law school, floundering, at loose ends until the war finally gave him what he was looking for. The army wouldn't take him with his shoulder, but Francis knew Donovan and it was arranged—the night train to DC, a job at the OSS. The first thing he did was recruit Simon as an intelligence analyst, pushing paper on Navy Hill while Frank practiced parachute drops in the Maryland countryside. But they were together, Washington another Cambridge, their oyster.

When the war ended, and the OSS with it, Simon moved with the other analysts to State, probably where he should have been all along. Frank hung on in the War Department, convinced Truman would have to replace Donovan's group with a new agency. His guess was right. The following year he landed at the Central Intelligence Group, Office of Policy Coordination, a euphemism for overseas ops, and their Washington life went on as before, official meetings and unofficial lunches at Harvey's, nights on the town, double dating. A special joint committee with the Brits to liaise with Baltic refugee groups and Ukrainian nationalists, Simon representing State and Frank the OPC, the heady pleasure of being in on things, part of something important, on their way.

And then, like a screech of tires, the headlines appeared one morning and everything stopped. Frank was gone. Just two steps ahead of Hoover, two steps ahead of treason. The Soviets' most successful agent, gossiping over lunch, picking Simon's brain, not just a leak at State, a spigot Frank could turn whenever he liked. Smiling, just as he had in the home movies. "You're the smart one." But not about Frank.

At the bottom of the stairs the military Russian introduced himself as Colonel Vassilchikov and with a quick nod dismissed the handler. Simon turned to say good-bye, then realized he didn't know his name, had never known it or forgotten, already failing DiAngelis's instructions: "Remember everything. Don't write it down, remember it. Everything. Even if you think it's nothing. Keep your eyes open."

Already failing. A name he should have remembered. A black car he should have seen, just over the colonel's shoulder—had it always been there? But in the curious half-light nothing seemed to have definition, the whole country somehow out of focus, behind a scrim.

"It is your first time in Moscow?" the colonel was saying, a standard courtesy, now oddly surreal. Did they see many repeat visitors, here on the moon?

"Yes, my first. That's all right—I'll keep that." His briefcase, the colonel reaching out for it.

"Contraband?" the colonel said smiling, an unexpected joke.

"The manuscript. Frank's book."

"There are other copies, you know."

"Not with my notes."

"Ah. I will be curious to see that," the colonel said, an insider, part of the editorial process. "What the CIA objects to."

"They're my notes."

"They'd better be." Another voice, behind the colonel, stepping out of the car. "The Simon touch." A laugh in the voice now. "That's what we're paying for."

Simon stared. The hair was receding, but not gone. The face tighter, lines spreading out from his eyes, lived in. But voices never change, the same flip intimacy that drew everybody in, and for a second the face matched the voice, lines smoothing out, the way he'd looked before, before all the lies.

"Simple Simon," Frank said, the old teasing name, his eyes suddenly soft.

Simon stood still. Simple Simon. As if nothing had happened. What did they do now? Shake hands?

"Frank," he said, light-headed. The same crinkly smile, someone who'd just been away for the weekend.

Frank nodded. "It's me," he said, as if he were reading Simon's mind.

"Frank—"

And suddenly there were arms around him, chest pressed against his, wrapping him in the past. Frank. Then he was being held by the shoulders, inspected. Frank tipped his head toward his glasses.

"Specs? Since when? Or are they just to make people think you read the books you put out?" He glanced at Simon's clothes. "You're dressing better. Hart Schaffner?"

Simon looked down at his suit, as if he'd just noticed he was wearing it. "Altman's."

"Altman's. And for only a few dollars more– Just like Pa." He dropped his hands. "You've met Boris Borisevich? Boris Jr., literally. I call him that sometimes, don't I, Boris?"

The colonel nodded, smiling, apparently a joke between them.

"Anything you need, he's your man. Driver. Tickets to the Bol- shoi. Anything. He likes pulling rabbits out of his hat."

Simon looked at him, disconcerted. The KGB as concierge.

"Of course he's really here to protect me. In the beginning, you know, we couldn't be sure–if the Agency might try something. I told them that really wasn't much in our line. But of course it is in their line, so naturally they'd think– Anyway, that was then. Now I just go about my business. But always nice to know somebody's got your back. Right, Boris? Here we go," he said, starting to get in the car, then turning, putting his hand on Simon's shoulder again. "It's good to see you. I never thought–" He paused. "Look at you. Gray." He touched Simon's temple. "And here I am writing memoirs. So when did that happen, all the years?"

Colonel Vassilchikov put the luggage in the trunk then sat up front with the driver, leaving Frank and Simon together in the back.

"In the beginning," Frank picked up again, wanting to talk, "before we knew we didn't have to worry, the Service gave us new names. Maclean was Fraser. Like that. No addresses, of course. No *Time* correspondent turning up out of the blue for a drink. That wasn't too hard. There's no telephone book in Moscow and nobody to tell them where I was. So in a way, I wasn't really here."

"Now you're Weeks again?"

"Mm. Whereabouts still unknown. I assume the Agency doesn't know where the flat is or I'd have spotted someone lurking."

Actually thinking they'd tail him now, twelve years later, a footnote to history.

"Like him?" Simon said, nodding to Vassilchikov up front.

"He doesn't lurk. He comes right in."

"He lives with you?"

"He visits."

"You know we've promised *Look* pictures. They'll want you in the flat. At home. How you live. All that. Is that going to be a problem?"

"No. In for a penny. My cover's blown now anyway. About time, I suppose."

"Blown how?"

"Well, you'll have to tell them. When they debrief you. You supposed to make a note or just keep it up here?" He put a finger to his temple.

Simon said nothing.

"Yermolaevskiy Pereulok. 21. You can write it down later. Very comfortable. My own study. Well, you'll see." He made a signal to the driver to start. "I got them to put you up at the National. They had you down for the Ukraina and I said no no, too far away from the flat. And the rooms aren't much to write home about. One of Stalin's wedding cakes. Not as bad as the Pekin, but still."

"What's wrong with the Pekin?" Simon said, playing along.

Frank smiled, enjoying himself. "Well, they built it for us, the Service. New offices. But that didn't work out for some reason. So, a hotel. Except the rooms can be a little—odd. Red light, green light over the door. To call a maid, they say now. But they were built as interrogation rooms. You know, red if someone was still being interrogated." He stopped, catching Simon's expression. "Anyway, the Chinese don't seem to mind. Very popular with delegations. Not a bad restaurant either. If you're in the mood for Chinese. We can go one night if you like."

"I'm not here that long."

"A week anyway. At least. And you have to come out to the dacha. Joanna's looking forward to it."

"Jo," Simon said quietly, another thing he seemed to have forgotten. Once all he thought about. "How is she?"

"A little under the weather. She wanted to come tonight, but I said you'd be there bright and early, no need to rush things. I think she's a little—nervous. Seeing someone from the States. What you'll think. You're the first. From before."

"But she likes it?" Somebody who'd been to El Morocco, her long hair swinging behind her when she danced. White shoulders, a broad lipstick smile. Don't be so serious, she'd say, pulling him onto the dance floor, anyone can do it. Not like her.

"Well, like. She doesn't *like* anything really, since Richie died," he said, almost mumbling, as if the words were being pulled out of him. "It's been hard for her."

"I'm sorry. I should have said first thing—"

Frank dismissed this. "It's all right. It's a while ago now. You think it'll never get better, but it does. Even something like this."

"He was sick?"

"Meningitis. There wasn't anything anybody could do. The best care. The hospital in Pekhotnaya." He looked over. "It's the Service hospital. The best care."

"The Service hospital. The KGB has its own hospital?"

Frank nodded. "I know what you're thinking. Maybe you're right. But when it's you—your son—who needs the privilege, you're grateful. You have to understand how things are here. All that," he said, waving his hand at the window, "you have to imagine what it's going to be. How far we've come. But the Service was always something—apart. Professional. Out there you wonder sometimes, does anything work? But inside, in the Service, everything works."

"You don't write about it. Richie. In the book. Or Jo. You never mention her."

"No. It's my life in the Service, how I managed to do it, play against the house. Jo's not part of that. She never knew." He looked at Simon. "It's not a soap opera. You haven't come to make it one, have you? Because I'm not going to write that."

"She never knew? But she came?"

"I didn't force her," Frank said simply. "It was her decision. But it's understood about the book? She's entitled to her privacy." He looked up at Simon. "I don't want to upset her. Not now."

"All right," Simon said, retreating.

"Anyway, there'll be plenty of other things to work on," Frank said, abruptly cheerful, switching gears. "Like old times. You whipping my papers into shape. What was the one we did for old Whiting? I left it to the last minute and—"

"The British Navy. In the seventeenth century."

"Your memory. The British Navy. A whole semester. On old boats." He shook his head. "Whiting. You had to have three people sign up or the course was canceled, so I figured he couldn't afford to lose anybody. All you had to do was show up. And then he got serious about it, wanting papers. Ass. But we pulled it off. Well, you did. So now this." He indicated Simon's bag. "You made notes?"

"Lots."

Frank smiled. "That bad?"

"No, just incomplete."

"You understand, some things can't be said. People still active. I'm not trying to get even with anybody. "

"Except Hoover."

"Well, Hoover has it coming. He hasn't done a damn thing

since he was swinging his hatchet at whiskey barrels. Just stamp his feet to see how fast people run away. And some blackmail on the side. You think I'm too hard on him? I just say what happened. What I knew personally. Why? He threaten you?"

"Not yet. He hasn't seen it yet."

"You think so? Then he's more incompetent than I thought. Anyway Pirie and the boys at the Agency will love it. They'll back you up."

"I'm not exactly popular there either. They think you want to make them look bad. Keystone Kops."

"Is that what you think I want?"

Simon looked at him. "I don't know. What do they want? Your people?"

"The Service?"

"They never talk. Never admit to anything. And now we've got Public Enemy No. 1 going on about the high old times he had in the war and how he fooled everybody, Hoover and Pirie and—"

"And?"

"Me."

"You're not in the book," Frank said quietly.

"And the Brits. And State. Why leave anybody out? But why say anything in the first place, if you're an organization that never says anything at all?"

"Why do you think?"

"I think they want to embarrass us. Maybe stir up a little inter-agency rivalry. That's always worth doing. Make trouble. And now I'm part of it. Helping you do it. Again."

"Jimbo." Simon James, another nickname, another hook from the past.

Simon turned and looked out the window. Nearly dark now, the beginning of the city, concrete apartment blocks and warehouses, an occasional church with onion domes. Anywhere. But not anywhere.

Not even Europe. Signs in Cyrillic. Everything in shadow, enemy territory.

"I never got much out of you, you know. If that's what's bothering you. The republic wasn't in any danger because of you."

"The republic didn't think so. I got the heave-ho."

"Yes, well, I'm sorry about that. You never know how people are going to react. Overreact."

Simon looked at him, speechless.

"Anyway, this suits you better. A book man. Very distinguished. And now it turns out, just what the doctor ordered. A book like this needs—a certain amount of respectability. Which is one thing you can say for Keating. Just the place if you're bringing a little notoriety to the party. Do they really think I'm that? Public Enemy No. 1? Like Dillinger?" Amused, or pretending to be amused.

"They used to. What did you think you were?"

"A soldier. That's all I ever was. I was proud to be in the Service. I still am. An officer now. You understand that, don't you? You must have seen that when you signed on for this. It's not a mea culpa."

"No, it's a 'see what a clever boy I am.' Is that how you pitched it to—the Service. Get them to okay it?"

"You've got it the wrong way around. It wasn't my idea. It was theirs. I'm still not sure they were right. But they were looking for *aktivnyye meropriyatiya*," he said, his whole voice changing with the language, suddenly a Russian.

Simon glanced up front. But Vassilchikov hadn't moved, just stared placidly out the window. Listening to both, English and Russian the same, so unobtrusive that after a while you forgot he was there, a human tape recorder, spools circling in his head.

"Active measures," Frank translated. "Something to show people how effective we can be. I had a pretty good run, you know. Nobody had a clue—Donovan, Pirie, any of them. If Malenko hadn't defected and brought his little CARE package of names with him, I might still be there. Who knows? I'm a hero in the Service. So why not tell my story?"

"Parts of it."

"Well, yes. And I suppose nobody's saying no to a little collateral damage. Some friction with MI6. Give Hoover's blood pressure a nudge. All that. But that wasn't the reason. It's an active measure. To show the Service—in a good light."

"Like a recruiting poster."

Frank shook his head. "These old stories? A lot of water over the dam since I was leading Pirie around in circles. Different world now. Not so many idealists these days. People here still want to be in the Service. It's a good job. But in the West— Now you have to buy them. They never had to pay me a dime. Any of us." He smiled. "Maybe that's why they think it was a golden age. We did it for nothing. Because it was the right thing to do."

"All of it?"

"I thought so. At the time." He paused. "Jimbo, if you're having cold feet about this, just say. It's not some piece of disinformation. The Service doesn't need to make things up. It's all true."

"But you need Keating to make it respectable."

"That's right." He looked over at Simon. "I want you to make me look good again. An A from Whiting. A B, anyway." He looked down. "And maybe I thought it was a little payback too. For all the trouble I caused you. The book's going to sell—that's what everybody tells me. So why not sell for you? Last year's figures—you could use the cash. Keating, I mean."

"How do you know?"

"Jimbo."

"You looked at our books?"

"Not me personally, no." He took out a cigarette and tapped Vassilchikov on the shoulder for a light. "So I thought, good for you, good for me."

"You could have got more money from someone else."

Frank waved this away with the smoke. "I don't need the money. I get eight hundred a month. That doesn't mean anything to you, but it's a generous pension here. I have everything I need. Anyway, *Mezhdunarodnaya Kniga* takes 70 percent, so how much more could there be?"

"Who?"

"The agency your people dealt with. That sells the book abroad."

"70 percent?"

Frank smiled. "The Soviets are very good capitalists when foreign currency's involved." He lowered his voice, serious again. "It's not the money. I trust you. I don't want this to be something for the tabloids. It's my life. I want to explain what I did. So it makes sense to people. To you. Maybe even to Pa."

Simon was quiet for a minute. "Have you been in touch?"

Frank shook his head. "I thought he'd write when Mother died. But he didn't." He paused. "How is he?"

"He still goes to the office."

"And the Symphony?"

"No. He doesn't go out much. You remember once you said his world was small? Now it's smaller. He dropped the Somerset."

"Because of me?"

Simon said nothing.

"Rotten food anyway." He looked away. "I'll bet nobody had to say a word. Just look. Christ. Boston." He drew on the cigarette. "I suppose you get the house now."

"I don't know."

"Well, he's not going to leave it to me. A little impractical under the circumstances."

"What would I do with it?"

"Live in it. No one else has ever lived there. Just Weekses. So now, you."

"I'm in New York, Frank." He looked at him. "I thought you hated the house."

"I hated what it stood for. The house– It's funny the things you remember. That leather pig by the fireplace. Nobody even knew whose it was originally, how it got there. The whole place was like that. Things nobody could explain. They'd just always been there." His voice trailed off. "I hate him thinking he's the last. It must kill him, to think that." He paused. "Does he ever talk about it? What happened."

"No."

"No, he wouldn't. He has the PO number here. I thought he might–but he never has. Mother did. Before she died. A good-bye letter, but she didn't say it–not a word about the cancer–so I didn't know. She said she never thought she'd be writing to a box number. There was a five-dollar bill for Richie. That's the last I heard."

Simon turned to the window again. Dark now, an occasional window light from the side of the road. "What a fucking mess," he said quietly.

"What?"

"All of it."

Frank was quiet for a minute. "I don't see it that way," he said finally. "Spain was a mess. The war was a mess. Pirie sending those Latvians in on some cockamamie suicide mission, that was a mess. I think things are getting better. I think we're building something here. And I helped." He turned. "I'm not asking you to agree with me. Just let the book speak for itself. That's all. Fair enough?" Closing the sale, everything but a handshake. "Here, try one of these," he said, offering the cigarette pack.

Simon inhaled. Russian smoke, so rough it clawed at his throat.

"It wasn't a suicide mission. Someone betrayed them. As long as we're telling the truth."

Frank looked at him. "Not all of it. Then we'd have to say

what they were planning to do. An assassination was involved, as I recall. Reprisal. In hopes that would lead to more trouble. All the old grudges. 'Destabilize' was the word Pirie used, wasn't it? But we knew what it meant. More people killed. Luckily they didn't get to start anything. Somebody stopped them."

"Somebody might have stopped them sooner. Before they left. Since the op was doomed anyway."

"Somebody might have. But that would have been revealing, wouldn't it? And who's to say they wouldn't have tried again? Not exactly angels, that bunch." He rubbed out his cigarette. "Look, you don't really want to pick at old scabs, do you? We had no business sending those goons in. What the hell did Pirie think was going to happen? An uprising? Pick up your pitchforks and march on Riga? This wasn't some client state. It was the Soviet Union. Russian soil. And we were sending in armed fighters."

"Who didn't think it was Russian soil. Who thought it was their country."

"Their country," Frank said. "So take on the Soviets. With us cheerleading in the background. Not to mention supplying the guns. You really want me to put this in the book? Hard to say who comes out worse. Pirie and his merry band of invaders or me, doing my job."

Simon said nothing for a minute. "I think it's important for the reader to know what you did. It wasn't just passing papers. Who said what at a meeting. It wasn't harmless. People got hurt. The reader wants to know how you felt about that."

Frank turned to him. "You mean you do."

"All right. I do."

"Which version would you prefer? How all this dirty business tied me up in knots? All those sleepless nights? Or the truth? I never gave it a second thought. What were the Latvians thinking? What were *we* thinking to let them think it? They wanted to make war. The Soviets had a right to defend themselves. All pretty clear-cut, as far as I could see. No trouble sleeping. Not over them." He took out another cigarette and toyed with it. "Still, I don't know that one actually wants to say that. In a book. Hard to get the tone right." He paused. "Christ. You're only here an hour and we're already doing this. Let's not fight. Tonight, I just wanted—to see you. Catch up."

"Like alums. A reunion."

"That's right. How's business?" A mock slap on the back in his voice. "How's the wife and kids?"

"Well, you know about the business. You've seen the books."

"They were just protecting their interests," Frank said, a little embarrassed.

"Did they actually break into the office to do it?"

"I wouldn't know," Frank said. "Let's hope things pick up next year. With *My Secret Life*. You like the title, by the way? You never said."

"I just got here."

"It doesn't feel that way, though. It feels like old times."

Simon looked at him. The easy grin, like turning on a light.

"Anyway, how *are* the wife and kids?"

"Diana's fine. No kids. She didn't want them." Just lovers, the ones Simon wasn't supposed to know about.

"I have to say, I'm surprised. That you're still together. You don't mind my saying that?"

"You've said it. Why surprised?"

"I never thought she was your type, that's all. But obviously I was wrong. Not the first time," he said, a kind of apology for the argument before. "And lucky for me. The boss's daughter. Just when I need you there. Making me respectable. Unless that's just a front. Is that it? Still working for Don Pirie?"

"I never worked for Pirie. You did."

"So I did. And he survived it. Well, shit always floats to the top. I have to say, the fact that he's head of section is one of the few things that gives me comfort in my old age. The Main Adversary doesn't seem as threatening with old Don in charge."

"The main adversary?"

"What we call the States. Sort of code name."

"Do you miss it?" Suddenly intimate.

"I don't think about that. What would be the point? I didn't buy a round-trip ticket. We're here." The words almost wistful, hanging in the air.

Simon said nothing, staring at him.

"And Moscow's a fascinating city. Lots of nooks and crannies. You have to see some of it while you're here. If I know the Service, they've booked you a Kremlin view, so that's a start." The concierge Service again. "And you know we travel, so I get around a fair amount."

"Travel where?"

"Black Sea. Budapest. Dresden last year. Anywhere I like, really. In the socialist bloc."

Simon nodded to Vassilchikov. "Does he go with you?"

"Once, to the Crimea. That was back when we thought some-one might try to take a potshot at me. Now it's usually just a local. To liaise. Help me with things."

"How does Jo feel about this? Having someone around all the time?"

"Well, it's not all the time." He looked away. "She doesn't always go. She prefers the dacha."

"That doesn't sound like her."

"No," Frank said. "Well, we change over the years."

But he hadn't. Simon watched him brush back the hair on the side of his head, a gesture so familiar that for a second you could believe he hadn't changed at all. Still Frank. Whoever that had been.

"Why didn't she want kids?" Frank said, a stray afterthought.

"She did. We couldn't have them. So she said that." Something he hadn't told anyone, not even his secret to keep.

"Not your fault, I hope."

"No." A botched operation neither of them talked about, not sure whose child it might have been.

"That must have been a relief. Remember when Ray had to go through all that? Sperm counts. God, how embarrassing. Beating off in a cup."

"What's the difference? Nobody's watching."

"Then you hand it to a nurse." He shuddered, playing. "And she's looking right at you. Ray told me." Another face, genuinely squeamish.

Simon smiled. "He look back?"

"What? Oh, at the nurse. Well, Ray. Not exactly Mr. Sensitive. He probably asked her out. Here." He held out an invisible cup. "Like it was roses. Something she'd go for." Both of them smiling now, Ray an old joke between them, the car easy again, no more scratchiness in the air. "Whatever happened to him anyway? Do you know?"

"Last I heard he was still at Bill's law firm. Trusts."

"Trusts. A guy who parachutes into France and makes it back. Funny how things turn out."

Simon looked at him, but Frank had moved on.

"That's the Kremlin. Almost there."

They were coming down a sweeping broad street, eight lanes, Simon guessed, curiously empty of cars, just a few black shapes gliding by. At the bottom an open square and behind it the familiar fortress walls and gate towers, each tower topped by a glowing red star.

"Gorky Street," Frank said, pointing to the road outside. "Stalin had it widened and then put these up." He motioned toward the huge apartment buildings, Russian neoclassical, sober as banks. "Everybody wanted to live here then. You know, Moscow's still medieval that way—people want to be close to the castle, to the center. Here we are."

The car had turned the corner and stopped in front of another neoclassical building, this one with doormen and sculpted nymphs and light pouring out from the lobby. "Lenin stayed here. So you're in good company. Don't bother. They'll get the bags." He held the car door, waiting.

Simon got out and looked around. Moscow. The airport had been nowhere. But this was Russia—the shadowy streets, the heavy stone laced with Soviet gothic, policemen in greatcoats on the corner, people glancing sideways at his foreign clothes. The Moscow he'd seen in movies, gray with menace. A car pulling up, men jumping out, taking him away. Hadn't it actually happened? Hundreds of times. Interrogated in a room with a red light over the door. On his own, not even an alphabet. Except he wasn't alone. He looked over at Frank. A man who'd betrayed everyone and now seemed a kind of lifesaver, something you could hang on to until the rescue boat arrived.

"Recognize the car?" Frank said.

"What?"

"The Zim." He nodded to the airport car. "It's a Buick. Same model anyway. They copied it. Something to make you feel right at home."

In the lobby there were oversized Grecian statues and a grand carpeted staircase that seemed to rise two stories to Art Nouveau windows. After the quiet street, the lobby seemed bustling, groups of men in bulky suits huddling like delegates, presumably plant managers from Rostov or Party officials from one of the Eastern Bloc countries, excited to be here, at the center, a little dazed by the luxury. He could see a few women in the restaurant, but only a few. More men in suits, box-shaped with loose sleeves. While Vassilchikov checked him in at the desk, Frank steered them to the bar, a tsarist fantasy of red flocked walls and velvet cushions, now worn, some of the threads showing, the air thick with stale cigar smoke.

"Well, as I live and breathe. I thought you *never* went out." An English voice, drawing room theatrical and loud.

Frank turned, ambushed. "Gareth."

"We've just been to the Bolshy and thought we'd stop by for a nightcap. Join us? You remember Sergei?" He turned slightly to include a man, at least twenty years younger, who nodded, awkward. "Sergei hates the ballet, but he indulges me. Of course, I indulge him too. Don't I? See the new jumper?" Feeling the sleeve of Sergei's sweater. "Won't go near a proper suit, so I have to do the best I can to make him look decent. Not easy. But of course worth it," he said, looking at the boy, "when you're so good-looking."

Gareth's suit, an old pinstripe with a handkerchief flowering out of the pocket, needed pressing. In fact everything about him seemed disheveled, his tie knot pulled away from his throat, cigarette ash spilling on his cuffs, an alcohol sheen in his eyes. Simon looked at him for another minute before he finally recognized him, the once wolfish face now softened with flesh.

"Gareth Jones," he said, blurting it.

Gareth tipped his head. "*Dans son corps.* Or what's left of it. But how nice. I thought no one had the faintest anymore. All these years."

Ten of them by now, caught in the undertow of Burgess and Maclean, another defector for the newsreels. Staring at Simon, curious, like the people in the street.

"And you are? Or shouldn't I ask? It's one of the things about this place—nobody introduces anybody." He looked at Frank, waiting.

"Simon Weeks," Frank said. "My brother."

"Your brother?" he said, almost a squeal. "You'd never know it. Well, if you look," he said, peering at Simon. "The jawline. And a little around the eyes. So you've come to see the sights? Or just this old non grata?" He poked Frank's chest. "Or something else?" This to Simon, almost taunting.

"Just Frank. And the sights."

"Such as they are. Of course, there's the body," he said, giving the word two syllables. "Macabre, if you ask me, but it's really remarkable what they do for him. Old Lenin. He looks better than I do."

Sergei laughed, then looked down.

"So disloyal," Gareth said to him, then turned back to Simon. "Of course you have to wait hours. Hordes, every day. But maybe Frank can jump the queue for you. Join us?"

"Can't," Frank said.

"Well, then we'll just have to chat like this," Gareth said, needling him. "Everybody wondering." He turned to Simon. "I didn't even know he had a brother. My God, what was he *like*?"

"The same," Simon said, smiling a little at Frank. And wasn't he? "People don't change."

"They do here. I wish I had your mirror. It ages you, this place. The cold. Nobody to see. The Russians won't talk to you—why take the risk?—and people who should see each other," he said, looking at Frank, "who have things in common, you would think—but they don't much either. It's a very stick-to-yourself town. At least for people like us. But there's the Bolshy, that's always wonderful. And friends." He turned to Sergei, touching him. "How do people live without friends? What else is there really? Well, I suppose if you won't join us we'd better push on. Maybe next time. Of course, there never is. Donald's just the same. Try to be friendly and you get a chill straight off the steppes." He made a brrr gesture. "Thank God for Guy. He's always up for anything. But then always making scenes. So you wonder if it's worth it. Nice to have met you," he said to Simon. "The Tretyakov Gallery's the thing to see. The icons. And tell this one not to make himself scarce. We should see more of each other, you know. We're all in the same boat."

"We're not in the same boat," Frank said, annoyed.

Gareth took a step back, as if he'd been struck. "Well, have it your way. He thinks he's one of them. The gendarmerie. But really we're just agents who've outlived our usefulness. That's how they see us. So we just *molder*." He glanced toward the bar. "And take our pleasure where we may." He turned, then spotted Colonel Vassilchikov heading toward them. "Oh. The sheriff," he said, his shoulders rising out of their slouch. "And not the gentle soul you think he'll be. Not at all nice to friends. Come on. Let's vamoose."

Sergei just stared at him, confused.

"The bar," Gareth said, taking his elbow.

Vassilchikov joined them, speaking Russian, his eyes following Gareth. Frank answered him in Russian, then turned to Simon.

"The room's ready. We can go up."

"What was that?"

"What?"

"The once notorious Gareth Jones."

Frank made a humph sound.

"Scrounging drinks."

"No. He's very well taken care of. The Service has rules about that. Taking care of your own. Otherwise it sends a bad message to the field. People have to know they'll always be taken care of. Brought home, if it comes to that."

Simon looked at him, surprised by the word. Home.

"It's just he's never made any effort. Never even learned the language. Look at Maclean—works for the institute, sends his children to Russian schools. He's made a life here."

"Is it true, though? That the—you know, the ones who've come here—don't see each other? You'd think—"

"Some do, some don't. It's a question of the wives, mostly. They're the ones who get lonely. Jo used to see a fair amount of Melinda, so I saw Donald. That's the way it worked. But Gareth? Why would I want to see Gareth? He was a nasty piece of work, even before. And now—"

"Nasty how?"

"His specialty was blackmail. After he got them into bed, had his fun." He looked away. "It takes all kinds."

Simon glanced toward the bar where Gareth was already tossing back a drink. Even the Service had its pecking order, some treacheries more acceptable than others, like prisoners who looked down on molesters but didn't bat an eye at murder.

"Come on, let's celebrate. I ordered caviar."

"Caviar?"

"Who's better than us?" he said, their grandmother's old line, usually before she clinked a champagne glass. "Besides, it's still cheap here. Not like it used to be, but still— You must be hungry. They never have anything decent on the plane."

He had ordered not just caviar, but a whole spread of food, laid out and waiting for them on a big round table in Simon's room, a suite with the promised Kremlin view. Smoked fish and caviar on ice and beet salad and pickled mushrooms, anchored by a board with black bread and sweet butter.

"*Zakuski*," Frank said, an Intourist guide. "In the old days they'd have a few appetizers put out before dinner to keep the hunger pangs away, but then it kept getting bigger and bigger until it became—" He opened his hand to the table. "*Zakuski*. Of course, most people had nothing. Kasha, if they were lucky. We forget that. Boris, some vodka?"

Colonel Vassilchikov, who had come up with them, opened the bottle and poured out three glasses. The room, like the bar downstairs, had red flocked wallpaper and antique furniture, an exercise in fin de siècle nostalgia, but seemed even more faded and musty, velvet drapes with lace trimming so old and fragile you thought it might come apart in your fingers. Simon looked up at the heavy chandelier, another relic from the tsars. Where DiAngelis had said there'd be microphones.

"Don't bother looking for them—you'd never get them all. Just assume someone's listening. They're all over the place. In the walls. The phone. That'd be easy enough, screw off the mouthpiece and there it is. But then they know you're looking. And you're not that kind of guy. You're someone—it wouldn't even occur to you, the bugs."

But now, looking up, he couldn't help imagining the listeners, sitting in some windowless room with headphones, recording every sound, the clink of vodka glasses as Boris welcomed him, a toast curiously official and secret at the same time, with no one there to hear it but the ears in the walls.

Frank raised his glass again. "The British Navy. In the seventeenth century." He nodded to Simon, smiling. "To making me look good."

"To making you look good," Simon repeated, hearing himself saying it.

"Here, have something to eat," Frank said, filling a plate, playing host. "Boris, what about you?"

Simon looked over at him. Here for the evening, apparently. A bodyguard who didn't stand outside the door, part of the family.

"I've been thinking," Frank said, handing Simon the plate. "About the Latvians. I can put them in, if you think I should." Shoptalk, directly to Simon, as if Boris weren't there.

"All right," Simon said, not sure where Frank was going.

"I'll have to clear it. The Agency might see it as a provocation. And we want to be careful about that. The line these days is make nice, hands together."

"That'll come as news to them."

Frank smiled. "I didn't say it was true. I just said it was the line." He looked over. "I won't apologize," he said quickly. "But I'll say what happened to them. My part in it. I had to, you know. They never should have—" He took another drink. "Well, water over the dam. So. Round one to you."

"It's not a fight."

"No. But I'll give you this one. Be the bad guy of the piece."

He fingered his glass, tracing a ring. "I'm sorry about—any trouble I caused you. The worst of it, all this business, is having to lie to people. To keep cover. It's nothing personal, you know. Just the way things have to be. Still." He looked up. "It's good to see you."

And suddenly, in a quick second, maybe the drink, it was. Simon felt a rush to his face, the old affection. An involuntary smile, sharing a joke no one else heard.

Frank looked away first. "Boris, caviar? Mustn't let it go to waste. Boris is a great one for caviar. Eat it every day if he could."

Boris said something in Russian. Frank laughed and answered back, a different voice again, as if the language put him in another body. He refilled Simon's glass.

"So did Pirie brief you himself?" he said to Simon.

Without thinking, Simon looked up at the chandelier.

"Don't mind about that—you get used to it. Half the time the tape just ends up on a shelf somewhere."

"And the other half?"

"Does it make a difference? I'm *in* the Service. Anything you tell me, you're telling them. So not Pirie?"

"No."

"Not even a hello? You'd think he'd take a personal interest. After all we've been through. Chip then? It's not a briefing you farm out. You'd want someone who knew me."

"Frank—"

Frank held up his hand. "All right, just asking. It had to be somebody. Or have I just slipped off the raft?"

"Guidelines for the book, that's all. They have to vet it. You know that."

"Mm. Their own special blue penciling. A courageous publisher would have told them to fuck off."

Simon nodded. "But you wanted a respectable one."

Frank looked up; your ad. "So not even a message? Something

cryptic to keep me guessing at night? I thought Don might want to have a little fun."

"No."

Frank made a face, then let it go. "Old Don. He's as crazy as Dulles. But predictable. Lucky for us. Whenever you want to know what they'll do, his section, just figure out the dumbest response and–bingo. Chip was all right, though. A good head on his shoulders. Which I suppose means he was never promoted."

"I don't know. Really. I don't work for the Agency. I never even go to DC anymore. So how would I hear?"

"I just thought you might–be in touch. You and Chip go back– the OSS days, for chrissake."

"I haven't seen him. People–scatter."

"So who do you see?"

"From that world? No one. If you want to talk about old times, I can't be much help. They're your old times, not mine."

Frank looked at him, then walked toward the window. "Well, some are yours too. I like old times. That's what we have now, isn't it?" He was quiet for a second, looking out, then turned. "Anyway, that's all the book is, old times, so one way or another–"

He stopped, jarred by the telephone ringing, something unexpected, his face suddenly wary. He nodded to Boris, now a secretary, who picked up the receiver and started talking in a lowered voice, as if Simon could understand Russian. Then more Russian to Frank.

"What is it?" Simon said.

"Oh, nothing. The battle-axe in the hall. You know, the one who keeps your keys. God knows where they get them. War widows, I suppose." His voice nervous, caught off guard. "Boris will fix it. Whatever it is." A forced easiness now, watching Boris leave, then turning back to the window. "Come look at this. I want to show you something." Distracting them both. "See the building over there? Catty corner. Hotel Moskva."

Simon looked out. An ugly big building hulking over an open square.

"See how the two halves don't match? Story goes they brought two sets of drawings to Stalin, to choose, but he just said yes, fine, and nobody had the guts to say 'which?' so they built them both, one on top of the other. That way nobody got in trouble." Talking just to talk, his mind elsewhere, out in the hall where something had happened.

"Did he ever say which one he liked? Stalin?"

"He didn't know there were two. He thought it was supposed to look like that. That was the joke."

Stalin jokes, whistling in the dark, pretending not to hear the knocking next door, years of it.

"I wonder what—" Frank stopped, his eyes fixed over Simon's shoulders. "Jo," he said, apprehensive.

"The old cow didn't want to let me in. So I had to tell her Boris was Lubyanka. That fixed it. That's all right, isn't it? I mean, it's not a secret—" She looked over. "Simon," she said softly.

"Jo," he said, rooted, not moving. The long Rita Hayworth hair now stopped at the shoulders, brushed back in an I-don't-care way, all of it gray, like one of those doctored pictures that show you what you'll look like old. A pencil skirt a few years out of style, the eyes tired, not as bright, or as ready to laugh. Not just an older version of herself, someone else.

"Simon," she said again, and now he saw her lying on a bed, dark hair spread out behind her, one leg raised, the hotel in Virginia, their one weekend. You never see a woman the same way afterward, knowing the body under the clothes, the way her skin feels. Someone you know, even years later, the look of her the same in your mind. One weekend, sweaty sheets, their secret, eating room service in robes, her throaty laugh, the way she gasped when she came, a whole weekend, just them, no one else. And then she met Frank.

"I thought you weren't feeling well," Frank said.

"I made a leap into health," she said, waving her arm a little. "Actually, a nap. That's all it took. So I thought I'd come. I couldn't wait," she said to Simon. "My God, how nice to see you. It doesn't seem real. Here, I mean."

She came up to him and hugged him, an awkward embrace, Simon not ready for it. Something off, lipstick not quite right, an edge to her voice.

"It's not fair. You look just the same. Except for these," she said, touching his glasses. "Very distinguished. All the better to see us."

"And you," he said, holding her shoulders, studying her face, her eyes moist.

"Liar," she said. "I look like hell. Always the gentleman. Oh, look. *Zakuski*. At this hour. Boris, would you pour me a drink?"

Boris looked over at Frank.

"Another?" Frank said gently. "It's getting late—"

"Are you counting them?" she said, almost snapping at him. "He counts them," she said to Simon, who now heard the slight slurring. "I'm no help. I never count. So he has to do it. Did he tell you that I drink too much? What else did he say? I'll bet he's been 'preparing' you. He does that. I thought I'd better get over here before he poisoned you against me."

"He could never do that." Intending to be light, but betrayed by his voice, like a soft hand on her cheek.

"Oh," she said, rearing back a little, catching it.

"He hasn't said anything," Simon said, covering.

Joanna looked at him, then went over and poured a vodka. "Maybe that's worse. Make me a nonperson. That's a specialty here. Lock me up in the attic. Like Mrs. Rochester."

"Jo—" Frank said.

"*Jane Eyre*," she said. "Not something you'd read. You know, I was an English major." She looked at her glass. "Now I'm just—whatever I am." She ran her hand along her blouse, as if she were taking stock. "And I wanted to look nice."

"You look fine."

She laughed. "Don't overdo it. I'm still steady enough to look in a mirror. Later it gets a little blurry, but we probably won't make it to that point. Frank will get me home, won't you, dear? Before I say anything. He worries about that. I don't know why. I mean, we never see anybody. Except the other spies."

"They're not—" Frank started, an involuntary wince.

"No, that's right, not anymore. Former spies. They hate the word. Agents. It's nicer. Not spies. But that's what they were. Busy as bees." She pursed her lips and made a series of whispering sounds, a kind of buzzing. "Spying on everyone. You," she said, nodding to Simon. "He spied on you."

"He didn't get much."

"Oh, is that what he says? In the book?"

"Haven't you read it?"

"No. I don't have to read it. I lived it." She sipped her glass.

"Maybe we should go," Frank said. "It's been a long day for Simon. Boris, would you call for the car?"

"I never thought you'd come. Why did you?"

"It's easier than doing it by mail. Working on the book."

"No, I mean why did you agree to do it? After he spied on you. Do you need the money?"

"So far the money's only going one way," he said, trying to be light, move away from it.

"No. I know you," Joanna said, holding up her glass, a pointing finger. "Something else. I'll bet you were curious. You couldn't wait to see—what a mess we made of everything."

"Joanna—" Frank said.

"I'll bet that's it. What happened to them? After all that? I know I'd be curious. But why come? Isn't it all in the book?"

"Not all of it."

"No. I'll bet. Just the good days. That's what the comrades like." She lowered her glass. "Well, who doesn't? So now you can see for yourself. How we're holding up." She stopped. "I thought you'd never want to see him again. But here you are. What did he say about you? In the book. That must have been strange—seeing the truth. Finally."

"I'm not in the book."

"No? Well, you're his brother. I guess there are rules about that. What about wives?" she said, half to Frank. "Any rules about us? What did he say about me? I've been dreading it, but I guess I'll have to know sometime."

"You're not in the book either. It's not like that. Personal."

A thin laugh. "So. Mrs. Rochester. Stuck up there in the attic." She looked at Frank. "Just think what you're leaving out. A real saga. The loyal wife who follows you to Russia. Russia. Maybe you should lock me in the attic. Anybody'd be crazy to do that."

"You're not crazy," Frank said, mollifying, familiar territory.

"No, just drunk. You can say it. Who knows us better than Simon?" She stopped. "Except you don't anymore, do you? What it's like. In the beginning it wasn't so bad. You know, I had Richie to take care of, so I was busy—"

"I'm sorry about that," Simon said.

Joanna waved her hand. "I know, I know. Everybody was. But it wasn't that. Frank likes to explain me. He thinks I blame myself. But I don't. Well, you always do in a way, but I know it wasn't anybody's *fault*. We did everything we could. The hospital too. It was just—he died. And we didn't. So now what was there? Make dinner? We have someone for that. Do the shopping anyway. Shopping takes all day here. Lines. Anyway, who do you have over? The other agents?" She underlined the word. "One cozy evening after another. Scrabble with the Macleans. Gareth throwing up in a taxi.

He's downstairs, by the way, did you see him? He wanted to gossip. Of course. Don't worry," she said to Frank. "I didn't say a thing." She turned to Simon. "You have to keep in mind who these people are, what they're like. It's their nature. Gareth gets people to talk—he's such a loose cannon people think he must be safe—and he reports them. That's what he does. Perry was all right. Poor Perry. He didn't notice things. What it's really like. But he had Marzena. Has Frank told you about Marzena?" A look between them. "No, he wouldn't. But you should meet. You'd like her. Perry did. Of course the question is—I'd love your take on this—does she work for the Service or not? They'd have to approve the marriage, but did they actually arrange it?"

"Arrange it?"

"To keep Perry happy. They like to keep their old boys happy. And keep an eye on them. This way they'll know his every waking thought. Even what he says in his sleep. They got Gareth a boyfriend. Why not a loyal wife? Mostly loyal anyway. They like doing that. Using someone close."

"The car is here," Boris said from the window.

"Oh, and we were having such fun," she said, her voice forced, then looked down. "I'm sorry. This isn't the way I wanted this to go. I wanted it to be—I don't know, like it was." She looked up. "I haven't changed so much, have I?"

"We've all changed."

"Not you," she said, patting his chest. "Don't disapprove. I couldn't bear that. I'll be right as rain in the morning and then we'll start over, okay?"

"That's an excellent idea," Frank said, getting ready to go. "Did you bring a coat?"

"A coat?" Joanna said, dazed.

"It's still cold, nights. Boris, take home anything you like." He nodded to the spread of food. "I'll send someone up to clear," he said, a show of normalcy, as if nothing had happened, just a drink and appetizers.

Joanna came closer. "So tomorrow? We can talk and talk. I want to know everything. Diana. Everything."

"Coming?" Frank said, almost at the door.

"Yes," Joanna said, then hugged Simon, putting her mouth near his ear, a low murmur. "He's up to something. I'm not crazy. You live with someone, you can sense it. He wants something. I don't know what yet. All of a sudden he wants you here. Why?"

"Maybe he wanted to see me," Simon said gently. "I wanted to see him."

"Oh, lovely Simon," she said, touching his cheek. "It's different here. You can't trust him. Any of them." She pulled back, a public voice. "Come early. There's so much to catch up on."

She followed Boris out, Frank lingering.

"I'm sorry," he said. "It's the excitement—your being here. Her sister came after Richie died and that helped. But no one since. Her family, anybody. Until you."

"Why not go see them? She still has her passport. She never renounced—"

Frank looked at him, then up at the chandelier, taking him by the sleeve and moving him out to the hall. Jo and Colonel Vassilchikov were at the other end, near the floor manager.

"It's all right out here," Frank said, voice low. "So you have been briefed. There's no other way you could have known that." Answering a question that hadn't been asked. "We'll take a walk tomorrow and talk. I do that every day. Boris won't think anything of it. Was it Pirie himself? I'll be curious—what he had to say."

"Frank," Simon said, dismayed, still hearing Jo, maybe everyone crazy.

"Be right there," Frank said to the others, raising his voice loud enough to carry, then turned back to Simon, conspiratorial. "We'll

talk. You forget. I know Don. I know how he thinks." Twelve years
ago.

"Frank—"

"By the way," he said, not listening. "Don't say anything to Jo
about—seeing her family. That's not really possible. You'd just upset
her. We're—we're here."

And then he was gone, the long overcoat flapping around his
legs. Simon watched them get into the elevator, then scanned the
hall. No one but the old woman who kept the keys. And no doubt
made a report. Boris listening in the car. Simon went back into his
room. Were they listening now? "Run water in the bathroom,"
DiAngelis had said. "The radio loud." He glanced at the telephone,
the light fixture again. Turn around. Leave. He went over to the window. Below Jo and Frank were getting into the car, a privilege, Boris
looking out for them. What had the Germans called it? Protective
custody. For your own good.

He looked over at the red stars on the Kremlin towers. A great
space, big enough for parades to rumble through. You could talk
there without running water. Line up to see Gareth's "bod-y."
Watched. Listened to. In prison, some vast Victorian panopticon,
so big you weren't aware of being inside. But if you kept going,
just walked out of the square and didn't stop, over the endless flat
land, reverse the trip he'd just made, you'd finally come to the visible fences—the barbed wire and attack dogs and watchtowers. No
glowing red stars there. No way to pretend the surveillance was for
your own good. One look at the wires and you'd know. He felt a
tightening in his chest. He could get out, do his time, a week or two,
and head back to Vnukovo, fly right over the barbed wire. But Frank
and Jo— We're here, Frank had said. A life sentence.

He glanced at his watch, then took out a cigarette and turned
on the table lamp next to the window. Open the window, DiAngelis
had said. That'll be the signal you're okay.

The spring air was soft but chilly. She hadn't brought a coat, not feeling it.

"Smoke the whole thing. By the window, like you're a tourist. Looking at things."

"What if he doesn't see me?" The street below empty.

"He will."

"Who is he?"

"You don't want to know that."

"I mean, is he a Russian or—?"

"You don't want to know anything. You're just a guy here to see your brother. And now you're having a smoke. Not one of us."

"I'm not one of you."

2

A RESTLESS NIGHT, UP TWICE, looking out at the deserted street. What did he expect to see? A man by a lamppost? Then morning coffee in the dining room, only a few other guests down this early, men in suits eating smoked fish and dark bread, buried in newspapers, columns of dense Cyrillic. He'd been told nobody read the papers—"propaganda sheets" according to DiAngelis—but here they were, as immersed and trusting as businessmen in Omaha. Outside the dining room windows the Kremlin, last night sinister and shadowy, was bathed in spring sunshine. Colonel Vassilchikov's car wasn't due until nine. He went out to the lobby, expecting to be stopped at the door, offered an escort, told he couldn't leave unaccompanied, but no one seemed to notice him.

He crossed the broad street by the underground walkway, then up past the Hotel Moskva, glancing over his shoulder. No one behind, just office workers streaming out of the Metro. Red Square. A place he'd seen in a thousand photographs, filled with tanks and military salutes and politburo members who disappeared from the pictures a year later, airbrushed from memory. He'd always imagined a gray ceremonial square, boxed in by Kremlin towers, but instead it was open and bright, flooded with light, the onion domes of St. Basil's at the far end swirls of color, GUM department store frilly and ornate, something a children's illustrator might have dreamed up. People hurrying across to work. Anywhere. He looked at the high fortress walls. Where Stalin had sat up at night putting check marks next to names on a list. Names he knew, names other people knew, names that struck his fancy. Terror had no logic. Check. Gone. Night after night.

Now a line was already forming outside the mausoleum to see him, the embalmed king, a primitive ritual as old as Egypt. Shuffling along patiently for just a glimpse. Except for the man with the hat. Simon looked again. Not moving with the crowd, using it as a kind of screen. Had he seen the hat before? Without even noticing? Maybe on the shallow steps of the Moskva, but maybe not. He hadn't felt anything, no prickly feeling at the back of his neck. But why stand there and not move with the crowd? To keep Simon in his sight line. He'd be one of theirs. "Nobody will contact you," DiAngelis had said. "All the embassy people are watched. Just give the okay sign at the window. If there's any trouble, or you need to make contact, go to the embassy. Ask for me." "You?" "The name'll get you to the right person. But only if you have to." So not one of ours. Unless he was imagining things.

He turned and walked over to GUM, then looked back. No hat, which was somehow worse, a man who could disappear. GUM wasn't open yet and in any case there'd be nothing to buy, so he kept walking toward St. Basil's, surprised that the square didn't end there but continued downslope to the river. He stopped and looked up at the onion domes, what any tourist would do. If in fact anybody was watching.

"Mr. Weeks?" An American voice. But nobody was supposed to contact him.

Simon turned. The same hat, now pushed back a little, a young man's gesture. A thin face with a permanent five o'clock shadow, someone in his thirties.

"Hal Lehman. UPI."

"Oh."

The man held up his hand. "Don't worry. Off the record."

"What is?"

Hal smiled. "It's not secret, is it, why you're here? You sent out a press release when you signed the book, so I figured—"

"How did you find me?"

"I took a chance they'd put you up at the National. There, or the Metropol. Big cheese place. So I waited to see who came out." Pleased with himself.

"And followed me."

Another smile. "At least I'm the only one."

"You sure?"

"Pretty sure. After a while you get a sense."

"Then how about letting me enjoy my walk. Off the leash. Really, I don't have anything to say. On or off the record."

Hal nodded. "That's okay. I was hoping you'd take a message for me."

"To—?"

"Your brother, who else? All these years, it's no, no, no. No interviews. But now. You do a book I figure you want interviews, some press. So why not UPI? We get picked up everywhere. I mean, you're his publisher. Don't you—?"

"That's really up to him." Simon paused. Not anybody. UPI. "Anyway, we've got a long time to go before pub. You're early."

"Look, just ask him. I've been trying to get this since I got here.

And that's eighteen months, so who knows how much longer? Two years would be a long run. They usually throw you out before that."

"Really? Why?" Simon said, curious.

Hal shrugged. "You're bound to write something that offends somebody in two years. Khrushchev's wife, somebody. And by then you might have some contacts, you might be able to do some reporting. So, out. New guy comes in, he's just got the press handouts to work with. They like it that way. You have a cigarette? They're hell to get here."

Simon hesitated, then offered him one from the pack. No longer a stranger asking for directions, if anyone was watching. A meeting, a conversation.

"So why the interest in Frank?" Simon said, watching him light the cigarette. "All this time. It's an old story now."

Hal inhaled. "Nice. You should see the stuff they smoke here. It's not just him. I'm interested in all of them. Not what they did—you're right, that's old news. What they're doing now."

"What they're doing now."

Hal nodded. "Now that they're ghosts. Kind of a ghost story."

"Why ghosts?"

"They're here and not here. Like ghosts. Look, you work for UPI you go to everything. Parties. Receptions at Spaso House. Everything. But you never see them."

"You really think the American ambassador is going to invite Frank to a Fourth of July? He's a—"

"Traitor. Right. So not the ambassador's. But there's other stuff, and you never see him. Any of them. You don't see them with Russians either. You don't see them at all. Once in a while you spot one at the Bolshoi, but that's because I'm looking. I'm interested. The others don't care. *Time.* The *Post.* You know they give us offices in the same building. Out on Kutuzovsky. So they can keep an eye on us, I guess. And that means we see each other all the time. So

I know. The Brits—they'll get to somebody like Gareth Jones once in a while. But the Americans don't care. They'd rather do rockets. The space race. But I still think it's a story. Being ghosts. I mean, what do they do all day? Gareth gets loaded, but what about the others? Do they like it here? I'm interested. So if he's going to talk to anybody, it would be great if it's me. I'd appreciate it, if you could help set it up."

Simon looked at him. "I'll give him the message. You should know that *Look* has serial rights. He can't talk before that. So it could be a while."

"It'd just be background if that's better for him. You know, with his people. You heading back? Mind if I walk with you?"

Simon smiled. "I was about to say it's a free country, but it isn't, is it?"

"No, but interesting. You have to give it a little time. Thanks for this," he said, indicating the cigarette. "I ran out a while ago, so I have to wait for the next Helsinki run."

Simon looked at him, a question.

"To get things we can't get here. Not even in the *Beryozka*—the hard currency stores."

"Helsinki. People can just come and go?" Simon said.

"Well, they can't," Hal said, nodding toward the mausoleum queue. "And you use your press visa too many times, you're asking for trouble, so we take turns. Maybe one trip a year. Everybody makes a list. And vegetables."

"You drive to Helsinki for vegetables?" Simon said, fascinated now.

"Try getting through a winter. They even run out of cabbage. You can have things sent in, if you can afford the dollars, but something always falls off the truck, so it's better to go get it yourself. Anyway, Nancy needed a new coat so we took the last run. My wife," he said, seeing Simon's expression.

"You're here with your wife?" Simon said, something he hadn't imagined. Vegetables and new winter coats and ordinary life.

Hal nodded. "I know. Everybody thinks it's a bachelor's job. And mostly it is. The Russians don't like it. It means a bigger apartment. Usually it's: here's your forty square meters and here's the key. Turn up this way. I'll show you around a little if you have the time."

"I should get back."

"Well, we'll make it short then. Just the highlights. It beats Intourist. They like to tell you how many tons of concrete the builder used. Look." He stopped, tossing the cigarette. "I'm not expecting Weeks to jump at this. He—doesn't. I mean, he never has. Just tell him it's not about—what he did. He can keep his secrets. Whatever they are." He looked up. "Unless he puts them in the book. But I'm not holding my breath."

They had already turned the corner at the north end of GUM into Nikolskaya, a narrower street with attractive nineteenth-century buildings whose plaster fronts were grimy and cracked. A few cars.

"It was Nancy who got me into it," Hal was saying. "The defectors. She said it would make a good story and nobody had done it. They get on a plane or a ferry or something and they just—vanish. But they don't. They're here. I mean, there she was, getting her hair done at the Pekin and Nancy recognizes her."

"The Pekin?" Simon said, trying to imagine it, a row of hairdryers, the remodeled interrogation rooms upstairs. Green light, red light.

"She likes the girl there. Anyway, Marzena was there too and Nancy recognized her so they talked and we got to know them a little."

"Who?"

"Sorry. Perry Soames and his wife."

"Perry Soames. The one Fuchs—?"

"Right. You can't get to them. Usually. The atomic spies. They send them straight to Arzamas and nobody talks there. Nobody."

Simon looked at him again, eyebrows up.

"The nuclear lab. Off-limits. Well, it would be, wouldn't it? Considering."

Simon thought for a minute. "But his wife's at the beauty parlor here?"

"Well, that's the thing. Of course, this is all later. After he moved to Moscow. But why leave Arzamas in the first place? I mean, people don't. Unless they're—"

"What?"

"Sick. Have a breakdown. I don't know. That's the story, no? Of course he wasn't going to talk to me, and his wife's careful, even with Nancy. They never tied him to the Rosenbergs, so it must have been a separate operation, sort of parallel tracks. Or the other theory."

"What's that?"

"They let the Rosenbergs take the fall to protect him. He gets here, they ship him right out to Arzamas, so he still must have had stuff for them. Then he checks out. So why? Maybe the science got ahead of him. Maybe he starts feeling guilty. That might do it, seeing the bombs every day, seeing what you'd done. But anyway he stops being useful to them. So Moscow. But what's he thinking all this time? That's the story."

"And what makes you think Frank can tell you?"

"He saw him that weekend. That's one of the things I want to verify. What did he say? What was on his mind? I mean, a guy shoots himself he must have said something. He's sorry, something. Or maybe not. Maybe he was just sleepwalking through it. But if he could tell me—I wouldn't have to quote him, I'd just like to know."

Simon stopped at the corner. "He killed himself? I thought he— was sick. That's what it said in the paper."

"That's what they wanted us to say. So we say it. Otherwise, you're gone. But suppose it's something else. Suppose he gets here and he realizes he did it all for this." He waved his hand to take in the street. "And now there's no way out. He runs to avoid prison and he just lands in a bigger one. That would be a hell of a story."

"If true."

"Well, you tell me. How does your brother feel about being here?"

Simon looked up at him, no more circling, at the point.

"You'll have to read his book and see. I'll tell you one thing, though. He doesn't feel like that. Putting a gun to his head. He thinks he did the right thing."

"Do you?" Hal said.

"No." He waited, an emphasis. "But it doesn't matter what I think. On or off the record. I'm not him. I spent years answering questions about Frank. What did he say to me. What did I say to him. What did he think about this. That. As if I knew. Wasn't that the point? Nobody knew what he was thinking. He fooled us all. But he wasn't thinking that. Maybe Soames was. How did they get to be such great pals anyway? I thought people didn't—"

"The dachas. In the country. They're in the same compound, so they got to know each other."

"Compound?"

"It's fenced. You don't see the fence." A country house, behind wires. "A KGB compound."

Simon looked at him. Their own hospital. Food store. Even countryside.

"So the papers just said he was sick," Hal finished. "Natural causes. No weakness. Not that shooting yourself is a sign of weakness—I don't know how you go through with it. But they think it is. Raises questions. They don't like that."

"Nobody does."

Hal nodded, touché, then cocked his head at the building on the other side of the busy square ahead. "Especially them. That's headquarters. The Lubyanka."

Simon gazed across. A tsarist office building with a yellow façade, so large it filled the entire block. A statue in the middle of the square, trucks lumbering by on either side. No black cars pulling up to the doors, no screams coming from the basement. Hoses to wash the blood off the walls. Thousands. More.

"It used to be an insurance company," Hal said. "Rossiya Insurance. They put in the prison in the thirties. Dzerzhinsky, the founding father." He nodded to the statue. "And now look." He turned to the big building on their side of the square. "*Detskiy Mir*. Biggest toy store in Russia. The kids love it."

"That's—" Simon said, unable to finish.

"Yeah, I know. But it's even stranger than that. I mean, they don't have a lot of irony here. It's okay about the store because that really isn't there." He waved to the KGB building. "It doesn't exist. None of it happened. Because if it did, if you started to see it—so nobody does. That's just a nice old guy looking down on the kiddies. Millions disappeared and no one saw them go. That's what it's like here. Things just aren't there, even when they are. So how did Soames feel about that, or Weeks, or any of them? That's what I'd like to know. When they saw who they were working for."

Simon looked across again. Walls of light mustard, almost cheerful. Frank's elite force, the country where everything worked.

"Of course, there's another possibility. About Soames. Maybe he didn't do it. Maybe somebody else did."

Simon waited a second. "Who?"

Hal made a wry face. "Who kills people in this country?" Looking across the square.

"One of their own?"

"Maybe they thought he was a double agent. Maybe he *was* a

double agent. They always worry about that. If the defector's a plant. Maybe he became a liability. Picked up the wrong intel at Arzamas. I don't know why. But if they did, it would make some story. They'd kick me out, but a story like that, you could write your own ticket back to New York." He glanced at Simon. "Maybe even a book."

Simon turned to him. "Frank's not going to talk to you about this. You know that, don't you? He works for the KGB."

Hal nodded. "But he might talk to you."

"To me?"

"I just need background. Confirmation. I don't need anything on the record."

"Is that what this little guided tour was about? Make me a source?"

Hal hunched his shoulders. "If you don't ask, you don't get."

"Not this time. I didn't come here for this—get you a byline."

"Look, we're on the same side here."

"As long as I set you up with Frank."

Hal took out a card. "This is where I am. Don't worry, it's not radioactive. Nobody'll think anything of it. Meet another American and take his number, that's all."

"At UPI. With him listening," Simon said, tipping his head toward the statue.

"Well, they do. Fact of life here. But what would they hear? You'd want the interview. It's good press for the book. You'd want to set things up early. Strictly business." He held up his hands to show them empty. "You should probably go back to the hotel alone, though. Just out for a walk. Follow left there. It'll circle back. Past the Bolshoi. Moscow's laid out in rings so you're always circling back. See the big pile down there? House of Unions. Where they put Gary Powers on trial. Poor bastard."

"You cover that?"

"Everybody covered it. If there's one thing they know how to do here, it's a show trial. One more cigarette?"

Simon offered him the pack, watching as he pocketed one.

"Just ask him about Soames and see what he says. If I'm right, I'd appreciate a call. Or maybe you see me at the National. At the bar. And we have a drink. Off the record."

When Simon got back to the hotel Colonel Vassilchikov was standing out front, annoyed but trying to mask it with a formal smile. He was wearing a business suit today, but everything about him—buzz-cut hair, the pulled back shoulders—was military, a soldier out of uniform.

"Mr. Weeks. You've been out?"

"I wanted to see Red Square."

"Ah. And what did you think?"

"Much bigger than I imagined."

Improbably, Vassilchikov's face softened, a patriot. "Yes, it's very beautiful. That's what it means, you know. The word for red is also that for beautiful. Nothing to do with the Soviets."

"I didn't know that."

"It was a market. There were stalls along the Kremlin walls. Well," he said, catching himself. "But if you had told me, I would have provided you with a guide."

"That's all right. Just a quick look around. I saw the Bolshoi on my way back. Very impressive too."

"Yes. Well, shall we go?"

"I'll just run up and get my bag."

"The briefcase? I took the liberty," he said, nodding to the backseat.

"Oh," Simon said, feeling someone had been through his pockets. "Mind if I ride up front? It doesn't seem right, you like a chauffeur. A colonel. Anyway, you can show me the sights."

Vassilchikov hesitated for a second, not sure how to respond, then opened the door for him.

"You didn't get lost," he said pleasantly, slipping behind the wheel. "Without a map?"

"No. But I suppose I should get one."

"Well, you know, it's difficult. There were no maps during the war. And afterward—"

"Then how does anybody—?"

"They live here. They know. But visitors—that's why it's so useful to have a guide. Someone who can help you. I would be happy to do it myself. Or one of my colleagues. Just let me know what you would like to see and we'll arrange it. Moscow is a big city. So easy to get lost."

They drove toward the Manège, then turned right. Simon peered at the street sign. Bolshaya Nikitskaya. He'd spent days memorizing Cyrillic letters but still felt he was decoding, translating letter for letter.

"The old university," Vassilchikov said, evidently taking the guide role seriously. "Down there, Moscow Conservatory. Very beautiful hall." He pointed to the statue in the forecourt. "Tchaikovsky. They say an excellent likeness."

"How long have you been Frank's—bodyguard?"

"I am his technical officer," Vassilchikov said, his fleshy face pulling back in disapproval.

"Sorry. I didn't mean—"

But Vassilchikov was waving this away. "A matter of terminology. I think in your Service you say case officer?"

"I wouldn't know." He waited. "I thought that was someone who ran agents in the field."

"Yes?"

"But Frank isn't in the field anymore."

"No, but I can be of use in many ways. You understand, Comrade Weeks is a hero of the Soviet Union. He is entitled to such privileges. In the beginning, it's true, there was a bodyguard—we didn't know if his life would be in danger. But now, it's a question of—general assistance. You see there on the right?"

Simon turned to a modern office building with a giant bronze globe hanging over the entrance.

"TASS," he said, the Cyrillic TACC easy even for him. "The news agency."

Vassilchikov nodded. "So you are learning Russian. It's good. Some of the others—"

"The others?"

"Western friends. Who come here. Still only English. Gareth Jones—you met him last night at the hotel. All these years and no Russian."

"Maybe he understands more than you think. Someone like him, that would be par for the course."

"Course?" Vassilchikov said, bewildered.

"Sorry. An idiom. I just meant, he was a spy. It might be in his nature to know more than he lets on."

Vassilchikov turned to him, his double chin moving up a little in a smile. "A generous assessment. No, he's like the others. A fish out of waters. That's correct? Except Comrade Weeks. And Maclean. He speaks Russian. His children are Young Pioneers. Sometimes, you know, the adopted land—you feel a powerful attachment. But Comrade Jones, I think not. Of course, that type—"

At the intersection with the first ring road they were stopped to let two black Zils race by, lights flashing, important.

"Kremlin," Vassilchikov said simply.

On the other side the streets became leafy, some of the houses even with grounds, a century away.

"Is here many embassies," Vassilchikov said. Classroom English.

"Nice," Simon said. "You don't expect somehow—"

"The future started with the revolution," Vassilchikov said, a practiced line. "But Russia was here before. A desirable district. Popular with writers."

"And Frank lives here?" Simon said, amused, imagining poetry readings, Village cafés.

"Near Patriarch's Pond. You'll see."

The houses became apartment buildings, slightly shabby but still attractive, neoclassical or creamy rococo façades. Europe.

"He is so pleased you are here. His brother. You were close?"

"Yes." Lunches at Harvey's. So what's happening at State? Who's going to the conference? Reporting everything back. Close.

"He vouched for you."

"Vouched for me?"

"With the Service. When he made the request for you to come. So it's important, you see, that no suspicion attaches to you. Even an innocent walk—"

Simon ignored this. "I thought it was their idea—your idea. The Service's."

"No. Comrade Weeks's. It's very serious for him, this book. His legacy. Of course, also a pleasure to see you. Patriarch's Pond," he said, lifting his left hand off the wheel.

Simon took in a park with a long rectangular reflecting pool, a playground at one end, a restaurant pavilion at the other.

"Vouched for me how?"

"Your purpose in coming. The editorial work."

"Why else would I be coming?"

Vassilchikov shrugged. "You were once in OSS, yes? It sometimes happens that an agent is reactivated. When an opportunity presents itself."

"You think I'm an agent? Don't your people have ways of checking that out?"

Vassilchikov smiled. "Yes, of course. But now another guarantee. Someone who takes responsibility for you."

"So it would be his fault if they're wrong?" He paused. "And what would I be doing here? If I'm—reactivated?"

"Comrade Weeks was a valuable agent. Perhaps the most valuable. A great embarrassment to the Americans."

"They think I'm here to bump him off?" Simon said, his voice catching, almost a laugh. "I'm here to make him famous." Then, half to himself, "I'm still not sure why."

"Brothers," Vassilchikov said quickly. "Comrade Weeks was sure you would come."

"Well, there's some money involved too."

"Yes, but for him, the blood. Family."

"You think so?"

"Mr. Weeks, I have been his technical officer for over five years. You see a man every day, you know him."

"I used to see him every day."

They had come to the end of Yermolaevskiy Street, before it curved and changed names. A concrete apartment building next to a vest pocket park that stretched all the way to the next ring road. Each section had its own entrance off the interior courtyard. Vassilchikov jumped out and swung open a high metal gate, then got back into the car and drove through. Number 21, Simon noticed. Moscow. Where he lived.

"Mr. Weeks," Vassilchikov said, oddly hesitant. "A word. It would be best not to mention last night."

"Last night?"

"Mrs. Weeks. It sometimes happens. A woman sensitive to

drink. Not a strong Russian head," he said, touching his own. "But then, the embarrassment. So, a politeness not to mention."

"How long has it been going on?" Simon said.

"Off and on," Vassilchikov said vaguely. "It's not a happy time now. One of their friends—a tragedy."

"Perry Soames."

Vassilchikov looked up at him. "You're very well informed."

"Everybody knows he died. What, and she's been on a tear ever since?"

"No. But a source of unhappiness. Their dachas are near to each other. So, friendly times. And now this. She was upset. Me, I think a holiday would be a good idea. Sochi. It's early for swimming, but the air is wonderful now. The flowers." Simon looked at him. The concierge Service again. What else did he do for them? "I have suggested this. Sochi. But of course she wanted to see you. Maybe you can persuade her—"

"To go to the Black Sea?" Sounding somehow like a joke.

"For a rest. You know the Service has a clinic there, to improve the health. It would be good for her."

"What does Frank think?"

Vassilchikov shrugged. "He says she can rest here. But maybe after you leave—then he can go with her. You know, he depends on her so much."

Simon looked at him, thrown slightly off balance. The KGB urging a rest cure, Simon trying to listen between words. A scheme? Or genuine concern? A girl who once went away with him. Long dark hair, body arched back toward the dance floor, everybody watching, maybe just him watching, holding her waist, in his hands. The memory of it here like a flash, then gone. Now a woman slurring warnings in his ear. Not to be mentioned the next day. It occurred to him then, looking around the dreary Moscow courtyard, that they had all thrown their lives away, everything they thought they were going to be. Or maybe Frank had done it for them.

"Are you going to stand there gossiping like two babushkas?" Frank was in the doorway. "Come in, come in. I thought you'd never get here. What was the problem? Traffic? Couldn't be. That's in the next five-year plan." He had put his arm around Simon's shoulder, guiding him in. "Careful here." He pointed to the concrete step, a chunk crumbling at the edge. "Lift is on the fritz today, I'm afraid. Well, every day. But much better for the health. Good exercise. It's only two flights. Keep the noise down, though. Madam has a headache." Raising an eyebrow, just between them, making a joke of it. "So what took you so long?"

"Mr. Weeks went for a walk."

"What, alone? Oh, you don't want to do that. Then Boris doesn't know where you are and he gets anxious. Blood pressure goes right up, doesn't it, Boris?"

"I wanted to see Red Square."

"Not the mummies, I hope."

"No, just walked around."

"Then you beat me to it. I was going to show you around later. I like to take walks in the afternoon. Boris too. Never mind, we'll go somewhere else. Lots to see. Ah, here's Jo."

She was standing in the open doorway, arms folded, as if she were holding herself in, a cigarette in one hand. A simple skirt and cardigan, a shy smile.

"There you are. How nice," she said, kissing him on the cheek. "The place is a mess. Ludmilla doesn't come till tomorrow."

But it wasn't a mess, just crowded, every wall lined with bookcases, framed pictures propped against some of the books, a couch and two tired club chairs, a professor's apartment. Not Mt. Vernon Street, not even the small house near the Phillips Collection.

"So many books," Simon said to Frank, a tease.

"Jo's a great reader," Frank said. "I'm still getting gentleman C's. But you know, now that I have the time—sometimes we just read all evening."

"This is the living room," Jo said. "Not much by your standards, but a lot of space for here. Frank's study is there—God knows what shape that's in. He growls if I move a paper. Used to be Richie's room," she said, her voice neutral. "Bedroom there. And kitchen. And that's it. Frank says I'm not to bother you when you're working, but let's have coffee first, yes? I can't just say hello and then not see you. How's Diana?"

"The same. Fine. She sends her best." A polite lie.

"Coffee okay? I suppose you've been up for hours. As usual."

"He went to see Red Square," Frank said.

"Did you?" she said. "And here we are, just out of bed. Come, help me in the kitchen and tell me everything. Boris, coffee for you too?"

"*Spasibo*," he said.

"My only word of Russian," Jo said. "Oh, and *pozhaluysta*. Covers practically everything, *spasibo* and *pozhaluysta*. Just use your hands for the rest."

"She's kidding," Frank said. "Her Russian is excellent."

"I have a woman comes once a week to talk to me. We have tea. In glasses. She looks at me with these mournful eyes—well, she probably lost somebody in the war. I don't dare ask, so we talk about the weather. Are the lilacs in bloom? Yes, the lilacs are in bloom. But not so many this year. And then I get the dative case wrong or something and she just *sighs*. Come. It won't take a sec. Boris, there's *Izvestia*."

Simon followed her to the kitchen, where she turned on the gas under a kettle. "There's some cake, if you like," she said, but was motioning with her hands for him to run the tap water, pointing and making twisting motions.

"No, that's all right," he said, turning the tap, his face a question mark.

She came closer to him. "They can't hear when the water's running. Interferes with the voices or something. At least that's what I heard. Anyway, let's hope so." She took a long drag on her cigarette and rubbed it out in the ashtray. "I'm sorry about last night. I do that now. I think I'm not going to and then I do. The worst part is that you're always apologizing."

"Not to me."

"No, not to you," she said softly. "You haven't given up on me, have you?"

"I don't know what you're talking about."

"You see it in their faces."

"See what?"

"Not that I see anybody anymore. You're the first since—"

She turned to lift the kettle, which was whistling now, and poured water into the coffeemaker, the sink tap still running.

"Remember Carrie Porter? Maybe you never met. We were at school together. So that far back. And she was here. Spaso House, no less. Visiting the ambassador. I don't know why—I suppose her husband does something. Anyway, she was at the Metropol. Frank likes to go there. The old world charm. So there we were having dinner, under the stained glass, and I look up and, my God, it's Carrie Porter. From school. And she sees me and at first she pretends not to and then she realizes I've seen *her*, so she comes over." She pushed down on the French press.

"What did she say?"

"Nothing. Well, what did she ever say? But that wasn't it. It was the look. She looked at me the way you look at a criminal. Nervous, a little afraid. Something you don't want to touch. And I thought, my God, that's what I've become. A criminal. Me, Ma Barker." She smiled a little. "But not so funny, is it, when somebody like Carrie can think it. It means everybody does. A criminal."

"You're not a criminal."

She shrugged. "And Frank? Carrie wouldn't even *look* at him."

"You're not him."

"But if I went back, they'd still throw me in the pokey. Anyway, I can't go back. No passport. It ran out. So how's it going to end?" She rested her hand on the coffeepot. "Well, we know, don't we? It doesn't. It just goes on like this."

"Jo—"

"Sorry. You weren't expecting this, were you?" She smiled to herself. "Neither was I. Sometimes I wonder how any of it happened. Was I there? I was going to be like Jo in *Little Women*, scrappy, take charge."

"Katharine Hepburn," Simon said.

"And here we are. In Yermolaevskiy Street. Getting plastered. Apologizing."

"Stop."

"Boris wants to send me to a sanitarium. For my health. No bars on the windows. Although what difference would that make?" she said, nodding to the running water. "And you know what? For about five seconds I thought about it. How bad would it be? Like the Greenbrier or someplace. Run by the KGB. Imagine Carrie Porter's face then. Palm Beach this year? No, Sochi." She looked down. "But Frank wouldn't like that. Who knows what I'd say once I got some brandy into me? I say things, apparently." She turned to Simon. "Don't stay here. I don't know what he wants, but he wants something. I know him." She stopped, folding her arms across her chest again. "Know him. I suppose if there's anything I didn't know, it was him."

"Jo, what you said last night—"

"That's the one good thing. I never remember. So be a gentle-man—be Simon—and don't tell me. I'm sure it wasn't good. Anyway, we'd better go in. You leave the water running and they get suspicious. At least I imagine they do. Where do you think they listen, anyway? Like mice in the walls."

"Your passport. Could I do something? Call someone at State? Maybe I could help."

She put her hand on his cheek. "I forgot how nice you could be. Oh, darling, there's nothing to do. Do you think they're going to jump up and down at State to issue me a new one? And if they did, then what? A whole room of Carrie Porters, a whole country? I couldn't face it. Five minutes at the Metropol was bad enough." She lowered her hand. "Anyway, I live here now. So. You take the tray. We can talk at the dacha. And you know what? The lilacs *are* in bloom. Just like the language lesson."

"Jo—"

"That's something anyway. Having you there. He'll be on his best behavior. Everybody will." She made a wry smile. "You're his good angel."

"Really? Since when?"

"Since always, I think. Up there on his right shoulder."

He picked up the tray. "So who's on the left?"

"Nobody. He's his own bad angel." She looked over at him. "But he'll make you think he's listening to you."

They sat drinking coffee for half an hour, Jo on the couch with her legs curled up beneath her, smoking, ashtray on her lap. The old liveliness was now just nervous energy—jerking the cigarette to her lips, brushing back hair from her forehead. Boris, still buried in *Izvestia*, said nothing, not there, another microphone in the wallpaper. Only Frank was eager to talk. So many years to catch up on, he had said, but the years had erased small talk, and anything larger, the reasons they were there, seemed off limits, not something you discussed over coffee. So they fell back on Moscow, what Simon should see—the Pushkin Museum, the Metro and its palatial stations.

"But first we need to work," Simon said finally.

"Simon Legree," Frank said pleasantly. "You never change. Okay, let's get to it. Come on." He stood up, about to head for the study. "Boris, I'll leave the door open, shall I? In case you want to listen in. He's interested in the process. Of course you're welcome to join us."

Boris made a dismissal sign with his hand, head back in the paper.

"What about you, Jo?" Frank said.

"I've got to pick up a few things for the weekend," she said, getting up too. "What about tonight? Do you want to go to the Aragvi or do you want to be in?"

"Oh, the Aragvi I think. We'll be in all day." He turned to Simon. "Georgian. Shish kebabs."

"And music," Jo said. "Lucky us. Do you have some currency for the *Beryozka*?"

"Not much." He took out his wallet. "I'm waiting for a fat check from my American publisher," he said, smiling at Simon. "Try the Gastronom first. They'll probably have everything you need." Then, catching her glance, "But just in case." He handed over some bills. "I hope we're not going to have a house full of people. We don't want to share Simon so soon."

"Just Marzena. Maybe the Rubins. Hannah wasn't sure."

"Saul Rubin?" Simon said, a headline name.

"Mm," Frank said, smiling. "The man who threatened the very existence of the Free World. To hear Winchell tell it anyway. Stamp collector. Like FDR. Not so easy here, since nobody writes him. He'll probably ask you to send some, but once you start—"

"Work hard," Joanna said, turning to go. No kiss good-bye. "Just ask yourself, what would Suslov say?"

"Who?" Simon said.

"Head of the International Department of the Central Committee. Party theoretician."

"Another okay? I thought it was just the Service–"

"Don't worry. Only to publish here. Then you'd need his approval. We're all right. Come on. I've got the Latvians. Have a look and see what you think," he said, leading Simon into the study. Boris turned a page of the newspaper, not even looking up.

The living room had faced the little park Simon had seen outside, but the study window looked west toward one of the Stalin skyscrapers.

"After a while you get used to them," Frank said, noticing Simon looking out. "That's the Foreign Ministry. Down near Smolenskaya. You have to hand it to him–he knew what he liked."

Simon glanced around. Another room of books. A big desk and a reading chair, no traces of Richie, no hanging pennant or single bed with a Navajo blanket, pieces of sports equipment. Whatever had been here had been taken away.

"Here, your Latvians." He handed Simon a sheaf of paper.

"Already? You did this last night?"

"No. I just fixed up the section from my debriefing. See if it works. It should. Everything's there–well, everything was there. I had to nip and tuck."

"Your debriefing?"

"I spent my first year here–almost two–being debriefed. Write down everything you know. Everything. So, my memoirs, in a way. That's why, last year, when the Service suggested it, I thought, well, I've already written the book. All I have to do is take out the names, do a little brushwork. Hope that doesn't bother you."

"What?"

"Publishing a KGB debriefing. That's what most of it is really, the book. My debriefing. A first for Keating, I'll bet." Said with a twinkle in his eye, having fun. "Take that chair. You'll be more comfortable. I'll have another look at the escape chapter. You had a question about that?"

"You said you got a phone call. So who was it?"

"Well, I can't tell you that."

"You mean he's still there?" Simon said, feeling uneasy, drawn into it, protecting someone.

"What does it matter who? I got a call. 'Now.' So I moved. And I got out. If Pirie put two and two together he could probably figure out who—at least where he was, who had access—but since he hasn't, I'm not going to tell him now. Do we need it?"

"It's the best part of the book, getting to Mexico. Like a movie."

"With the Bureau nipping at my heels. So does it matter who's on the phone? You just want to see what happens. If I make it." He sat back. "I was lucky. I admit it."

"And you were tipped off."

He looked at Simon. "I can't, Jimbo." He paused. "So how about the Latvians?"

Simon started to read. It was all here, the joint project with the Brits, meetings they'd both attended, moments from his own life, but seen now from the other end of the table, Frank's side of the looking glass. The plan details, copied and passed on. The Latvian recruits, the list of names. The meeting with Frank's control. Getting the signal that the mission had started out. The landing at night. The radio transmission suddenly cut. The frantic attempts to make contact, already knowing it was too late.

Simon looked up. "You don't say what happened to them."

Frank stared back at him. "The whole pound of flesh? But as a matter of fact none of us knew. I'm just writing what happened at the time. I wasn't there, in lovely old Riga."

"But you do know. Now."

Frank said nothing for a minute, his eyes on Simon. Finally, he reached for a cigarette. "All right, how about this? 'As for the Latvians, we never knew what happened to them. But I can make an educated guess.'" He lit the cigarette. "Does that make me a big enough shit?"

Simon held his gaze for a moment then started to write. Outside, Boris turned another page, not glancing in their direction, maybe not really listening either.

"No regrets?" Simon said, still writing. "You led them into–"

"We've been through this," Frank said. "They knew the risks."

"They didn't know it was rigged."

A silence so long that Boris looked over to see what was wrong.

"I'm not sure what you mean by this note," Frank said, pointing to the page in front of him, moving on. "Here, pull up a desk chair and we can go through it together. Your handwriting–it's like a doctor's these days. I need a translator."

Simon put the Latvian chapter down and went behind the desk, pulling up a chair next to Frank.

"That's better. Like old times," Frank said. "You still circle things?"

"I don't get to do much editing these days."

"Now that you're a plutocrat. Buying off the rack at Altman's."

"What it *says*," Simon said, pointing to the question, "is 'what after Spain?' You tell us you're recruited there–you even tell us by whom, for a change."

"He's dead."

"And then you go back home and it's fuzzy until you join the OSS."

"Well, it was fuzzy in real life. The Service knows how to play a long game. I kept thinking they were going to drop me. I'd meet with my control and I'd have nothing to tell him. But they hung on. Then Wild Bill fell into my lap–or I guess I fell into his–and we were off and running."

"You don't say how you fell into it."

"You know how it happened. All Pa had to do was make a call. Which I didn't think made anybody look good, so I left it out."

"With everything else. Before Spain. Don't you think a brief sketch—?"

"What, family history? The old Brahmin stock? Like something out of Marquand. You know I met him? During the war. He was at OWI, doing God knows what. I never got a thing out of him. I wonder what he thought later. Anyway, it doesn't explain anything, all the Yankee stuff. This is *My Secret Life*. If we go with that title. That begins in Spain. You know what it felt like? Years you're looking through a kaleidoscope, everything mixed up. And then one turn and all the pieces fall into place. Everything makes sense. The way things are. The way they should be. That's where it began. Before that didn't matter."

"So one turn and you're a Russian spy."

"Spy. That's somebody looking through peepholes. Like a house detective. I was an agent. Of the Party. The Service." He looked over. "I still am. Is that so hard to understand?"

"You'd make it a lot easier if you told people who you were before, why everything clicked into place in Spain."

Frank was quiet for a minute. "Maybe. But I can't do it. Do that to him. It would kill him, being in the book. As far as he's concerned, I'm not here. His son died during the war. Waving the Stars and Stripes. Anyway, he's not part of the story, any of it. That starts with Spain. My secret life."

Simon looked at him for a second, then turned the page. "Well, think about it."

"Is that a way of saying 'all right' without saying 'all right'?"

"It's a way of saying 'think about it.'"

"Stubborn."

"Anyway, what do you mean, if we go with that? You having second thoughts about the title? What's wrong with *My Secret Life*?"

"I don't know. It sounds like one of those articles in *Confidential*. The love child I won't acknowledge. The benders. You know. What do you think of *The Third Department*?"

"What does it mean?"

"It's where I worked. The Third Department of the First Chief Directorate. In charge of intelligence operations against the West. It's in the book. Don't you remember?"

"My eyes probably slid right over it. So will the reader's. Keep the love child."

Frank smiled. "The siren call of the dollar."

"We can call Chapter 2 'The Third Department.' That's where you begin working for them. During the fuzzy period."

"But it was fuzzy. Do you think there's something I'm not telling you?"

"Well, there we are in Spain. And you meet Paul on the road to Damascus—or Barcelona or wherever it was. The conversion. But we don't tell anybody about it. The opposite. We don't join the Party. We don't go to meetings. We go to the other side. Except we're still meeting someone on a park bench every once in a while. Was it a park bench, by the way?"

"It varied," Frank said, enjoying this. "The seals at the zoo. Like that."

"And what would we say? Nothing, you say now. Nothing until the war. Then there's lots to say. But that's a few years. When things were fuzzy. And the Service is happy to wait."

Frank nodded. "They know how to do that. Be patient. It's one of their strengths."

"So you just gab about this and that. The state of the world. And watch the seals."

"More or less." He looked over. "Why? What do you think we talked about?"

Simon said nothing.

"You must have an idea or you wouldn't have brought it up. So, what?"

Simon looked toward Boris, still reading the paper, then met Frank's eyes.

"I think you were talking about Pa. His friends in the administration. Maybe what they were like. Maybe more if you happened to come across something. I think you were spying on him."

For a minute there was no sound but the clock, Frank's face ticking over with it, as if he were trying on responses, see which one would keep the mechanism going.

"That's a hell of a thing to say," he said finally, voice low.

"Is it true?"

"No. I never talked to my control about Pa. Why would we? He was out of government by that time anyway." He paused. "We never talked about him."

"I'm glad."

"But you thought I did. Or might have. You really think I would do that?"

"I never thought you'd do what you did to the Latvians, but you did." He held up his hand. "I know, they had it coming. I'm just saying I don't know what you did. Except what's in the book," he said, touching the pages. "Which I assume is true, more or less?"

"More or less."

"I don't mind you covering your tracks. Everybody does that. But I don't want to publish lies either. Be a mimeograph machine for the KGB. So I need to ask questions."

"About Pa."

"You're in law school, then here and there in Washington, very junior. Pa knows Morgenthau, Hopkins even. Who else was there to talk about?"

"You really want to know? We talked about my friends. People we might bring along. They already had people to tell them about Morgenthau. I was talent spotting the future. Little acorns with promise. I doubt they got much out of it. But it kept me busy. And it kept me compromised. Reporting on my friends. So after a while the only friend you really have, the only one you haven't–spied on–is your control. That's the way it works. I'm not saying they were wrong. They played me. But I wanted to be played. We both got what we wanted. But I never talked about Pa. Or do you think this was worse?"

For a second Simon imagined himself on Frank's shoulder, about to whisper the right thing in his ear. Whatever that was.

"I guess that would depend on what you said."

"Not much," Frank said easily. "Which means there's not much to say now either. So fill in the blanks with me learning the ropes. How the meetings were arranged. Dead drops. The tricks of the trade. And then we're in the OSS and now it matters, what I'm saying on the park bench. And we tell them. Beginning of story."

Simon nodded, a tactical retreat. "So all that time they were just waiting– for something to happen to you?"

"And it did. I told you they know how to wait." He took out a cigarette and lit it. "And they knew something would. I was–well placed. It's touching the faith they have in that. Got it from the English, I think. It worked that way there, so why not with us? Capitalists being all alike. And they weren't far wrong, were they? One phone call."

"Which they told you to make. Or have Pa make."

Frank took a second, looking at him. "They didn't tell me to make it. They suggested it would be very valuable if they had someone there. On the inside. So I took the hint." He paused. "I asked him to make the call."

"To plant a Soviet—"

"I think you're making this worse than it was. Yes, I worked for the Soviets. No, he didn't know. And neither, God knows, did Bill. But what harm did it do in the end? We were on the same side. We just didn't like telling the Soviets what we were up to. So I did. And probably a good thing. They'd know they didn't have to worry about us. They do worry, they're suspicious, it's their history. But everything was about the Germans. Not them. Not then, anyway." He looked away, tapping ash off his cigarette. "So I asked him to make a call. He thought he was giving me a leg up. In my career. And he was. Just not the one he thought. I did a good job for Bill, you know."

"I know."

"So where was the harm? Look at Ray. Evan. Who made calls for them? They probably did more damage than I ever did. They thought it was still Friday night at the Porc. Fun and games."

"They weren't passing documents."

"No," Frank said, stubbing out the cigarette. "So where were we? What was the question?"

"How you felt asking Pa to do it. Knowing—"

"Was that the question? I don't remember you asking that."

Frank got up and went over to the window, looking out to the back courtyard, Stalin's high-rise in the distance.

"You know, it's good, you playing devil's advocate. Good for the book, I mean. Push-pull. But it's not always going to be what you want to hear. You want me to say I had mixed feelings—using Pa. Deceiving him. Maybe I should have. But I didn't. Not for a minute. They needed someone inside. There was an old boy network ready to put me there. I used it. Not a qualm. I was fighting to keep a system alive. Something I believed in. I didn't have time for– So I did it. There was a war on. Things were different later. But the OSS chapter? You want me to be sorry or—what? feel guilty? I didn't." He stopped, then turned to face Simon. "Not then. So let's keep Francis Weeks Senior out of this, shall we? He wasn't in it. Anyway, why complicate things? How many chapters like this do we have? All the Rough Rider stuff. I thought maybe we could use 'Wild Bill' as a chapter title. What do you think?"

Asking something else, an odd truce.

"Perfect," Simon said with a slight nod.

"A vote of enthusiasm," Frank said with a smile.

"No, it's fine. Bill's always good copy. You're right about the chapter. Once we get you in, everything just sails along." He looked up. "So let's move on."

"Do you want a break?"

"No, let's get through the OSS anyway. See if we can finish this week."

"Listen to you. You've just arrived and you're halfway out the door."

"I have a business to run. We're publishing a few other books this year too."

"Not like this," Frank said, putting his hand on the manuscript.

"That's what every author thinks."

Frank dipped his head. "I'm just being greedy. Having you here. But we want to get it right, don't we? Anyway, I thought you might want to see something of the place, as long as you're here. How many times are you likely to come? I thought we could go up to Leningrad. St. Petersburg as was. Would that interest you?"

"What?" Simon said, surprised.

"A shame to leave without seeing the Hermitage. Of course we'd need to get permission, but that shouldn't be too hard to arrange. There's an overnight train. All the comforts. Better than a Pullman."

Simon was staring at him now. Frank had turned away, not

looking at him, his voice pitched somewhere else, to Boris, to whoever was listening in the walls. When he finally met Simon's eyes, the question in them, he said, "Jo would like it, I know," keeping his voice even, and Simon understood that for some reason he was meant to go along, play to the unseen galleries.

"Well, the Hermitage–" he said, neutral.

"After we finish. A kind of treat. Unless you really have to go back," Frank said, eyes steady.

"Let's see how we do. The Hermitage." Being persuaded.

"Of course there's lots to see in Moscow. All work and no play. After we finish this we'll take a walk. It's so nice out. We could have a picnic. What do you say, Boris?" he said, raising his voice, as if Boris had been out of range before.

"A walk is good. For the mind."

"If Ludmilla were here, she'd make sandwiches. There's some salami. But we can pick something up."

"I can make," Boris said.

"That's okay."

"Pickles?" Boris said, paying no attention.

Frank opened his hands, a conceding gesture.

They were another hour, then left by the far end of the courtyard, a passageway leading out to the Garden Ring.

"We'll make a little circle," Frank said, turning left.

Simon moved closer to him. "Leningrad?"

"Well, it's an idea," Frank said, dropping it.

Boris, carrying a string bag, walked with them and not with them, a few steps behind, a courtier's distance. When they rounded a curve in the road, another Stalin skyscraper came into view, closer than the one they could see from the study window.

"Kudrinskaya," Frank said. "That one's apartments. Pilots."

"Pilots?"

"Housing authority likes to bunch people together. I don't know why. Maybe they think it gives them something to talk about in the elevator. Anyway, lots of air ministry people. American embassy's just down from there, past the square. I suppose you'll have to check in?" Another veiled glance, his voice pitched to Boris.

"At some point," Simon said vaguely, waiting for a cue.

"We'll have Boris fix you up with a lift. Right, Boris? But it's just down there, if you want to walk. Ugliest building in Moscow. And that's a hard contest to win."

They were almost at the square when Frank pointed to a two-story house on their left. Faded pink plaster, a side entrance through a gate.

"Take a look. Chekhov's house. Where he used to see his patients. There's really nothing much left, but it's his house, so at least they won't tear it down. Put up something else."

They turned down Malaya Nikitskaya and walked to the end of the block. Another house, this one pale blue, partly hidden by a high wall. "Beria's house," Frank said. "They say this is where he brought the little girls. Eight years old. Nine. Nobody said a word. You wonder if the neighbors heard anything."

Boris said something to Frank in Russian.

"Boris doesn't approve. Bringing you here. Raking up the past. So, on to better times. We'll swing back this way," he said, leading them down the side street. "But imagine. Chekhov, Beria. Just one block away. You wouldn't see that anywhere else."

"You wouldn't have Beria anywhere else."

"Yes, you would," Frank said calmly. "Lots of variations on that theme. He just had a longer run than most of them. A monster. But he gave Stalin his bomb."

"He had help."

"Not from me, if that's what you're asking. The Service, yes. We gained a few years. A matter of time, that's all, not science. But Stalin couldn't wait. That's all he could think about then. The bomb. When? We had to have it."

"And now you do. Pointing right at us."

"Well, it takes two, Jimbo. Somebody puts a gun to your head, you better put one to his." He paused, glancing toward Boris. "Anyway, he got it. And that bought Beria a little time. And then, once Stalin was gone—" He let the thought complete itself. "Everything ends sooner or later. Even Beria."

They were coming up to the park Simon had passed in the car, the long rectangular pool bordered by allées of linden trees.

"Patriarch's Pond. There used to be more, three of them, I think. But now just this. Beautiful, isn't it? I think it's my favorite place in Moscow. I come here and sit—read, if the weather's nice."

"With Boris?"

"Oh, Boris isn't always around. He's just making sure of you. That you're on the up-and-up."

"As opposed to what?"

"I'll be right back."

He huddled for a minute with Boris, who moved off in the direction of the playground, still carrying the string bag with lunch.

"I said we'd meet him on the bench near old Krylov," Frank said, indicating a big bronze statue.

"Who?"

"Children's stories. A kind of Russian Aesop. What a lot you don't know. He can keep an eye on us from there, so he'll sit tight. And we can talk."

"It's like having a nanny."

"Oh, don't underestimate Boris. Political officer during the war. At the front. Pure steel. They say the troops were more afraid of them than the Nazis."

"The bayonet behind you. Still hard to believe they'd do that. To their own people. While the war's–"

"Nobody deserted. It was a different time." He caught Simon's look, but ignored it. "Come on. We don't have long. Just a walk around the pond."

"What did you tell him?"

"That I wanted to talk to you about Jo. It embarrasses him, anything personal. So we have a little time. It'll get better, once you're familiar to him. Sometimes I go off, pick up the mail or something. As long as he knows where I am. Where I'm supposed to be. Play up the Moscow angle, by the way. That you want to see things. So you'll have an excuse to be here and there. Different places."

Simon looked at him, puzzled.

"The embassy, for instance. Now he knows you're supposed to report there, so he won't be suspicious when you go."

"And when's that? What's going on?"

"Walk this way. So what did Pirie actually say?"

"What?"

"When he briefed you. We can talk now."

"Frank–"

"He must have said something. An opportunity like this. A perfect chance to make a pitch."

"I don't know what you're talking about. Honestly."

Frank looked at him. "Jesus Christ, he's dumber than I thought. Not even a trial balloon? So somebody else briefed you. Remember everything. Don't write it down. Simon, I helped write that rule book. I know how it works. So what's the offer?"

"The offer?"

"For me. The double cross. They'd have to take a run at it. How could they not? They finally have access to me. Right now. No filters. How can they not at least try?"

"I'm not with them."

"You are as long as you're here. So Pirie didn't talk to you and whoever did had nothing to say to me, is that right?"

Simon nodded.

"Christ."

"I'm not sure I'm following. Why would they ask? You'd refuse. What's the point?"

"Or maybe he isn't as dumb as I think," Frank said, half to himself. "He doesn't want to give me any leverage." Abruptly he changed voices. "But it's a little early for Sochi."

Simon looked up. A woman was passing, a blonde wearing a tight skirt and high heels, the first Simon had seen, an unexpected erotic flash after all the sturdy sandals and shapeless sundresses. She smiled at them, then made a motion with her unlighted cigarette. Frank took out a match and lit it, saying something in Russian as she bent down to the flame. A quick jerk of her head. More Russian, then a kind of sneer before she moved off.

"What was that?"

"What you think."

"In the middle of the day?"

"It's known for it, the pond."

Simon looked around. A few people lying on the sloping banks with their shirts off, or eating in the shade, an Impressionist leisure, not the people in posters with their sleeves rolled up, building dams.

"I thought there wasn't any prostitution in the Soviet Union."

"Or crime," Frank said, distracted, thinking, then shaking his head. "No, he is that dumb. And I'm going to make him a hero. The high point of his career. Such as it is. The last thing he deserves. But sometimes you get lucky. Donald Fucking Pirie."

"What high point?"

"Me."

Simon stopped for a minute, trying to take this in. "You."

"The ultimate catch. And he caught me. And didn't even throw out a net. He'll say he sent you to do it and you might as well go along. You'll both look good. I'll make you a hero too. You were the persuader."

"What did I persuade you to do?" Simon said, watching him, fascinated.

Frank turned to him. "Defect."

Simon stopped, rooted, things suddenly in slow motion around him.

"No, keep walking. Boris will notice. I know, you're surprised. But we don't have much time. I thought you'd be coming with an invitation, but never mind, I'll just invite myself. I still have you. You're the key."

"Me?" Simon said, still trying to absorb this.

"You have a reason to be here. Boris has seen you work. That's why I wanted him there. The perfect cover. I can't contact anybody. I need to send a messenger. And they'll believe you, that it's a real offer."

"What is?"

"To come back."

"Come back," Simon said, as if repeating it would make it real. "Nobody's ever done that. Come back."

Frank nodded. "So nobody here will be expecting it."

"Come back," Simon said again. "Just like that."

"No, not just like that. You know what I mean by the Thirteenth Department?"

"Like the Third?"

"Except they're in charge of retribution. To defectors. The minute I start this, I'm in the crosshairs. Then they track you down. And kill you. As a lesson to the others. That's why we have to arrange a new identity. That has to be part of the deal."

"What makes you think Pirie would do this?"

"You playing devil's advocate again? I'm the biggest defector the Agency ever had. To get me back would be—bigger. Even if I didn't know anything. But I do. I know everything. That's part of what I do here. Train agents who are being sent to the States. How to act, what to say, what would an American do in a given situation. How to be like us."

Simon looked at him, his stomach suddenly queasy.

"I know who's on the ground there. Some of them anyway. And I know who's here. The whole Service organizational chart. Personalities to be filled in at the debriefing. Maybe you don't know what this is worth, but Pirie will. The minute you tell him."

"I tell him?"

"Get word to him. There's somebody at the embassy who can send a smoke signal to him, right? They must have given you a name."

Simon just looked at him.

"Jimbo, it's what I do. I know how this works."

"And why would he believe you? After—"

"Well, that's the point. He'd be suspicious. And careful. And he'd take his own sweet time. But we don't have that kind of time. You're only going to be here for—"

"Me?"

"I can't do this without you. It's got to be while you're here. He may not believe me, but he'll believe you. And just to hurry things up a little, I'm going to give him a—a little something down. Kind of a deposit."

"What kind?" Simon said, suddenly not wanting to hear. The park, the sunny day, had become surreal, swirling slowly around him. The yellow pavilion. People eating ice cream. Maybe overhearing, maybe not a prostitute, the signs in Cyrillic, cipher letters, Frank about to run again, with Simon caught in his slipstream.

"A name. In Washington. To prove I'm for real. Of course, he can just take that and walk away, leave me here, but I'm betting he'll want more. And there is more," he said, as casually as putting a chip down on a table.

Simon stared at him. "A name. One of yours."

"Well," Frank said, unexpectedly thrown by this, embarrassed. "I don't have much of a choice, I have to give them something."

"So first you give the Service us. How many, by the way? Scribbling away for two years. Everybody in the Agency you ever took a piss with? And now you're going to give us them. Your new people. Time now to cash them in too. All these years, whenever I thought about it, what you did, I'd think, well, but he believed in it. Like some religion. Like it is in the book. But it turns out—"

"I do believe in it," Frank said quietly. "I believe it's just, the system. And I believe it's going to win. This doesn't change that. But I'm almost done here. They're going to retire me and what's the difference when you're retired?"

"So cut and run. And throw a bomb behind you on your way out. The way you did last time. I thought this was what you did everything *for*," Simon said, spreading his hand to take in the park, Frank's life.

"It is. But it's a different time. Things are better now. We survived the war. And Stalin. Beria. We survived the Americans, all the loonies flying around with their bombs. We're sending satellites into space. We're catching up. One beat-up old agent switching sides isn't going to bring the house crashing down. If it ever would have. Sometimes I wonder how much any of it mattered. At the time you think—but then you look back and it's gain an inch here, an inch there, but the whole thing really just rolls along whether you're there or not. If I hadn't done any of it, would things be different?" He looked over. "Or maybe I'm just getting older. But I don't think I'll be undermining the future of Communism. Maybe give it a little bump in the road. The Service will recover. Of course, we don't want to say that to Pirie. He thinks it all matters, he has to, that's why he gets up every day. And now we can hand it to him on a platter, the club he's been looking for. To beat the Service with."

"And you'd give that to him."

"I'd have to. None of this comes free. Immunity from prosecution. Actually, there was never any evidence against me, anything they could use, so that's a moot point."

"Other than turning up in Moscow."

"But a new identity," Frank said, not stopping. "That won't be cheap. Expenses. The exfiltration."

"The exfiltration," Simon said, the word itself surreal.

"I can't just book the next Aeroflot out. There have to be arrangements. Don't worry, I've got it all worked out."

"You."

"You don't think I'd leave it to Pirie, do you? Put my life in his hands." He looked up. "This is going to be the tricky part. Getting out. You need a Houdini, somebody who knows how the locks work."

"Like you," Simon said, hearing the bravado in Frank's voice, his next astonishing act.

"And you," Frank said, looking at him. "I'd be putting myself in your hands."

Even the air seemed to stop now, nothing moving at all.

"To get you out," Simon said, so softly that it sounded only half-said.

"I'm very good at what I do, you know. You just take a message. That's all. It's no risk to you." Looking him in the eye as he said it.

"And then what?" Simon said, still softly.

Frank shook his head. "First we put out the line. Then we take it one step at a time, in case—"

"In case it does go wrong. And somebody asks me. With the red light over the door. But no risk to me."

"There won't be. I've been planning it. It can work. Do you think I'd ask you if I thought—?"

He looked over Simon's shoulder. The woman in high heels, circling back around the pond. She smiled at Frank, a tease, exaggerating her hip movements. The rest of the park seemed to come back to life with them, out of Frank's vacuum, people looking up at the sun again, licking ice cream.

"What makes you think I'd do this?" Simon said, no longer in an echo chamber. "Any of it."

Frank nodded, a question he'd been waiting for. "First you'd be doing something for your country. That always has a certain amount of appeal. Like I said, I don't think it'll matter very much in the scheme of things, but the Agency won't think that. They'll think they won the Cold War and you helped. Then there's the book. With a brand-new last chapter. Which I promise to write. Remember when I left? How big a story that was? So think about me coming back. You do the numbers. If Keating counts that high. You'll even be the hero of the piece, if you want to be. I'll do it however you want. If I know the Agency, they'll nickel-and-dime me on the pension, so I'll need the royalties. And no sharing with Mezhdunarodnaya Kniga. Just my own account somewhere. Which I'll help you set up." He stopped, then put his hand on Simon's arm. "Look, this is just talk. Why would you do it? I was hoping you'd do it for me."

"For you."

"It's always been the two of us, hasn't it? I couldn't tell you—what I was doing. You know that. I thought it was for the best, all of it. I didn't think things would end up this way, me walking around Patriarch's Pond—where the hell was that anyway? But they did." He looked up. "I don't want to die here."

"And what do you think it'll be like there?"

"I know what it'll be like. They keep me in a safe house somewhere near the Agency. And we debrief. They don't trust me, they trust me, they don't trust me. Months, longer. I'm not having dinner at Harvey's, I'm not seeing anybody, I'm in jail. With guards, so nobody pops me. They hope. I hope. And when they're finished squeezing the lemon, they send me somewhere as somebody else. Somewhere warm, by the way, would be nice. After here. And then I live there, wondering if anybody back at Langley screws up and slips where I am. Because then I'm Trotsky, waiting for the hatchet in my head. Wondering if anybody recognizes me when I go out to get the mail. Locking the door, making sure. And that's my life. What's left of it."

Simon was quiet for a minute, slowing his steps, the end of the allée just ahead, Boris on a bench somewhere.

"Then why do it?" He looked around, people in the sun. "You're better off here."

"Maybe. But Jo isn't."

"Jo?"

"Why do it? I should have started there, I guess. So it makes sense to you. It's killing her, this place. She'll never get better here. Jesus Christ, a sanitarium in Sochi. Can you imagine what that's like? What it would do to her? So why do it?" He looked directly at Simon. "Because I have to. You know us better than anybody. You were there. Before we were—what we are now. We got through so much—coming here, Richie, we even got through that, but now she's coming apart and I'm just sitting here watching it happen. I can't. She's only here because she followed me. I have to do something. So why? The oldest reason in the book, isn't it? It always comes down to something like this. They teach you that in the Service—look for the Achilles' heel, the soft spot. So, mine. I don't think the Service knows it. They've never tried to use it and they would, that's what they do. Boris thinks I'm annoyed with her. He doesn't see it's eating me up, what's happening. But you know her. How she used to be. And now look. You saw her at the National." Her breath in his ear.

"Why not send her home? Without all the—?"

Frank shook his head quickly. "Even if State gave her a new passport, which they won't, the Soviets would never let her leave. She's my wife. She knows too much—even if she doesn't. They think that way. They'd lose face. So they'd—deal with her."

"Sochi."

"Somewhere. A rest. And she'd never get well." He glanced toward the playground. "There's Boris. So it turns out we *are* talking about Jo. If he asks, say you'll mention the clinic to her. But he won't ask. He listens." He looked at Simon. "Jimbo, I know this is a lot all at once. But you're smart, you get things right away. You'll be a messenger, that's all. It's me. And Jo. I have to get her out. I won't always be here to—"

"What do you mean?"

A quick glance up, caught. "Don't react. Boris will see. I'm sick."

"Sick? What do you mean, sick?"

"Well, Dr. Ziolkowski—who has a gift for words—calls me a walking time bomb. Not very precise, but vivid."

"Jesus, Frank." He lowered his voice, just conversation. "What is it? Cancer?"

"My heart. Don't worry, I'm not going to peg out on the way home. But if anything happens, she'll be here on her own. It's one thing, both of us here. But if she's alone— So if I have to sing for Pirie, I sing. The deal is for two of us. Two."

"Are you sure? The doctor—"

Frank nodded, then looked up. "But Pirie doesn't know about this, understood? He's a prick. He'd just as soon let me rot if he thinks I'm damaged goods. Might die on him."

"Frank—"

"I know. Don't," he said, looking at Simon's face. "I only told you so you'd see why—I need to do this." He stopped, letting his voice linger between them for a second before it drifted away. "I know you. How you worry. But I'll take you step by step. I know how to do this."

"Houdini."

"Nobody'll believe it. That we pulled it off," he said, his voice eager, another Frank scheme, Simon trailing after, his accomplice. "Right under their noses. Even Boris's." He nodded toward him and Boris got up, opening the string bag. "I'll have your back. All the way," Frank said, in a hurry now. "Go to the embassy. Today. Tell whoever it is you want to get a message directly to Pirie. They'll use a secure line that's routed through Vienna. And it is secure. Today."

Simon raised his eyebrows.

"I have to protect both of us now. But I can't risk more than one day. Somebody's bound to wonder. Tell Pirie you want a meeting. And tell him he's right about Kelleher. Try an account at Potomac Trust under Goodman. Got that?"

"That's the name. Kelleher," Simon said, dismayed. Part of it now, one walk around the pond, Frank that sure of him.

Frank nodded. "That's all you have to say. He'll know. Then we wait."

"I'll have to tell them. About the secure line. Now that I know. If I don't, I'll be working for—your people. I won't do that."

Frank shrugged. "We're not working for anybody now. Just us. But if it makes you feel better, fine. You'll still need some way to get to the Agency, though. After tomorrow. Tell them to route a secure line through Stockholm. We don't have anybody working the lines there right now."

"And how would I know that?"

The sides of Frank's mouth began to go up in a grin. "Don't tell them anything. You like to play things close to the vest. Where you got your information. They'll be grateful. People have gotten medals for less," he said, almost jaunty. "Boris, still here? I thought you'd be off with the *shlyukha*. What's the matter? Too expensive? She's just your type. Blonde like that."

"From a bottle," Boris said. "A disgrace, in such a place. With children to see." The family watchdog. Ready to send soldiers to a gulag for making a Stalin joke.

"Well, they won't know what they're looking at. Is that tea?" he said, pointing to a thermos.

"Tea only."

"You see how he looks after me? No spiking the tea if you're working. How's the salami?" he said to Simon.

"Fine," Simon said, taking a bite, wondering if he could do it too, slip into someone else, a quick-change artist, and then he was doing it, talking to Boris and munching on sandwiches as if nothing had been said on the walk, the secret there, his skin warm with it, but unseen. Every look now, every sentence a kind of lie. Without even saying yes, he had become Frank, being careful, hiding in plain sight.

It was Simon's idea to ask Boris to walk him to the embassy, make it a KGB excursion. They left Frank at the pond and went out to the Garden Ring, curving down, not talking, Simon trying not to look over his shoulder, see a black car pulling up behind, the movie scene. And wouldn't they be right? Not just an embassy visit, an act of espionage. Exposing an agent. A show trial, or just a quiet disappearance, Diana asking State to make inquiries. Don't look back. His skin still warm, itchy. When they came to the pedestrian underpass, he felt he was crossing more than a street, Boris waiting behind, outside the range of the surveillance cameras.

The embassy was as ugly as Frank had promised, a custard pile with some graceless decorative brickwork, its roof bristling with antennas. Oddly enough, it reminded Simon of the Lubyanka, the same era and bureaucratic heft. There were Marine guards outside and a high gate blocking the driveway, which swooped around down in back. Not a building, a compound.

DiAngelis's name worked, the indifferent clerk snapping to attention and immediately picking up the phone to call someone down, all the while staring with curiosity. Simon, still nervous, looked away, fixing instead on the framed picture of Kennedy behind the desk. In minutes, a man was coming toward them off the elevator.

"Weeks? Mike Novikov," he said, presumably an immigrant son but as American as his crew cut. Simon thought of Boris, standing across the street, hair shorter but similar, another doubling effect, like the buildings.

"We're on six," Novikov said, pushing the elevator button. "Everything all right?"

"Fine. Just wanted to report in. Is the Vienna line open?" Breezy, confident, the way Frank would have played it.

Novikov nodded, a knowing military respect, Simon now a fellow cold warrior, DiAngelis's man.

"Did you make contact? With your brother?"

Simon nodded. "We've already started. On the book. No problems."

"Is he—? Excuse me. Just curious."

"Is he what?"

"Still—active. We haven't been able to get a bead on that. Whether he's retired. He doesn't go to the office."

"Really?" Something Simon hadn't known. "I think he keeps his hand in, though," he said, covering. "Training agents, for one thing. He mentioned that. The ones going to the States. How to act."

"Christ. We should have done something about him years ago."

Simon looked over, startled.

"Sorry," Novikov said, embarrassed.

"Not so easy in Moscow," Simon said, letting it go.

"No. Not the way things are."

Meaning what? The KGB presence or hands-off rules from Langley?

"Our new best friends," Novikov said.

"And all ears," Simon said, looking up. "We'll need to send this in code. You have a–?" What was it called?

"All set up," Novikov said, cutting him off. "This way."

He led Simon past two desks crammed into a corridor-wide space, then into a windowless room.

"We can talk here. We sweep for bugs every other day, so it's about as safe as you can get. You want to cable DiAngelis?"

"Pirie, actually. Eyes only. But I suppose that would have to go through DiAngelis anyway," Simon said, guessing.

"From here, yes. I can set you up. Not much traffic today. I assume you want to send it yourself."

"Please," Simon said. "Pirie's orders. Not my idea."

"No, that's right. If you learn anything at this station, it's 'be careful.' Even in the building." He looked round at the bunker-like room. "Except here. This way. I'll just put in the routing codes for you, then leave you to it."

"Thanks," Simon said, following him into a small room with what looked like a jerry-built Teletype machine, its keyboard connected by wires to a big console behind. "By the way, have somebody check this line tomorrow. At the Vienna end. You might think about routing an alternative line through Stockholm."

Novikov looked at him, suddenly conspiratorial. "This information good?"

Was it? He imagined Frank having puckish fun snarling the Agency's communications, pulling connector plugs out of an old switchboard. What if none of it was true, another feint to confuse the enemy? Except they weren't the enemy anymore, or wouldn't be.

"Check it and see," Simon said, in the part now. "Tomorrow. We're all right today."

"That's pretty precise," Novikov said, fishing.

"Or the next day. Keep checking."

Novikov dipped his head, backing off, a kind of salute. "I'll just set you up."

And in minutes it was done, everything Frank had asked him to do, Kelleher's name typed into the machine like a judge's sentence. And why not? If Frank had the name, he was one of theirs, burrowing in. But Simon's fingers stopped for a second anyway. Not just judge, executioner. One click. Now the bank account name, the evidence. A few more clicks. And Kelleher was gone, a game piece wiped off the board. Wondering if he'd given himself away or—

"All done?"

"That'll do it. Thanks. I'd better run. I'm just supposed to be checking in with the visa section."

"You have an exit date yet?" Agencyspeak.

"Not yet."

"You don't want to overstay the visa. That's always trouble," Novikov said, walking him to the elevator.

"Even when the KGB's sponsoring you?"

"Officially you're a guest of the Writers' Union. KGB have a funny way of disappearing when you need them. Who me? So I'd keep the visa date. Be on the safe side. Here we are," he said, opening the elevator door. "Thank you, by the way. For the information. Appreciate it."

"One for our side," Simon said, nodding a good-bye, then heading past the Marine guard to the broad street, where Boris waited, on the other side.

3

THE ARAGVI WAS IN THE HOTEL DRESDEN, just a few blocks up from the National, but Boris had sent a car anyway, part of the Service cocoon.

"Dolgoruky," the driver said, pointing to the equestrian statue in the square fronting the hotel.

Simon just bobbed his head, something everybody knew, and stepped out into the soft spring air, the sky still light. After the hulking apartment buildings on Gorky Street, the Dresden seemed as sensuous and baroque as its namesake city, topped with an elaborate cornice of carved fruits. Frank and Jo were already at the table, pouring vodka.

"Who's Dolgoruky? Outside, on the horse," Simon said.

"Founder of Moscow," Frank said.

"That's who it is? I always wondered," Jo said. "I must have passed it a thousand times. Don't I get a hello?"

Simon bent down. "Still the prettiest girl in the room," he said, kissing her on the cheek.

"This room," she said.

She had dressed for an evening out, lipstick and earrings, a brooch, cheeks pink with blush.

"We've already started," Frank said, "so better catch up."

He poured out a glass for Simon, then took a drink from his own, his eyes shiny, and Simon realized, something he hadn't seen last night, that they drank together. He had somehow imagined Jo off by herself, melancholy, not clinking glasses as she was now, both of them loose, the way it must have started.

"Catch up and overtake," Frank said. "That used to be the slogan, remember? Catch up and overtake. The West. In industry. Production."

"Oh, don't start," Jo said, but pleasantly. "Another five-year plan. How about five years of gossip? Tell," she said to Simon. "Don't be discreet. Nobody here gives a damn anyway. So busy catching up."

"But not yet overtaking," Simon said and smiled. "Who do you want to know about?"

"You. Tell me about you. All the gossip."

He shook his head. "No gossip. That I know of. I'm boring. Editorial meetings on Mondays. Lunch at the Century. Book parties. Canapés passed twice. No shrimp. California wine. The author usually makes a pass at somebody. I make a toast. Then we all go somewhere like this," he said, looking around. "Except French."

"I think it sounds wonderful," Jo said.

"You wouldn't if you had one every week."

"So why do it?" Frank said.

"To get something in the columns. Sullivan. Lyons. One of them. Put the book out there somehow."

"*My Secret Life?*"

"Well, probably not. No party without the author. And you have to feed them if you want a mention."

"Winchell will mention you," Jo said. "Winchell hates Frank," she said to Simon. "Hates him."

"I know."

"Course you do. I forgot. You were there. " She looked down at her glass, then brightened, determined to enjoy the evening. "Anyway it doesn't sound boring to me. It sounds—distinguished." She reached up and touched his glasses. "Who would have thought? A man of letters. Do you meet people? You know, Hemingway, people like that?"

"Yes, but not the way you think. Business. Not table hopping at the Stork."

"So how do you do it?" Frank said. "Put the book out there?"

"In your case? You're a news story. Everybody will want to take a swing at it. Reviews. Off-the-book-page pieces. Editorials. We don't have to worry about coverage with you."

"Just what they'll say," Jo said.

"They've already said it," Frank said, touching her hand. "We're used to all that."

She moved her hand, not making a point, but moving it. "You are."

"Anyway, we won't see any of it. Not unless Jimbo sends the clippings. Will you do that? I'd be curious, what people say now. Whether anything's changed."

Simon looked at him. But he'd be there.

"Sure. If you'd like," he said, feeling back at lunch with Boris, playing a part. What it must have been like for Frank all those years. Every meal a performance. Saying one thing, knowing another. Something no one else knew. The meetings with the Brits, the only one at the table who knew. Enjoying himself, the sheer technical skill of it, the way a juggler takes pleasure just keeping things in the air.

"I don't want to see them," Jo said. "Go through all that again. How terrible you are. And what does that make me? Ah, finally," she said, seeing the waiter. "If I keep filling up with cheese bread, I won't have room for anything else."

"Cheese bread?"

"A Georgian specialty. Very good here," Frank said, taking a menu from the waiter.

Simon looked at his. Cyrillic. Across the room, waiters in Georgian clothes were carrying kebabs and platters of rice, trays of vodka glasses for the long, full tables. Who were they all? Intourist groups? Party officials? Who went to restaurants in Moscow? He'd imagined them all like workers' canteens, with surly resentful waiters. But here at the Aragvi, men in white shirts and tunics slipped like dancers between the tables, popping corks and sliding meat off skewers. He looked at the Cyrillic again. Like an eye chart he couldn't make out.

"You order," he said to Frank. "You know what I like."

Frank said something in Russian to the waiter, who nodded and started collecting the menus. "How did it go at the embassy?" he said smoothly, the other Frank now.

"Fine. They saw me right away."

"What did they want?" Jo said.

"Nothing. They like you to check in, that's all." The other Simon.

"Maybe they're afraid you'll go over the fence. Once you see how wonderful it is." She took another drink.

"More like a French hotel, I think," he said lightly. "Keep track of the passports."

"A French hotel," Jo said, smiling at the idea. "Remember those keys, with the tassels? It's true, they were always asking for your passport."

"The police keep a record."

"I wonder if I'm still on an index card somewhere. Still suspect."

"A dangerous character."

"And you'd never think it to look at her, would you?" she said.

"No. You never would."

"Hoover would. A file this high, I'll bet," she said, raising her hand. "Well, never mind. Tell me about Diana. It's so good to see you," she said, taking his hand, sentimental. "Do you know what I miss? When we all used to go out. Remember? When we went dancing. I used to love that."

"Yes. You did," Simon said. Her hair swinging behind her.

"The last time—well, I suppose we were still in the States. Nobody dances here. Remember Natasha in *War and Peace*? When she dances to that Russian song? It's supposed to be a symbol of Russia. According to Professor Davis. Turns out she was the last one. I don't think anyone's danced since."

"And the Bolshoi?" Frank said.

"Oh, the Bolshoi."

"Is that Boris?" Simon said, spotting him at the door. "I thought he had the night off."

"He does," Frank said, putting his napkin down, ready to get up.

"What do you think he does? Off duty?" Jo said. "I can't imagine. Actually, I like Boris. He's all right. In his very peculiar way."

"I'd better go see," Frank said, leaving.

"He puts in a full day," Simon said.

"He's devoted to Frank." She smiled to herself. "That's one way of putting it. But I think he is, really. I used to think he was just a—I don't know, guard. But it's not that. He looks out for Frank."

"And you?"

"Me? I look out for myself. Doing a wonderful job too." She turned to him. "Tell me something. I'd like to know. Are you happy?"

"Happy?" he said, surprised, thrown by the question. "I don't know. I never thought about it. Not like that. I suppose so."

"You must be, if you never think about it." She took out a cigarette. "I notice you don't ask me if I am. Too late," she said quickly, stopping him before he could speak. "Besides, what could I say? No? Yes? Would it make any difference?"

"I'd like to think you were," he said, lighting the cigarette for her. "Think of you that way."

"I was. For a while. Even here. It's funny, you don't know it when you are. Just when you're not. I never blamed Frank. I came because—I was his wife. We had a child. And things were the way they were then. In the States. How horrible people were. Calling you names. In front of your child. To tell you the truth, I thought Frank was half-right. Not the spying half. I'm not making excuses for him. But I thought his reasons— Well, it was another time. The thing is, I was in love with him. You know."

"Yes."

"Think how easy if it had been someone else." She smiled faintly at him.

"But it wasn't."

"No. So here we are. It was nice, though. You were nice. And what a thing you had for me," she said, playing.

"Jo—"

"I know. Asking my old beaux to flatter me, tell me I'm still— God, how embarrassing. Who's the fairest in the land? You are." She looked at her drink. "You know, when I heard you were coming, I thought, he's coming to rescue me. I actually thought that. Then I saw your face last night. When you saw me. It's different for men, isn't it? You get older and nobody thinks anything of it. But the ladies— So no rescue this time. Anyway, it's a little late. Not too many candidates. You were it. But sometimes you like to think—how it might have been."

"There was no might have been. It was never me."

She looked at him, then rubbed out the cigarette. "And I made my bed. So to speak. And now I get to lie in it. Do something for me, though? For old times' sake? Tell them we're happy. Frank and me. I don't want to give them the satisfaction of–"

"Who?"

"Whoever you're talking to at the embassy. Nobody goes to get his visa checked. That's something the Russians do, not us. So you must be talking to somebody. What do they want to know? What we have for breakfast? How many drinks at night? I never thought it would be you doing that–" She shrugged. "Spying on us. But I suppose you didn't have a choice. Imagine what you could pick up, all day in the flat. All the little details they like for the files. Although I can't imagine what for. At this late date. But it's what they do. So tell them we're happy, would you? It can't matter to anybody anymore. Except me."

"I'm not spying on you. I'm just here to get the book–"

"Then why go to the embassy? It's not a French hotel. They're not checking passports."

Well, why?

"Don't lie to me. Please. Everybody lies to me. Not you. I couldn't take that, not you too."

"All right. I promised I'd report in." Trying it, keeping the balls in the air.

"Report in."

"Not like that. Not about you. They just want to know if I get approached."

"Approached?"

"By the KGB."

"They *are* the KGB. Boris and Frank."

"Anyone else."

"And were you? Approached?"

"How? I was with Frank all day. They're just suspicious, that's all. They can't figure out why the KGB is letting the book happen. Whether there's something else going on. So they want to know who sees me. Who says what. Not you." He paused. "Not you." Said easily, almost second nature now.

"But they've already seen the book. So what—?"

"I didn't say it made any sense. They just want to know if anyone makes contact."

"The usual way that happens is a lady in the bar at the Metropol."

"Yes? That's something to look forward to, then."

"Mm. Those pictures you didn't know they were taking. And the next thing you know, you're—"

"Working for Frank. Is that the way he plans to recruit me?"

"It's not funny, though. They do that." She refilled her vodka glass. "Well, maybe a little bit funny," she said, almost giggling. "I think it would be more ideological with Frank. Anyway, he doesn't do that. I guess. Who would he meet? To recruit. We're not allowed to see anybody. Except the others in the Service. Maybe they're afraid somebody'll try to recruit *us*." She lifted her glass. "Smoke and mirrors. They think everybody's like them. So I don't think he's in the recruiting business. I don't know what he does exactly. He's always home. Not that he ever went in much. It makes them nervous, foreigners at headquarters."

"Their foreigners."

"Still foreigners." She looked down. "Frank said people were coming to take pictures."

Simon nodded. "From *Look*."

"To see how we live. Instead of a jail cell. I'd better get Ludmilla to tidy up. Put a good face on things. Cover that hole in the carpet. God. This wasn't your doing, was it?"

"It was part of the deal. First serial excerpt."

"What's that mean?"

"Magazine runs a piece of the book before it comes out. They like to run pictures with it. So—"

"So open house on Yermolaevskiy Street. Smile for the camera."

"You don't have to, if you'd rather not."

"You mean only Frank has to. They don't care what's happened to me."

"I just meant—"

"I know. But I must have a certain curiosity value. We'd want to do right by *Look*. Just give me fair warning, will you? I'd have to get my hair done. After a certain age, it's all about hair." She picked up a spoon and turned it over, hesitant. "Simon, do people think I helped him? That I did it too?"

"Some people."

"You?"

"No."

"But you wondered. Everybody did. How could I not have known? His wife. Sometimes I wonder myself. But you weren't supposed to ask. During the war. If things were secret. So I didn't."

"We can put it in the book if you want. Clear it up once and for all."

"Who'd believe Frank? He'd lie to protect me." She took a drink. "The least he could so. Considering. No. Keep Carrie Porter guessing. Who cares?" She glanced around the room. "They don't care. They don't even know who Frank is. See, here he comes and nobody even notices. Now what? He looks like the cat who swallowed the cream. What did Boris want?" she asked him, back at the table.

"Something at the office," he said, then looked at Simon, pleased with himself. "One of our people overseas."

Simon raised an eyebrow, another conversation without words.

"What happened?" Jo said. "Do you have to go?"

"No, no. Just a general APB for the Department. They could have waited until tomorrow but people like to know things. Makes them feel important." His voice unconcerned, nothing to do with him.

Simon stared at him, imagining the scurrying at the Lubyanka, cables landing on desks, worried phone calls, an agent betrayed, the balls moving faster in the air.

"Shall we have some wine?" Frank said, looking at him again.

They had two bottles, a rough Georgian red that went well with the lamb and made Simon's face feel hot. They talked about Moscow, other restaurants, and the weekend, Boris's office crisis put aside. Except by Simon, who kept calculating time zones, how many hours it had taken for Pirie to move, the surprising speed a kind of vote of confidence in Frank. Kelleher now in a room somewhere, wondering how much they knew. Put there by a few clicks of a keyboard. His. And for a moment he wondered how he should feel about that, which of his selves to ask. Something Frank had learned years ago.

There was sticky phyllo pastry for dessert, then thick Turkish coffee, an endless meal. It was only after they ordered brandy and Jo excused herself to go to the ladies' that Frank and Simon could use their real voices.

"So he bit," Simon said.

"Right away too. I thought he'd sniff around for a while, but no, just snatched it off the line. Maybe Don's getting decisive in his old age. So. Let's see what it buys us."

"Jo doesn't know," Simon said.

"Not yet. Nobody," he said. "I told you, we have to do this right. Not even a hint."

"Was that all Boris wanted? You'd think the Service would want to keep it to themselves."

Frank looked over at him, appreciative. "You might have potential. No, that wasn't all. In time-honored fashion, they've already begun an investigation. Desks upside down, all of it. Boris wanted me to know. No surprises."

"They suspect you?"

"No, no. I had nothing to do with Kelleher. I knew who he was, but so did other people in the department. First you work on his control, then you move out from there. By the time they get to me I'll be—well, that's the plan anyway."

"But you're the only one with a brother who sent a cable to the Agency."

"Did you? Boris doesn't know that. And he was right there with you. Nobody knows. It was a secure line." He picked up his brandy. "I'm beginning to get the feeling you don't think I know what I'm doing."

"You'd better know."

"Jimbo," he said, making a toasting gesture with his glass, "I'm famous for it. Look, stop worrying. Right now they're hoping against hope he gave himself away, did something stupid. What usually happens. But what if? That would mean one of our people sold him. Which means somebody's been turned. Here or in Washington. What's the logic? It's a lot easier to turn somebody there. And if they've got a rotten apple, the whole barrel— So they'll start there."

"And what if they talk to Boris. About my little trip to the embassy?"

"He was *with* you. It would never occur to him now that you— He thinks you're here about the book."

"I am here about the book."

"You see? An innocent. And you stay that way. No intrigue. No double backing. Getting on and off buses. You never try to shake a tail because you never think anybody might be following. Why would they? Boris can read all the signs and you're not flashing any. Besides, he likes you."

"Me?"

"You're my brother," he said simply, looking across at Simon, another wordless conversation.

"And any brother of yours—?"

Frank took up his glass. "I saved his life."

"Saved it how?"

"His name was on a list. I got it taken off. A while back. When things—" He downed the drink. "God, this stuff takes the lining off, doesn't it? Armenians. They swill it down." He paused, a grimace from the burning brandy. "How did Jo seem to you?"

"All right. It wasn't so bad tonight, the drink."

"You weren't counting. See how her lipstick looks when she comes back."

Simon glanced over at him. Every detail. Watching without watching.

"She said you don't go to the office much anymore."

"Well, they mostly come to me. Nice in the winter. One of the privileges of age."

"Age."

"Seniority. And the book kept me home. All of which plays out nicely for us just now. My name won't be on any cable traffic to Kelleher. No connection."

"Who is he anyway? American?"

Frank nodded.

"Why did—? A true believer?"

"Too young. We were the last of those," he said with a wry smile. "We turned him. Demon rum." He held up the brandy glass. "It's a hell of a weakness. Makes you sloppy about everything. He fell right into a classic honey trap. That usually goes with the booze. So we had him. Never a very happy situation, though. He couldn't stay away from it," Frank said, tapping his glass. "And like I say, he was getting sloppy."

"So throw him over? I thought you said the Service—"

"The Service didn't throw him over. We did."

Simon looked up, Frank's eyes steady on him. "What'll happen to him?" he said, a spasm in his stomach, not the brandy.

"After the debriefing? Depends on whether they want to go public with it. A trial? Twenty years."

"For being bait."

"No, for betraying his country. Don't look like that. He did, you know. For years. So don't waste your sympathy. You should be glad he's caught. America can sleep just that much safer tonight."

"And what does the Service do now?"

"Deny it. It's Washington. You don't want people sent home. An incident. So we never heard of him."

"Or his bank account."

"The piece Don was looking for," Frank said, pleased.

"And if he talks?"

"He will. He's the type. But he won't have enough to buy himself anything. Just his control. Who's probably packing right now."

"So he's on his own."

"With lots of time to contemplate his sins." He looked over. "It was just a matter of time. Don may be an idiot, but once you start sniffing around like that—Kelleher's days were numbered. We just hurried things along a little, that's all. In a good cause."

"And now he'll spend the rest of his life—"

"He should have thought of that when he agreed to work for us."

"Agreed."

Frank brushed this aside. "There's always a choice. He made it." He looked at Simon. "It's not publishing. It's not a gentleman's profession."

Simon said nothing, staring at him, hearing the sounds of the restaurant around them. How long did it take? To become like this?

Frank glanced over, reading his face, then looked down, fingering the glass.

"Would you mind not doing that? That look. You make a choice. He knew that. I knew it. And then you have to—do things. Then more. But I don't want to anymore. Does that surprise you?"

Simon said nothing.

"It wouldn't if you knew. You've just had a taste. Kelleher? Nothing. But after a while it gets harder to live with. The ends justify the means. You have to believe that, to be able to do it. And they do. I still think we're on the right side of history. It's just—in the beginning you don't know about the means. Not all of them. Not until you're in it." He looked at him. "I said it was for Jo. It's for me too. I want out. Don't worry, I'll pay. But I want out." He put his hand on the table, a miming gesture, reaching. "Don't go soft on me, Jimbo. I need you. To make it work."

Simon looked at the hand. Just get up and walk out. Past the Georgian waiters, Dolgoruky on his horse. Their lives, not his, dulled with regret and brandy. And if Frank was caught? On his own, like Kelleher. No, worse. Willing to risk that, a different floor in the Lubyanka. The first step already taken, irrevocable. And then the moment was over and Frank was moving his hand back, smoothing the tablecloth, as if he had just taken a trick.

"You know why Don moved so fast on this?" he said. "I've been thinking. It's because he trusts me. I know, after all the— But we used to work together. You put in years like that and— He hears the bank account and he knows he can trust it. No double-checking. He knows it's right. That kind of trust—that's coin of the realm. Coin of the realm."

"And now?"

"Now they'll want a meeting. They'll want to hear it from me. Coin of the realm or no," he said, a small smile. "I suppose I'd better be disillusioned. That always plays with them. They can't imagine what you saw in it in the first place." He glanced over at Simon. "They'll contact you to set it up. Interesting to see who they send. And then we meet with them."

"We?" Simon said, feeling the spasm again. "I'm the messenger. I sent the message."

"I can't just meet somebody in Gorky Park. You're the cover. We're all over the place, showing you Moscow, looking at this, looking at that. Boris is used to it. Nobody thinks twice. I'm with you."

"And we just happen to run into–?"

Frank nodded. "The most natural thing in the world."

"And when does this happen?"

"That depends on them. They have to send somebody out. To make the deal. But look how fast Don– Soon. So meanwhile we see some sights. Set up a pattern. Do what we'd be doing anyway. How about the Tretyakov tomorrow?"

"You want the meeting there? The art museum?"

Frank shook his head. "No, the Tretyakov wouldn't work. With meetings, there's a kind of–choreography. You have to work out where everybody needs to be. Entrances and exits. There's a flow to it."

"So where?"

"Let them make contact first," Frank said calmly, reassuring. "I'm just being careful. Then nothing goes wrong. For either of us. I'll pick the place. One guy, not a posse. Someone who has the authority. Pity they can't send Don. But everybody in the Service knows that face by now. And I don't see him showing up in a fake nose, do you? He'd never get out of the airport. So somebody else. One meeting. We need to be clear on that. One meeting. Otherwise, we start pushing our luck."

"And if they say no? They're not interested?"

Frank shook his head. "They're not coming all this way to say no."

"Look who I found," Jo said, suddenly next to the table, her voice brighter.

"The bad penny," Gareth said, next to her. "Imagine twice in two days. Even for me. You'll think I'm *stalking*. But I promised, just one brandy and we'll vanish." He made a swooshing motion with his hands.

"One," Jo said. "I know you. One."

"Scout's honor," he said, raising his hand. "Guy, you hear that? We're on our honor."

He stepped aside to make an opening for the man behind him. Simon looked up, surprised. "Guy Burgess," he said. A man whose picture he'd seen for years, forgetting that it was the same picture, young Burgess down from Cambridge, not the bloated figure in front of them. If anything, he was even more slovenly than Gareth, clothes rumpled, his face puffy, the flesh pushing up to his eyes.

He nodded his head, as if they'd been introduced, and unsteadily sank into the chair Gareth had pulled out for him.

"We were out having a few drinks," Gareth was saying. "And Guy wanted to go to the Praga, didn't you, and I thought, I can't face another dumpling, why not here? But imagine seeing you. You never go out."

"You say that, but we are out," Jo said, a little insistent, and Simon saw that Frank had been right, the lipstick was slightly uneven, the eyes not quite focused.

Frank signaled for more glasses, clearly annoyed. Gareth now pulled up another chair.

"Very kind of you," Burgess said to no one in particular.

"I love this place," Gareth said. "It reminds me of the Gay Hussar. Don't you think, Guy?"

"Don't know it," he said, sitting up as Frank poured out his drink.

"Of course you do. Greek Street. Just down from Soho Square."

Burgess drank, then shuddered a little. "After my time."

"But it's been there forever."

"No. No such place when I left. You forget, it was years before you did," he said into his glass. "Years before."

"Certainly a lot more sensational," Gareth said.

Burgess stared into his drink, apparently not hearing, all the old notoriety and insouciance now slack and vague. But the good posture was still there. Eyes half-closed, he sat with his shoulders back, as if he were waiting for a valet with a clothes brush.

"That's the trouble," he said. "You think everything will be the same and it's all changed. I don't think I'd recognize it now, London."

"Oh, are we planning to go, then? Get tickets from Cook's?"

"Don't be an ass," Burgess said, reaching for the bottle. "Do you mind?"

"Quite a welcome that would be. Bands out and everything. Handcuffs more likely."

"No, I don't think so," Burgess said, his voice serious, considering this. "The last thing they'd want. A trial. Think who'd have to take the stand. Admit they hadn't the faintest clue. For years. Very embarrassing. They hate being embarrassed. Calls the whole thing into question."

"So you'd just slip in on the quiet, is that it? Go see Mum. Maybe a few drinks at White's. And then what?"

"I don't know," Burgess said, his eye on Gareth. "Maybe better just to stay here. It's nice, being able to come and go and nobody notices. Best thing about Moscow. Of course someone always *is* noticing. Bless their suspicious hearts. But not the general public."

"Why would they be suspicious of you?" Simon said.

"You know, I don't know. It does seem a waste of manpower, doesn't it? I mean, I cashed in my chips years ago. But there they are, keeping an eye. Like a bloody great *croupier*," he said in exaggerated French. "Except he's supposed to watch who's winning. Not—" His voice fell, letting this drift.

"Well, they're not watching here. Nobody's even looked at the table," Jo said.

"And you call yourself a Service wife," Burgess said, dipping his head, courtly.

"You mean they are? Where?" She looked around the room.

"They're not supposed to be obvious," Gareth said.

"Well, one," Burgess said. "Then you don't notice the other. Check the sight lines to the table, bound to be somebody taking an interest. Didn't they teach you that? But you'd get him soon enough. You're supposed to. It's the one you're not supposed to see you have to watch out for."

"And where might he be?"

Burgess smiled. "I'm much too drunk to know that. Anyway, he's not watching me. I booked at the Praga. Probably some lonely comrade there still waiting. Fuming. One of the nice things about getting drunk–you don't see them anymore. They're in some blur on the margins."

Gareth, who'd been looking out at the room, suddenly stood up.

"Back in a sec. Have to use the Gents. Right back."

"Which way is he going?" Burgess said, not turning in his chair.

"Toward the bar."

Burgess sighed. "It's a wonder he didn't get caught sooner. The Gents. Don't they train them anymore?" he said to Frank. "We're agents, we're supposed to know how to do these things. Be discreet. But that's Gareth, isn't it? Anything for a leg up. He wants to be part of it all. Not tossed in the bin. Let me guess. He's talking to someone at the bar now?"

"Yes."

"And if I were still in the game, I wouldn't look. Too obvious. But what the hell." He turned. "Ah yes."

"You know him?"

"I've seen him. Gareth's always running over to him, eager to help. Share some tidbit. Much good it will do him. He can't accept that it's over. A field agent without a field. What could be more *de trop*?"

"Man at the bar seems happy enough to listen to him," Simon said.

Burgess looked over, slightly surprised, as if he'd just noticed Simon was there.

"To all his very important state secrets. What could they be, do you think? Whisper, whisper. About who?" He paused. "About *whom*. Not me, that's one mercy. Washed-up old snoop. Maybe you," he said to Frank, then looked at Simon. "Who's this, anyway?"

"His publisher," Simon said, formal.

"Oh, the memoir. *My Deceitful Life*. What a lot of mischief you must be up to," he said to Frank. "All those skeletons in the closet. But I suppose they have to stay there, don't they? The Service wouldn't like it. You ought to do his other book," he said to Simon. "All the bits he's left out of this one. Quite a read."

"So is this."

"Really? Well, quite a career. I guess there's enough there to pick and choose. You know he got the Order of Lenin? The rest of us got—well, Gareth got little Sergei, but the rest of us got fuck all." He made a soft burp. "And the honor of helping the cause, of course. Maybe I should write my memoirs. Would you be interested? You could start a series. Trouble is, it all seems so long ago now. God, the Foreign Office. I remember people in cutaway coats, actually in cut-aways." He was quiet for a second. "But to tell you the truth, I doubt I'd have the energy. I quite like being washed up. It's a soft life. I enjoy the leisure. Not Gareth. Look at him. The game's still afoot. Still hoping to get back in. It must be about you," he said to Simon. "New girl in town. Mind what you say to him. It all goes right back."

"There's nothing to tell."

"Well, that's always best, isn't it? Make him work for it. But imagine, right out in the open. In my day that wouldn't have been allowed. We were trained."

Simon looked out at the room, Burgess's voice like a radio narrator's. Who was anybody? Maybe there were watchers everywhere, people glancing away, then back. Gareth at the bar now, eager to report in, like one of Winchell's runners, and suddenly, absurdly, the room seemed like the Stork, everyone people spotting, feeding items to the columnists, the room dotted with them, KGB Winchells and Sullivans. He sipped the brandy. But no one knew the real story. How much was Jo drinking? Would Burgess make a scene? Was the American publisher just what he seemed? No one knew. A cable sent, a man already betrayed, just the beginning. He looked over at Frank, still listening politely to Burgess. No one knew. In this room of gossip and lapdog agents, only Frank seemed to sit in a calm center. Back where he'd spent most of his life, above suspicion.

They left Burgess with the rest of the bottle and made their way to the door, Jo leaning on Simon's arm, Gareth still at the bar, his face slightly alarmed as he saw them leaving, as if something had slipped out of his hands. A car was waiting at the curb.

"We'll drop you," Frank said.

"That's all right. I'll walk."

"No, we'll drop you," Frank said, an order.

Jo, still holding on to Simon's arm, swayed a little, unsteady.

"Here, let me help," Frank said, maneuvering her into the car.

"I'm *fine*."

They all sat in the back, Jo patting Simon's hand.

"Like old times. But we never talked. There's so much I want to know." She stopped, looking down, slipping into a private conversation. "But maybe not. What, really? What happened to everybody? Well, what did? The usual. Except me. Imagine the class reunion. Everybody coming up to say hi and looking—" Her voice drifted off.

Frank glanced over at him, a signal to let it play itself out.

The driver swung into Gorky Street, heading down toward Red Square. One or two cars, the sidewalks deserted, even on a late spring evening, the doorways pools of dark now, everything in shadow. They were at the National in minutes.

"Get some sleep," Simon said to Jo, kissing her cheek.

"Oh, sleep," she said, her head already nodding.

Frank got out with him.

"Same time tomorrow?" Simon said.

"You never change. I can still read your face," Frank said, a fond smile, the intimacy of drink.

"Yes? What's it saying?"

"You're worried. You don't want to take your hand off the checker, until you're sure. Remember how you used to do that? No move until you thought it was safe."

"This isn't checkers."

"No." He paused. "It's safe for you. The board. I promise."

"Well, it's done now. The message."

Frank nodded. "Which means from now on I'm a dead man here. You realize that, don't you?" He put his hand on Simon's arm. "I need you to stay with me on this. Keep your head. It's going to work."

"This is why you wanted me to come, isn't it? Your plan. What if I hadn't?"

"Jimbo, it's *us*. Of course you'd come. So would I. I never thought I'd have to ask, involve you, but–" He looked up. "I didn't think it would end like this."

Simon was quiet for a minute. "How did you think it would end?"

"I didn't. I didn't think it would end." He looked around, toward the darkened Kremlin. "Oh, in the triumph of socialism, I suppose. And it did. It just didn't end that way for me. Sometimes you get– taken by surprise."

Simon looked at him. Move the piece. "Tomorrow," he said. "Get some sleep."

He was halfway across the lobby when Novikov, evidently waiting, came out of the bar.

"Nightcap?" he said, the American voice somehow at odds with his Russian bulk and features.

"No, thanks. I've had enough."

"Have one anyway," he said. "Just one." He guided him toward the bar and signaled the bartender, who brought two small brandy snifters. "Armenian," he said. "The vodka will make you blind."

"This a social visit?"

"Delivery." He took an envelope out of his pocket and handed it to Simon. A thick cream-colored invitation with an embossed American eagle at its top. The ambassador requests your presence—

"Spaso House. I'm moving up in the world."

"Bring the invite with you. They check them at the door."

"Any idea why?"

"Me? I'm just the delivery boy. To make sure you get it. Make sure you come."

"To meet—?" He looked at the name on the card.

Novikov shook his head. "That's who the reception's for. Theater people. My guess is somebody else wants to meet you."

"Your guess."

"That's what I've been doing all day. You come in, send a cable, and the next thing I know the telex is going like you just started World War III. Did you?"

Simon smiled. "Not yet."

"And that's as much as you're going to say."

"Sorry."

"Well, I like working in the dark. Keeps you on your toes. Look," he said, suddenly serious, "you need anything, you just ask, right?"

Simon nodded. "I appreciate it."

"And maybe someday you tell me what it was all about."

Simon took a sip of brandy. "Who am I supposed to meet?"

"Tomorrow? Just show up," he said, nodding to the envelope. "My guess is, he'll find you."

The embassy had been ugly and barely functional, but Spaso House, the ambassador's residence, was a handsome mansion in a quiet Arbat square, just a block or two off the noisy main street. Simon had taken a taxi, which he assumed was the same as riding with Boris but at least gave the illusion of independence. They swept past a church with a tall white bell tower and pulled up to the residence's outer gate. People were already spread across the lawn and a circular porch ringed with Ionic columns. A soldier checked invitations.

The reception was being held for a visiting American theatrical troupe, and the sounds from inside, almost a tinkling effect, seemed livelier than the usual diplomatic cocktail party with its polite bows and apologies for missing wives. There was an informal receiving line, easily ignored, and waiters passing with drinks trays. Simon stood for a minute, looking around the reception hall, a two-story room so large that the rest of the house seemed an appendage, the vast space sitting under a gold and crystal chandelier that looked as if it required a special staff to keep it gleaming. There were a few gray-suited Russians, presumably from the Theatrical Union, talking to each other, and a good turnout of what Simon guessed was the expat community, correspondents and embassy workers. And Pete DiAngelis, leaning against a pillar with a drink in his hand, watching him. Simon took a drink from a tray and waited.

"I didn't expect you," he said when DiAngelis came over to him.

"That was a pretty powerful smoke signal you sent. Pirie thought I'd better come see what it meant. What the fuck is going on?"

"You get Kelleher?"

DiAngelis nodded. "So to what do we owe the favor?"

"Have you seen the lawn?" Simon said.

"A few days and he's a field op. Okay, let's go have a smoke.

You're here but that doesn't mean the ambassador wants to pose for any pictures with you."

"I'm not Frank."

"Close enough. And now you're going to embarrass everybody with his book. That puts you right off the guest list."

"Unless you put me back on. And who are you? Here, I mean."

"GSA. In town to go over the embassy books. Make sure your tax dollars are going where they're supposed to. Light?"

They walked across the porch, past women in cocktail dresses and pearls, and onto the lawn.

"How old do you think it is?" Simon said, looking up at the giant shade tree, one of whose lower branches was propped up with a pole.

"So what was Kelleher?" DiAngelis said, ignoring this.

"A down payment."

DiAngelis drew on his cigarette, eyes squinting, taking this in. "What's the joke?"

"No joke. He wants to go home."

DiAngelis said nothing, his expression blank, preoccupied, as if he were rifling through a card catalogue of responses.

"This your idea?"

"His idea."

"I mean, we didn't send you here to talk him into—"

"You didn't send me here. I told you I'd keep my ears open, that's all. It's the last thing I expected."

"What makes him think he can do it?"

Simon shrugged. "He thinks he can. He didn't tell me how. The question is what kind of reception committee does he get at the other end."

"Why would we want him back? His intel's about ten years late."

"Why did you come then?"

DiAngelis dropped his cigarette, rubbing it out with his shoe.

"He said Pirie would know what it meant—when he gave you Kelleher. What else he knew. What he could tell you. Isn't that why Pirie sent you?"

"And he's going to give us the whole organization chart. All his buddies. Why? He doesn't like the winters here anymore?"

"His wife is sick. He thinks she'll get better there. This would be for two. And new identities when they get there. Protection."

DiAngelis nodded. "He's going to need it. So what's he offering, exactly?"

"Ask him. I don't know. I'm just supposed to set up a meeting. One. Someone with authority to make an agreement. That's you, yes?"

"It could be."

"It better be. Or you'll lose him. You don't want him to get away again."

"And what if it's a trick? A little disinformation for the Agency."

"It's a little late for tricks. Once he leaves— But you decide. I don't think so."

"Why not?"

"I've seen his wife. And—I know him. He wouldn't ask me to do this if he didn't mean it."

"And nobody knows about this but you."

"And you."

DiAngelis looked at the ground, thinking. "Nothing thicker than blood, is there? So he gets you to front this."

"No. He talks to you. You work it out between you."

"Nobody's ever done this before," DiAngelis said, still looking at the ground. "A switch back." He smiled to himself. "The Russians will go out of their minds. Right out of their minds. Almost worth it, just to see their faces." He looked up. "Nice for you too, huh? With the book. He'll be famous again."

"In hiding. With you. Different kind of famous."

"How's he going to do this? We can't exfiltrate him. Operate on Russian soil."

"I don't know. He says he has a plan."

"Something he worked out in his leisure time. And now he drops it into our laps. You know what I think? I think it's going to be a fucking mess. And for what? Kelleher? We were going to get him anyway. KGB ops on the ground in 1949? Some old boy network stuff. Maybe a seating plan for the Third Directorate. The current one, or the one used to drive Pirie nuts? While your brother was taking notes—" He stopped. "Fuck. He'll want to do it, won't he?"

"Who?"

"Pirie. He never got over that time. None of them did. And now your brother's going to bring it back for them. Who did what to who and who gives a fuck? They do." He looked at Simon. "Let me talk to Washington. I'll have all the authority he needs. When's all this supposed to happen, by the way? He got his suitcases packed yet?"

"I don't know. The important thing is for the two of you to meet. Work things out."

"What, and then you negotiate the fine points?"

Simon shook his head. "It's not a book contract. I wouldn't even know what to ask."

"But you're a quick study." He smiled. "Christ, we ask you to keep your ears open and the next thing, we've got this." He looked across the lawn, hesitant. "You know what I said before, nothing thicker than blood? You don't want to forget who you're working for."

"I'm not—" He stopped, not worth it. "I'm not working for anybody. You or Frank."

"Right now it looks like you're working for both of us. It's hard, working two sides. It gets complicated."

"Let's keep it simple, then. Do you want this meeting or not?"

DiAngelis nodded. "My boss would."

"I'll let you know where, then. Where are you staying?"

"Here," DiAngelis said, nodding toward Spaso House. "Some place, huh? We figured if the GSA cover got too thin, they'd still cut me a little slack if I'm here with the ambassador. Nobody wants to make trouble. You see inside? A fucking palace. Must annoy the hell out of them, the Russkies. They're living in barracks and we're—"

"So how do I contact you? I can't come here again. I'd have no reason."

"Give me a day. Work things out with Washington. Then maybe a few of us have a nightcap at the National. To celebrate, but they don't know what. You could run into us. It's that kind of place."

Simon nodded. "Tomorrow night. Keep in mind, when you talk to Pirie, it's for two people. He won't leave without her, so it has to be for two."

"I'd still like to know how he plans to pull this off."

"He says he has it worked out. He didn't want to leave it to you."

"Nice."

"He just meant he knows it here. How things are." He paused. "He's working for you now."

"He did that before."

They went back to the house separately, Simon circling around the porch with a now empty glass. More people had crowded into the reception hall. How long before he could decently go? The ambassador didn't want him there anyway, tainted now by Frank. But in a second he was trapped by the telltale clinking against glass, the signal for a toast. People on the porch stood still, half-listening. A meaningful cultural exchange, a bridge between two great peoples. Meanwhile canapés floated by. Nothing particularly fancy—cheese puffs and triangles of tea sandwiches and water chestnuts wrapped in bacon—but here, in the dreary, gray city, a spread of defiant opulence. A Russian from the Cultural Ministry was welcoming the troupe's director.

"Mr. Weeks." A voice to his side. "I didn't expect to see you here. Hal Lehman, remember?"

"Of course. I'm getting you an interview. After *Look*."

"Funny you should say that, because he's here. *Look*, I mean. Oh, my wife Nancy. Nancy, Simon Weeks. You remember I told you—"

"That Weeks? As in Francis?"

"Guilty. Except I'm not."

She half-laughed, not sure where to go with this. Blond, teased hair and a flowery summer dress with a full skirt. A nice open face, someone you might meet at a barbeque. Who drove to Helsinki for lettuce.

"Simon's a publisher, honey."

"But you're his brother?" she said, not letting it go. "What was that like? I mean, when it happened."

"It was a rough time. For the family. But that's a long time ago."

"And he lives here now? All these years. I've been here a year, more, and I've never even seen him."

"Well, he doesn't go to a lot of parties at Spaso House," Simon said pleasantly. "In fact, neither do I. I should be going."

"No, wait, meet Tom."

Simon raised his eyes.

"Tom McPherson. *Look*. The photographer."

Hal craned his neck, then signaled that he'd be right back.

"I'm sorry. I hope I didn't— He's your brother. I didn't mean—"

"That's all right. It happens."

"And you came here to see him? What was that like?"

Simon hesitated, as if he were thinking this over. "What you don't expect? You still have the same jokes. You laugh at the same things. The way you always did. Of course, it's sad too. You see him and you think, I'll probably never see you again."

Embroidering the cover story, seeing how well it fit.

"You won't come back?"

"I'm here on a special visa. No guarantee they'll—"

"No, they're like that. Even for family, I guess. So unfair."

"Well, he's the one who came here," Simon said gently. "I can't blame them for that."

"No," she said, confused now.

"Here he is. Tom, Simon Weeks."

"Pleasure," the man said, shaking his hand. Young, not yet thirty, hair looking as if it had been combed by a hand brushing through it, shirt open, the only man at the party without a tie. "I was going to leave this at your hotel, but now you've saved me the trouble." He handed him a business card. "Mr. Engel was hoping I could get the pictures while you're still here. He said you knew what we're looking for. Kind of thing that'd go with the excerpt."

"In other words, run interference with Frank."

McPherson grinned. "Well, I was told he might be shy."

"No. He knows about this. Let me check with Jo. His wife. Give her time to arrange the furniture."

"Just the way they usually are," McPherson said. "A typical day—"

"I know what you want."

Frank in his study, Frank and Jo having breakfast, comfortable, not going anywhere. Boris in the other room, taking it in, the cover holding.

"I'll set it up. Promise."

"And then the interview?" Hal asked.

"I'll ask."

Frank would object, but why not? Another stitch in the cover, a man with a book coming out, at home in Moscow. As settled as he'd been in Washington.

The next morning they worked on Frank's escape to Moscow—the tense race to the airport, the last-minute change of flights, the car to Mexico.

"I was terrified the whole time." He looked over at Simon. "But I'm not going to say that."

"Were you?"

"Well, that's part of the game, isn't it? Get the adrenaline flowing. Beat the clock. Anyway, we did."

"How did you feel when you got here? Your first impressions. You don't say."

"I was relieved. I thought they saved my life, the Service. And gave the finger to Hoover, which was a nice bonus." He looked toward the living room, Boris deep in *Izvestia*. "I was excited. The whole thing had been—"

"A once-in-a-lifetime experience," Simon said, looking at him.

Frank caught the look and held it for a second. "Well, how about some lunch? Boris," he called to the other room. "What say we go to the university after, show Simon the view. Take the Metro. Look at a few stations."

"Komsomolskaya is in the other direction." Evidently a showcase.

"Plenty on the way. Arbatskaya, Kropotkinskaya. You'll be impressed," he said to Simon. "Best subway in the world."

It turned out that Boris's father had once worked for the Metro system, so he took a proprietary interest and loved showing it off. They stepped out onto ornate station platforms to see the design, then caught the next train, the next station, like field agents hopping on and off to lose a trail. The university, the tallest of Stalin's gothic wedding cakes, was a hike from the station, through a formal park.

The tower sat on the top of the hill with a lookout terrace just below and in front, all of Moscow beyond, dotted with more Stalin sky-scrapers. A couple were being photographed from a tripod, the girl with flowers in her hair, the boy in a boxy suit and tie.

"Newlyweds," Frank said. "They come here right after the cere-mony."

"Quite a view."

Frank nodded. "The highest point in the city. The Lenin Hills. Khrushchev's building a children's center over there." He pointed over to the right. "Near the circus. God knows what they'll call it. They have a mania for naming things. These used to be *Vorobyovy Gory*," he said, the Russian deep, a voice change. "Sparrow Hills. Which, with all due respect to Lenin, fits them better. But there you are."

Boris had drifted toward the end of the rail, as absorbed by the view as the newlyweds.

"We can talk now," Frank said. "What was all that about a once-in-a-lifetime trip? You don't think I can do this?"

"You act as if nothing could go wrong."

"You have to stay positive with something like this. Keep look-ing over your shoulder, you might trip."

"It's more than that. You're enjoying it."

Frank looked at him. "All right. I am. I want to see if I can pull it off."

"It's a hell of a risk to prove—whatever you think you're proving. You've got a life here. What are you going to have there?"

Frank was quiet for a minute, looking out to the skyline. "You know, when I first came here, the Foreign Ministry was still being built. Now you look—it's a different city. Or maybe I'm different."

"You're older."

"Not yet." He turned. "I'm still me, not one of those men you see at the Pond, sitting on a bench. But it's a different city. I don't fit in anymore. It's time to move on."

"And take their files with you."

Frank smiled. "Airfare, that's all."

Simon turned back to the view. "And what kind of life is she going to have there? Hiding."

"Only at first. She's been through it before. You don't go anywhere. A Russian identity. You're not *here*. But gradually you adjust. They adjust. It gets better."

"But it hasn't for her."

"No. But that was about Richie. Everything's been about Richie," he said, his voice quieter. "Not Moscow. You can't blame Moscow for that." He turned and moved closer to Simon. "Point at something, so Boris thinks you're sightseeing. I wonder who my new Boris will be. Eddie. Joe. That's one thing about this life, you're never alone."

"Frank—"

"You want me to recant," he said, lingering on the word. "You want that to be the reason. Lost my faith. Finally came to my senses. Oh, don't bother," he said, holding up his hand before Simon could speak. "I know you. That would make everything right. Instead of the way it is." He leaned against the balustrade. "But I can't. Then there'd be nothing. All of it for nothing." He looked up. "But I'll give you this. A little doubt. Of course there is no such thing. As a little. Once doubt comes into it, the whole thing's in play." He forced out a small smile. "Or it makes you stronger. That's what they say anyway."

"What did you doubt?"

"Well, not the revolution," he said, wanting to be light, then turned away from Simon's stare. "When Richie was sick. The best hospital. The Service hospital." He pointed to his forehead. "In the front part of my mind I knew we were doing everything we could. Logically. It wouldn't have made any difference in Bethesda, wherever we were. I knew that. But in the back of your mind, you think, what if? What if we could have saved him at home? No sense to it, but once it starts—and where do you go from there? He's here because of me. I killed him—"

"Frank."

"I know. I know it's not true. Maybe it's just—to distract you, take your mind off what's really happening. Which is that he's dying. Nothing prepares you for that. Not other people dying, even family. It's not the same. A child. He's not supposed to die. So, at the back, it starts nagging you. Your fault. Your fault. This place. The system. What else? Who else can you blame?"

"Frank," Simon said, putting his hand over Frank's on the rail. "Jesus Christ."

"I know. But you still think it. Jo did. She says she didn't, but she did. We cleaned out all his stuff. Just kept some pictures. But he's still all over the place. He's here. My fault. Until you want to be someone else. That's when I started thinking about all this. Leaving. Be someone else. So give me a name. Joe Blow. Harry Houdini. Somebody else. Then I don't have to think about it. Let them stash me somewhere, that's okay. It takes a little time. And Jo will be someone else too. A new life. How else to do it? Live with this." He looked at Simon, the moment suddenly close, as if they were embracing. "It's worth the risk. Worth it to me. I'm sorry that it probably means I won't see you." He tried for an ironic smile. "No family visits if you're an alias. But maybe you'd prefer it that way. At least I wouldn't be here. With the enemy."

"Don't."

"Jimbo, I wish—" His shoulders slumped, as if the years had weight. "Well, I wish. I wish. But that doesn't make it happen. We're going to lose each other again. But who else would have helped me? It's a hell of a thing, isn't it? There's nobody else I can trust. All these years and nobody else. And after everything. After I wrecked your life."

"You didn't wreck my life," Simon said, then turned away. "You wrecked yours."

Frank stepped back, as if the words had actually hit him, surprised. For a moment he said nothing. "Maybe I did," he said finally. "And Jo's. But maybe I can fix it." His voice wrapping around the words, the way it did in Russian, drawing Simon closer, an undertow pull. "It's not too late," he said, a kind of question.

"No," Simon said, lowering his eyes, ending it. "Where's the meeting?"

Frank hesitated, wanting to say more, then pointed down the steep wooded slope. "There," he said, finger out. "That's why I brought you here. So you could see it."

Another wedding party had arrived and they moved to avoid it.

"See the onion domes? There by the curve of the river. Past the stadium. The Novodevichy Convent."

"You want to meet DiAngelis in a convent?"

"Former convent," Frank said, smiling at this. "Although somebody told me there are still nuns there. But you never see them. Invisible nuns," he said, toying with it.

"Let's hope you're invisible too. Why there?" he said, peering down. A red brick bell tower, high white cathedral, a few other churches and outbuildings, all surrounded by fortress walls. Trees between the buildings, an enclave.

"It's a major attraction. Sort of place we'd go. Or DiAngelis, if he has to explain himself. The iconostasis is famous. See outside the wall over there? The Novodevichy Cemetery. They're connected through a gate. Lots of exits. Here comes Boris. DiAngelis sees you tonight? Let's say Friday, that gives us an extra day's cushion. After lunch, two. In the cathedral. The Virgin of Smolensk."

"The Virgin—?" Simon said, the name suddenly implausible.

"Don't be disrespectful," Frank said, enjoying himself again, a commando leader.

"And if Boris sticks close?"

"He won't. He's a good Soviet, hates anything religious. He'll wait in the grounds somewhere and have a smoke. I'll take care of him. Just tell DiAngelis to be inside, waiting. We won't have much time. Just a few minutes overlap, coming and going."

"And what if there are other people there?"

"They'll be praying to the icons. Relax, Jimbo, it's going to be fine. The nuns will look out for us."

"In a church?" DiAngelis said at the bar. "In public?"

"Get somebody from the embassy to take you sightseeing. No taxis. Maybe the Kremlin first, your pick. But be at Novodevichy before two. We're only talking about a few minutes."

"No. We have rules in Moscow. Three cars, safe house, two tails. There's a protocol. You think we don't know how to do this?"

"This time, his rules. He knows how to protect himself."

"Right out in the open. What is this, the fucking Hardy Boys?"

"You talked to Washington. Everything's okay?"

"That depends."

"On what?"

"How he wants to get out of here."

"He says he has a way."

"So let's go meet in church and discuss it. Let's let everybody know."

"He's KGB. He knows what he's doing. Give him that. If you're that worried about being seen, what are we doing in the National bar?"

"You're not him. We talk, it could be anything. Me talking to him? Either I'm here to kill him or turn him." He looked at Simon. "I could still go either way."

"Be early then. You'll need the time."

4

THEY TOOK THE METRO AGAIN, a quick walk down the Garden
Ring to Krasnopresnenskaya, then a change at Park Kultury, all
orchestrated by Boris to show off more stations. "No car," Frank
had said. "There's only one parking lot and the embassy car will be
tailed. We don't want to go anywhere near it." Their stop, Sport-
ivnaya, served the big stadium nearby, but the street itself was leafy
and unassuming, a quieter Moscow. At the end Simon could see the
bell tower and onion domes of the convent grounds. At the first big
intersection a small convoy of trucks rumbled by, followed by an
official Zil.

"You can take this straight back to the Kremlin," Frank said.
"Different names. Same street. Here, Bolshaya Pirogovskaya," he
said, the Russian easy, matter-of-fact. They began to follow the big
street down to the convent, past the entrance. "We'll use the back,
through the cemetery. Nobody sees us go in. Take a look at the
parking lot. Anybody we know? Diplomatic plates?"

But they were walking too quickly to pick out any detail. A car.

A school bus, presumably for visiting students, and a battered utility truck toward the end. The high convent wall was to their right now, beyond it the famous octagonal bell tower, blood-red with white trim.

"That must have been their car," Simon said. "By the bus."

"Let's hope so. They should be here. Seeing things. You want to know something?" Frank said, his voice suddenly low. "I'm nervous. Shaking. It's been a while. Being in the field. It's the kind of thing—you don't want to get rusty. Not now. Christ, look." He stretched out his hand to show it trembling.

Simon slowed a little, then put his hand on Frank's arm, squeezing it until the hand became steady, not saying anything. Boris, already ahead, didn't turn.

"You know what it means if anything goes—"

"It won't," Simon said quietly. "You've done this before."

"Not over here." He stopped, then looked away. "Well, listen to me. A little case of the willies," he said, sounding embarrassed, young.

"Now what?" Simon said, straightening his shoulders, body language.

"The cemetery," Frank said as they passed the end of the convent wall. "Chekhov's here. Gogol. Lots of generals. See the back entrance there? Under the church. It had to be big enough for a hearse."

Simon looked up. More domes, one gold, the others green.

"If you need to get out," Frank said, almost a whisper, "use this gate. Not the main entrance. They'll block the parking lot." He touched Simon's shoulder. "Here we go."

They passed through the street gate into the cemetery, leaving Boris outside on a bench with a newspaper and a full pack of cigarettes. There were some maintenance buildings and after that rows and rows of graves, some topped with elaborate statuary or, in the Russian fashion, with a photograph of the deceased embedded in the stone.

"You'd think he'd have used an earlier picture," Simon said, pointing to a jowly face.

"Maybe that was his best," Frank said, almost playful, some scheme they were cooking up in their grandmother's yard, laughing at the neighbors.

"Who gets to be buried here?"

"The great and the good. Maybe me. If I stayed. Well," he said, shrugging this off. "Through here."

He led Simon along the passageway under the church and into the convent grounds, old trees lining the paths, moving a little with the breeze, the only sounds birds and a groundskeeper's shovel, uprooting something near one of the other churches. Across the compound a few children's voices heading back to the bus.

"No guards," Simon said.

"No. Stalin gave it back to the church. For loyalty during the war. So officially it's church property." He raised his arm to the white cathedral that was the centerpiece of the complex. "See how high the gables are? Like the Cathedral of the Assumption in the Kremlin. See anybody?"

"They're supposed to be inside."

"Walk around to the bell tower first. Let's see who else is here."

But they seemed to be alone, even the children's voices now gone, nothing but birds, the quiet of a churchyard. Frank glanced at his watch, then pointed up again at some architectural feature, another gesture. But what if no one was looking? It occurred to Simon, a kind of dismaying joke, that Frank, all of them, might be acting for cameras that weren't there.

The cathedral was built on a raised piece of ground, its own natural dais, so they had to walk up to enter. At the doorway there was the usual clerical gloom, the far aisles in dim shadow, then flickering candles, and a cluster of massive columns soaring up to the onion domes, their sides covered with frescoes, an Oriental swirl of color.

Farther in, a bright center nave held a chandelier shining on the five-tiered iconostasis, each holy face framed in gold. DiAngelis was standing in front, looking up with a tourist's wide eyes, fingering the brim of his hat. Novikov was at his side, his bulk somehow incongruous in all the filigree. They both turned at the sound of footsteps.

"My brother, Frank Weeks. Pete DiAngelis," Simon said, an unnecessary introduction. "And Mike—what was your last name again?"

"Novikov."

"I hope you don't mind if I don't shake hands," DiAngelis said. "Around the Agency you're—"

"Let's make this fast," Frank said, all business. "We might pass each other in here, but we don't stay long enough to do anything else. You have authority from Pirie?"

"You're speaking to him. Through me."

"I wonder what that's like. For you," Frank said, a sly look to Simon.

DiAngelis hesitated, not getting this, then said, "I have all the authority you need."

"Good. Would you mind?" he said to Novikov, a sign to move away.

DiAngelis nodded. "And yours?" he said, as if Simon and Novikov were seconds at a duel.

"My witness. Since we won't have anything in writing." He didn't wait for DiAngelis's reaction. "Basics, I think already understood: my wife comes with me, so two of us, immunity from any prosecution, new identities, security coverage for at least a year, more if we think we need it. Agreed?"

"Go on."

"A pension. Just enough to cover living expenses. I won't haggle. Pirie will just lowball it anyway. I'll take base. I'll be swimming in royalties." He smiled at Simon. "From an account they can't trace.

The book, by the way—I want your guarantee you won't interfere. I want Simon to come out ahead on this, whatever happens."

Simon looked at him, oddly pleased, part of Frank's plan.

"And what do we get?"

"Whatever you can squeeze out of me during our cozy fireside chats. Don may want to do that himself. For old times' sake. A little ancient history."

"So, out-of-date intel."

"No, that's just for Don. New intel for you. For a start, I'll update your Who's Who. Of the Service. Thumbnails, bios, you'll have a field day, don't worry."

"Agents?"

"I gave you Kelleher."

"We could leave it there, you know," DiAngelis said, glancing at him, a poker look.

"But you won't," Frank said, meeting his eyes.

"We'd need the agents."

Frank nodded. "I don't know everybody. Just out of my department. It's set up that way. So those, yes. In the States. I can't give you a roll up, just those."

"How many?"

"How many would you like?"

DiAngelis glared, offended.

"Look, we don't have time to do this here," Frank said. "I'll give you the DC names, the ones I know. You have my word."

"Your word."

"Then not my word. My self-interest. By the time Don gets his sweaty hands on me, I won't have a lot of leverage. So, yes, agents. What else?"

"How are you going to do it? Get out of here. Everyone's curious about that."

"You're going to help. You're going to pick me up."

"Here? Are you crazy?"

"Not here," Frank said, a small smile. "That would be impractical."

"We don't exfiltrate. We don't set foot on Russian soil."

"Because you can't. I know. But you'll still have to pick me up. I can't swim to the States."

"Where?"

Frank hesitated. "I'll let you know. Not here. There's a great big socialist empire out there. I'm allowed to travel. Maybe even take my brother on a trip."

Simon looked up at this, surprised.

"Are we talking about Eastern Bloc countries? And how is that supposed to be better than Russia? You still have the KGB crawling all over the place."

"Or their sister agencies. Always a little intimidated. Always cooperative. Especially if it's a Service operation. So eager to liaise."

"If what's a Service operation?"

"My little scheme. I'm going to run it. For the Service. The KGB's going to get me out. They don't know it, but who better? Then you pick me up."

"You're going to set up a KGB operation to get yourself out."

"It's the safest way. Nobody suspects. My operation. I direct it. Everybody cooperates, gets me to where I need to be." He looked at DiAngelis. "Then you get me out. Agreed?"

"In the West?"

Frank shook his head. "I can't manage that. So you're going to have to get your feet wet a little. It's a risk, but not a big risk. I wouldn't set it up this way if I didn't think you could do it. That's the deal." He looked over at DiAngelis, waiting for a reaction.

DiAngelis stared at him, as if he were reading his face for clues.

"A penny for your thoughts," Frank said.

"I'm just wondering if you're worth it. We do this, we could end up with a mess on our hands."

"And I could end up dead. So who's taking the risk?"

"For some old intel and maybe a cypher clerk in a basement somewhere."

"What did Pirie say? He's not interested?"

"He told me to use my own judgment."

"Then use it. We've already been here too long."

"You set up a KGB operation, a front, so nobody thinks you're trying to fly. And it gets you somewhere near us and you just slip away. With our help. Do I have that right?"

"More or less."

"What's the operation?"

"Some dissidents we suspect are getting Agency backing," he said, turning his head toward Simon.

"So it's an operation against us."

"Of course. You're the Main Adversary, as we say. I'm going to swoop down and pick your team up. Except, instead, you pick me up. And I disappear." He made a movement with his fingers. "Thin air. A triumph for the Agency. Their first defector in years. Except for Sokolov. And he was a plant."

DiAngelis jerked his head up. "What?"

"That's my second payment. On account. Don can stop wondering. If he's still wondering. So. Agreed? Is there a problem?"

"I don't like operating anywhere behind the Curtain."

"Well, technically you won't be behind it. Just nearby. I said you'd get your feet wet a little. In the boat. You pick me up on the water. Open sea, not Soviet territory. That safe enough for you? The question is, do you want me or not?"

DiAngelis stared again, not saying anything.

Frank took a quick look at his watch, then sighed. "All right, shall we sweeten the pot? How about a Who's Who at Arzamas?"

DiAngelis blinked. "The nuclear facility? How would you have that?"

"I didn't. I had a friend who had it." He pointed to his temple. "Up here. He drank, we talked. I made notes. He died. So now I have it." He touched his head again. "And a few papers he took with him. Which he shouldn't have done. He was going to get them to the West. A great believer in the scientific community. Disarmament. But he only got them as far as me. Of course, strictly speaking, I should have turned them over right away to the Service. And I would have. Except I thought they'd make a nice calling card. Overcome any—qualms you might have. Do they?"

"Perry," Simon said, half to himself, watching Frank, a new prickling on his neck.

Frank pretended not to hear. "Do they?"

DiAngelis turned to the icons, as if, oddly, he were looking for spiritual guidance.

"Where do we do this? When?"

"Soon. I'll give you time, don't worry. Meanwhile, we communicate through Simon." Simon looked up, but said nothing. "We should set up a dead letter drop. Nothing fancy. Simple. Say the men's room at the National bar. Last stall. Use one of your people in Moscow. Not him," he said, nodding toward Novikov. "Not embassy."

"We don't have anybody on the ground in Moscow."

"Pete," Frank said, sarcastic, drawing it out, then moved on. "If you need to talk to Simon for any reason, use the bar. Simon will make it a point to be there. But only if you have to. Meanwhile, arrange for the boat. Stockholm or Helsinki, either would work."

"You're coming out on the Baltic?"

"You need a boat big enough to cross and fast enough to get the hell out after the exchange. And armed. It's the only tricky part, how my colleagues are going to react. You want to have enough firepower to make them think twice about any heroics. Problem?"

"No."

"Good. When I have the exact time and pickup point, you'll

have it too. Want to shake now?" He extended his hand. DiAngelis looked at it for a second, then took it. "How do you like working with the Service? Everything planned. Clean."

"You're a real piece of work, aren't you?"

Frank looked at him for a second, then dropped his hand. "Just get the boat ready. You come, by the way. Nice if Don could be there, but I suppose he's beyond all that now. I want a face I know. Let's see if you can get this going without making any noise. Pirie only. Nobody else at the Agency, not until it's done. Or it won't happen. The Service has lots of ears, some even I don't know about. So you be as quiet as you can. We do have one advantage. If you fuck up, I'll hear about it. I'm inside. But it's not much of an advantage. If they find out what you're up to, they'll start connecting the dots back to me. So, quiet. Understood?"

"We know how to run an operation."

"I'm counting on it. Anything else?"

DiAngelis just stared.

"Better get going then. Skip the cemetery. Just go back to the car. Anybody tail you?"

"I assume. You're supposed to be good at that."

"The best."

DiAngelis, unsure how to react to this, signaled Novikov.

"I'll see you on the boat," he said to Frank, then put on his hat and walked toward Novikov.

Frank watched them go, eyes following them out the door, making sure. A sudden silence, broken only by bells from one of the other churches, maybe calling the sisters to prayer.

"Take a look at the ciborium," Frank said. "Wood. Mention it to Boris."

"Shouldn't we go?"

"Let them get to the car." He paused. "You trust him? You think he'll do it?"

"Yes." He looked over at Frank. "Now it's dead letter drops. Meetings at the bar. I'd be in real trouble if—"

"I know," Frank said, cutting him off. "I said I'd have your back." He stopped for a second. "I need you out there."

"Your field agent."

Frank smiled a little. "That's right. I'm running you." He put his hand on Simon's sleeve. "I know what I'm doing."

They moved toward the outside light of the entranceway, white after the soft yellow of the candles. At the door they heard running footsteps, someone racing up the stairs to the church. Frank stepped back, out of the light. A girl in uniform, knotted kerchief at her neck. A Young Pioneer? Some youth group. She stopped short, almost bumping into them, then lowered her head. "*Izvinite*," she said, indistinct, a whisper, then hurried along the outer aisle, looking for something. A minute later she stopped and picked up a knapsack. Simon watched as if he were seeing a spool of silent film, no sound, everything in her face. She turned toward the frescoed columns and went still for a second, eyes wide. A quick intake of breath to cover her surprise, then she glanced toward Simon and Frank, trying to work something out. Nothing else, just a girl's expression, seeing something. Someone. Frank froze, putting his hand up, quiet, more silent film. The girl lifted the knapsack onto one shoulder and ran back, ignoring them, eager to be outside. Simon looked at Frank. Frank mimed a *shh* signal, then cocked his head, listening. No footsteps, no sounds at all. But not alone, the air filled with it now, another presence.

He signaled to Simon to go where the girl had been, then stepped carefully toward the center, paralleling Simon but coming up to the columns from behind. He passed the first, and waited for Simon to come into his line of sight before going on. Almost where the girl had been. He stepped softly around the next column and stopped. A man was pressed against its flat side, his head turned toward the outer aisle where Simon was moving, footsteps faint but audible.

Frank could feel him holding his breath, straining to hear. Not some casual visitor, wandering around the icons. Hiding.

As Simon came closer, the man crept backward, clearly intending to slide behind the column, out of sight. How long had he been there? What had he heard? Another step, his back still to Frank and then stopping, aware now of someone behind him. Simon stepped into view, eyes surprised, someone he knew. Trapped now, between them, the air alive, almost trembling, a frightened rabbit about to leap away. Before he could bolt, Frank grabbed him by the shoulder, turning him, hand at his throat, pinning him against the column. The sound of panting, then an involuntary squeaking noise, a trapped rabbit again. "Don't." Frank pushed him harder against the column, choking him, so that he sputtered. "Stop." Finally staring at him, Gareth's face pale, skin pushed back, twisting under Frank's hand.

Everything went still for a second, even the birds. Simon felt the tips of his fingers tingle, as if the blood had drained away, rushing to his head. He could see it all at once—the terror in Gareth's eyes, Frank's panic, both in it now, caught.

"What the hell are you doing?" Frank said, low, hoarse.

"Stop," Gareth said, a gasp. He moved his hand up to grab Frank's away, and Frank relaxed his grip for a second, letting Gareth's head move forward, gulping air, then shoved him back again, in a vise now, his head hitting the column. "Stop."

Simon saw them scrambling against each other, twisting, like the two scorpions in the story, locked in a bottle, safe if neither of them attacked the other. But one always did.

"What are you doing here? You followed us?"

Gareth shook his head, then signaled that he'd talk if Frank loosened his hand.

"I live here," he said, rubbing his neck where Frank's hand had been, his voice breathy, still racing. "Up the street. As you'd know if you'd ever accepted an invitation."

Frank looked at him, disconcerted, the answer surreal. He dropped his hand. "What?"

Gareth's eyes darted past him, the relaxed hand the opening he'd been looking for, and lunged left, starting to run. Without even thinking, Simon stepped forward, blocking him, then pushed him back against the wall, holding one shoulder while Frank held the other. Gareth kept gulping air, almost whimpering, looking from one to the other.

"You too," he said to Simon. "Get off. What do you think you're doing?"

"That's your question," Frank said. "What?" He shoved him again. "Now."

Gareth winced, looking at his shoulder. "Beast. It was an accident."

"What was?"

"Being here." He looked at him, suddenly defiant. "Though not in your case. 'See you on the boat.' Now, what boat would that be? The one down the Moscow River? Kremlin views?" His breath still ragged, but no longer gasping.

"What are you doing here?" Frank said again.

"I told you, I live here. Just up Pirogovskaya. Very handy to the stadium, though in my case–" He stopped, aware of Frank's eyes. "I can see across to the parking lot. Look, if you want to hear this, take your hands off. We're all friends here," he said, trying it.

Frank said nothing to this, another surreal moment, but dropped his hand.

"And you?" Gareth said to Simon. "The good brother. Just beavering away on the book. Nothing else. Really."

"Talk," Frank said, his calm a kind of menace.

Gareth blinked. "So I take a look from time to time. Being an old snoop. It passes the time. And then today, what? An American embassy car. And who? Novikov. What's he doing here? I said to myself. Come to see the nuns? And who's that with him? I had to take a look, didn't I? It's my job. So I came down and there they were, looking at icons with the Girl Guides or whatever they call themselves and I thought, I'd better find out who he is, the new man. The Service would want to know. They didn't come to see the Virgin of Smolensk. It must be a meeting. And so it was. But I never thought—it was an accident."

"But now it isn't."

"No," Gareth said, looking up. "Maybe best forgotten."

"But you have such a good memory. You think you know something."

Simon glanced over, Frank's voice a disturbing low register.

"No I don't. Really. Maybe it's your brother meeting with his people. They would, wouldn't they?"

"But I wouldn't be here."

"No."

"So what do you think you know?"

"Look, it's not me meeting with the Americans. You act as if I were the one—"

"But that's exactly what I'd have to say."

"What?"

"Until about five minutes ago, you thought you'd struck gold. All those years with your little bits of gossip, snitching on this one and that—finally, a real strike. Isn't that right?"

"I didn't hear anything," Gareth said, eyes alarmed now.

"But that's not the way it's going to play out."

"Frank, I—"

"Nobody's going to say anything."

Gareth shook his head. "No."

"I should. I should report this. But you know what it would mean. We both do. I don't want to do that to you."

"Do what?"

"Report your meeting."

"My—?"

"Try it this way. The tail on the embassy car saw two things—Novikov and his friend going in and then you going in a few minutes later."

"Frank—" he said, jumpy now.

"Funny thing. When Simon and I came into the church, what did we see? The three of you, thick as thieves, so I thought I'd better listen in. I couldn't quite get it all, but the new guy was American, making some kind of deal. With you. I thought, why not a Brit? That would be the obvious thing. But that's where you're clever. Nobody would think you'd go to the Americans. With your little bits of business. And you almost got away with it. If I hadn't been here. I'd have to do my duty."

"Your duty."

"And who do you think they'd believe? You or me? With the Order of Lenin?"

"You wouldn't."

"I'd have to. I'm sorry. I know what it means. Afterward. Not pleasant."

"Except I know what really happened. What you're planning to do."

"So you did hear. I needed to know that."

"Frank—"

"Of course you'd be grasping for straws at that point. Any story that pops into your head. Even an implausible one. Why would I do that, when I'm so well settled here? Yes, it would be just like you to make trouble for me. And yes, to be on the safe side, they'll watch me closely for a while. But when nothing happens—and it won't—they'd be right back where they started. And who would they believe? Your word against mine."

"They'd kill me," Gareth said quietly.

"Yes. I'd look for another way out if I were you."

"Such as."

"I'd keep my mouth shut. Could you do that, do you think?" he said, staring at him, reading his face. "Keep quiet? That's the question, isn't it?"

"Keep quiet. I was a spy, for God's sake. You don't have to—"

"But this would be such a coup for you. The Service would be so grateful—if they believed you."

"Take your hands off me," Gareth said, rallying. "Nobody has to say anything." He looked up at him. "You'll never get away with it, you know. Sticking it to the Service. They won't need me. You'll never make it to the boat." He looked over at Simon. "And you. Do you have any idea what they're going to do to you?" he said, his mouth twisted, almost sneering.

"Leave him out of it."

"They won't. No, they'll have a lovely time with you. Think of the trial. Like Mr. Powers. The great pilot. Oh, they'll love that." He turned to Frank. "I admit I was surprised. To see you. The great Francis Weeks." He let out a pretend sigh. "It's a wicked old world, isn't it? You never know." He started straightening his coat. "All right. No proof anyway. Your word against mine. So, checkmate. Nobody says anything."

Frank looked at him, considering. "I don't think you can do it," he said slowly.

Gareth's eyes darted from Simon to Frank, then around the room, trapped again.

"So what do we do?" Frank said.

"Don't be ridiculous," Gareth said, twitching. "That's not really in your line, is it?"

"No, but it's nothing to Boris. He's just outside."

Gareth gulped some air, taking a deep breath, then suddenly pushed away from the column, knocking Simon aside, and started to run back toward the entrance.

Simon leaped after him, catching his coat, pulling on it, both of them staggering down the aisle, Frank now behind. Gareth twisted, trying to wrench free, the coat twisting with him, pocket turned upside down. Something metal fell to the floor, a clang echoing in the empty church. Simon looked down, then let go of the coat and scooped up the fallen camera.

"No proof!" he shouted, imagining the pictures inside, trial exhibits.

Frank swept past him, catching Gareth and shoving him up against the first pillar, smashing his head back, arm at his throat, Gareth going limp, like a doll. "No proof," Frank said, then to Simon, "Open it." Simon flipped open the back, pulling out the film, exposing it. "Now where's your proof? Bastard."

"Stop. You're—"

Frank pushed harder. Gareth made a choking sound, trying to pull Frank's arm away from his throat, then pushed at his face, ducking to get away. Frank brought up his knee, a fast kick that made Gareth crumple, raspy screams, pulling at Frank until they both toppled over, on the stone floor now, rolling. Simon shoved the camera into his pocket, stuffing in the loose remnant of film. A shine of blood on the column where Gareth's head had been. Simon could feel his heart beat, breath coming faster. No pulling back. Not just a show trial, his life at stake. Frank's. He looked down. Frank was sitting on him now, knees on either side, his hands on Gareth's windpipe, Gareth gasping, making sounds, a kind of gurgling. Then he stopped, his head moving to one side, and Frank moved his hands away, shaking, his whole body shaking.

"Oh God," he said, to himself, to nobody.

Simon stepped over and took his hand, helping him up.

"I've never done that," Frank said, his face distant, hands still shaking, the last few minutes now one spasm rippling through him.

"There's some blood over there. I'll wipe it off," Simon said, taking out a handkerchief, hearing himself, not really there.

Frank stood looking at Gareth. "I had to, didn't I? He would have—"

"Put the coat under his head. In case there's more blood."

"Still," Frank said, eyes fixed on Gareth. Who would have ruined everything. The scorpion striking first, his nature.

Suddenly there was a faint moan, indistinct as a night sound, a slight movement of Gareth's head, and Frank involuntarily reared back. Simon looked at Gareth, beginning to move, then at Frank, still stunned.

"Finish it," Simon said, seeing everything in a flash. The men in leather coats, the fast car and back entrance, the beatings in the cell, the trial, after. "We have to finish it."

Frank stared at him, shaking. Simon dropped to his knees, what had to be done, hands on the warm neck, thumbs pressing into the windpipe. Gareth's eyes opened, maybe a panicked recognition, maybe just some abstract disbelief as air left him, struggling a little, kicking his feet against nothing, Simon pressing down now, what had to be done, harder, the last gasps barely audible, no wind, the eyes rolling back, closing, and suddenly the only things moving were Simon's hands, pressing, everything else still. He stopped, staring down, the lifeless face slightly contorted, not peaceful. What murder looked like.

He got up, staggering on one knee, unexpectedly weak, drained. Frank was staring at him, still dazed, someone at an accident.

He looked down again. Not just still, dead, a different stillness, skin already going gray, mouth open, unnatural. In one second. No. Take it back. Not dead, a figure in a First Aid manual. Drop to your knees, spread your hands against the rib cage, push, don't panic, a rhythm, in and out, be his lungs, the face turned to the side for the water to run out, your hands breathing for him until you heard the choking sounds, signs of life. Take it back.

"We have to get him out of here," Frank said, matter-of-fact, coming back.

"Should I get Boris?"

Frank shook his head. "Nobody. But we can't leave him here. They'll find him."

"They're *going* to find him."

"But not yet. No connection. Take a look outside. See if there's anyone—"

Simon half ran to the door, grateful to be doing something. The grounds were quiet, no Young Pioneers, no nuns, not even the groundskeeper, gone for a smoke or a siesta, leaving his wheelbarrow near the uprooted shrub by the red church.

"There's a wheelbarrow," he said, coming back.

"No. How do we explain it, if anyone comes? Grab his other side. Ever carry a drunk?"

Simon put one of Gareth's arms around his neck and lifted, grunting at the weight.

"We just have to get him to the cemetery," Frank said, beginning to move. "Did you see the sheds? Near the wall. We can put him there."

"They're still going to find him," Simon said, hoisting the body against him, the feet still dragging.

At the entrance Frank stopped. "Check again. If there's anybody. Lean him here."

They backed Gareth against the wall. Simon stepped out, looking around. Still no one, a cloister stillness. He went back and slung Gareth's arm around his shoulders again.

"Ready?" Frank said.

"What if someone's in the cemetery?"

"He passed out. We're getting some help." He looked at Simon. "I don't know."

They stepped out into the light, the gate church just across a stretch of lawn, open, the shade trees all next to the church.

"Come on, quick," Frank said, heaving the weight on his side, then stopped, turning his head, listening. Some voices coming from the cemetery. No, the same voice. Coming from the underpass now. They lugged the body back, not quite there when the voice came through the gate. The groundskeeper, carrying a heavy pair of gardening shears, drunk or just talking to himself. He looked up, as if he'd heard their breathing, but gazed at the other church, where he'd been working. A louder stream of Russian now, some private rant of complaint. In a second, they were back through the doorway, Gareth hanging between them. The Russian was still talking, crossing the lawn, heading right for them, swinging the clippers in one hand. Another step back, out of the light.

The groundskeeper stopped, a dog sniffing the air, and looked at the entrance, leaning his head forward, peering, his glasses catching the sun. Simon stopped breathing, his eyes fixed on the Russian's glasses, little flashes as he moved his head. Could he see? What? Three men, holding each other up in the church's gloom. A disturbance in his world. Something off. No sound. Another step, still peering.

And then, just as he was approaching the entrance, he gave it up and veered off on the path to the bell tower, behind the cathedral. Another minute, listening, then the sound of steady clipping, the shears attacking some unruly shrubbery. But where, exactly? Could he see the lawn? They looked at each other, panting under the weight of the body. In a minute another bus could arrive or someone with flowers for an icon, mourners in the cemetery, the whole complex come to life with people who would see them. Frank nodded and they hoisted the body again and started across the lawn. Out in the open. But no shouts, no voices disturbing the quiet, just their own heavy breathing, their ears filled with it. How could the groundskeeper not hear? When the bell in the tower started ringing, the clanging tearing through the air, they jumped, almost dropping the body, as if they had set off an alarm. They began to move faster, their breathing, any sound, covered now by the bells. Was anyone actually ringing them, looking out high in the tower? In another minute they had reached the gate church, Gareth's shoes now scraping against the floor of the underpass. At the other end the cemetery seemed deserted, no widows paying respects. But for how long? Just to the shed against the wall. Their luck held. The caretaker had left it unlocked.

Inside there were tools, odds and ends, even slabs of tombstones leaning against the wall, loose cobbles to repair the paths between the rows of graves.

"Over there," Frank whispered, nodding to the shadowy far end of the building.

They gave the body one last heave and dropped it in the corner, hiding it behind a pile of tools, the caretaker's mess an unexpected cover.

"Wait," Frank said, seeing Simon turning to go. He squatted, loosening Gareth's belt buckle, then dragging his pants down.

"What are you doing?"

"Why he was here. Someplace out of the way. The Service is funny about people like him, they'd rather not know. If they believe it, they'll cover it up."

The pants down, Gareth's white body exposed, caught in the act. Now his wallet, cash taken out and the wallet wiped for prints and thrown back, what might have happened. Frank went over to a pile of cobbles and picked one up, carrying it back to the body and raising it above Gareth's head.

"What—?"

But the arm had already come down, a crack as it smashed into Gareth's head, opening it.

"It won't fool anybody if they really look—the marks on his throat, and the blood's stopped. But they may not want to look. Disgrace to the Service."

"And the police?" Simon said softly, looking at the body.

"The Service will take this over. One of ours. I'll make sure."

"What are we doing?" Simon said, a question to himself.

Frank looked at him, but said nothing, moving them to the door. He poked his head out. Still no one. Outside they took the path nearest the wall.

"Stalin's wife," Frank said, pointing to one of the graves. "You can tell Boris you saw it. The writers are down here."

They were walking quickly, hurrying to the entrance. Out of the corner of his eye Simon could see a woman with a headscarf at the far end, kneeling at one of the graves, but she didn't turn. They were still invisible.

"I can't stay here," Simon said suddenly. "I have to get out before they—"

Frank stopped, holding him by the shoulders. "Listen to me. By the time they find him they won't be able to establish time of death. He said he lived down the street. This is just the kind of place he'd use—to meet people." He gripped Simon's shoulders. "No one saw us."

"I can't," Simon said, light-headed, as if he were about to float away, held back by Frank's hands on his shoulders.

"Yes, you can," Frank said calmly. "It's going to be all right. If you leave now, you'll make it worse. For both of us. No sudden moves. Everything the way it should be."

Except for the body in the shed. Simon saw the face again, the startled eyes. But what he heard was the calm excitement in Frank's voice. It's going to be all right. What he'd done all his life, maybe why he'd done it, the risk.

"I'm not going to jail, not here."

"Neither am I," Frank said, trying for a tentative smile. "I have an alibi. You. And you have me. We're fine, if nobody gets spooked."

Simon felt the hands like a grounding rope, pulling him back.

But then he saw, a flash of horror, that Frank and he had become the scorpions. Both safe until one—

He nodded his head and Frank dropped his hands, then took out a handkerchief and wiped his forehead. "All that weight," he said, the same hand he'd raised in the air with the stone.

"You have to do it soon," Simon said. "We can't stay here. I won't."

"I know," Frank said, soothing, brushing Simon's jacket as he spoke. "You okay?"

Simon took a breath. "Which one is Stalin's wife?"

"Over there," Frank said, pointing.

But when they told Boris they had seen it, his face clouded with disapproval, something inappropriate for Simon, any Westerner.

"Was it well tended?" he said, polite conversation.

Simon nodded. "The cathedral was beautiful. You should have come." Nothing in his voice to give anybody away.

Boris shrugged. "The opiate of the masses," he said flatly. No irony, no self-consciousness.

Simon looked at him, a good Soviet man, and suddenly wanted to laugh, about to fly off again, another not funny joke, the whole country full of them, the women in the hotel hallways, the listening chandeliers, the men plotting in the Kremlin, Stalin feeding on his own, check mark by check mark, a city without maps.

They were crossing the intersection. Simon looked up at what he guessed was Gareth's building, with its view of the parking lot. A high rise with concrete beginning to crack. Did Sergei live there too? Waiting for him to come home. He looked over at Frank, who was talking to Boris in Russian, idle chat by the sound of it. I have an alibi. You.

Now the Metro again, the palatial stations. If he stayed on, could he go all the way to the airport? And then what? Visas and questions about why he was leaving. So soon? Before the book was done? Why was that? And for a second he felt what everyone here must feel, living under house arrest. For imaginary crimes. And he had just killed a man, a real crime, and no one knew. All the grisly apparatus of a police state and no one knew. An outing with Boris, on the KGB's watch.

During the war, at his desk on Navy Hill, he had wondered what combat would be like, how it would feel to kill somebody, whether he could go through with it. But it had been easy, an instinct, even when Gareth's eyes opened. Save yourself. Only now his stomach was filled with it, churning with dread. It's going to be all right. Was it? Frank had thought that before and ended up here. If nobody gets spooked. Simon clenched his fist, some gesture of control, as if he could hear Frank's tail scratching against the bottle.

To his surprise, it was Tom McPherson who turned up for DiAngelis at the National bar.

"Doesn't *Look* give you enough to do?"

"In Moscow? Everything happens behind closed doors. No access. Ever. So a little moonlighting. Makes it more interesting."

"Does *Look* know?"

McPherson ignored this, his pleasant, bland features turning serious, full of purpose. "We need to set a date for the shoot. I'm going to have a package for you and they don't want to use the dead letter drop. Direct handoff."

"Monday. We're away this weekend. What's in the package?"

"No idea. I'm just the mailman. Ordinarily I'd guess visas, papers, kind of thing you don't want to leave in the men's room. But in this case—I don't know. You already have yours. So it must be—whatever you're talking to the Agency about." He turned to the bar, ordering a brandy. "Mind if I ask you a question? Were you close, you and your brother?"

"Why?"

"It's unusual, that's all. You being with him. And working for the Agency. Does he know? No offense. I was just curious. What time Monday?"

"Ten," Simon said, then, "He doesn't tell me anything."

McPherson shrugged. "But here we are. And you've got a delivery coming. Don't worry, I'm not looking for a story. It's strictly pictures with *Look*. Lehman's the one you want to watch out for. He's been trying to get a story on the defectors since he got here."

Simon looked up, a sudden thought. "He do this kind of work too?"

"Not that I know of. But then I wouldn't know." He finished his drink. "Look who's here," he said, his voice lower, glancing toward the end of the bar where Gareth's Sergei was questioning the bartender. "Mr. Jones must be out on a toot."

What people would think, the body still not found. Simon looked at Sergei, his face troubled, not sure what to do. Had Gareth done this before? It must be a small circuit of watering holes. Moscow wasn't New York. The National, the Metropol, the Aragvi. But then what? The apartment suddenly quiet, empty. People like Sergei didn't go to the police. Simon imagined him sitting alone, waiting. Getting up to look out the window. Now he noticed Simon, a flicker of recognition. For a second Simon thought he'd come over, ask if he'd seen Gareth, another layer of lies, but evidently the bartender's word was all he needed. He turned and darted out of the room, heading for the Metropol.

"They say the KGB fixed them up," McPherson said. "Keep Jones happy."

"Who says?"

"People. You know. Must have taken, though. It's been years."
Now over, cut off like the air in Gareth's throat.

"I'd better go up," Simon said. "Anything else?"

"You tell me. I'm here, if you want to get word to anyone."

"Monday at ten."

"We might want to do another. Shoot. It's a good excuse to
talk." He put down his glass. "Sorry about before. It's just the logic
of it. If you're not reporting on him, what are you talking to the
Agency about?"

He looked at McPherson, the eager, open face.

"This and that," he said.

5

THEY DROVE WEST OUT of the city on Kutuzovsky Prospekt, a showcase street lined with new apartment buildings.

"The Friday ritual," Frank said, looking at the swarm of black cars, the first traffic Simon had seen in Moscow. "Even in the rain."

It had been drizzling all afternoon, the air heavy and wet, forming condensation on the car windows.

"It's supposed to clear up," Joanna said, next to Frank in the back. "Anyway, it's good for mushrooms."

"Mushrooms," Frank said, dismissing this, not worth talking about.

"It's all wasted on Frank. The country," Joanna said, smiling. "When they offered us the dacha he didn't want to take it. At first."

"What made you change your mind?" Simon said.

"I didn't want anybody to think I was ungrateful. It's considered a privilege."

"The vegetables are," Joanna said. "In the summer you can eat out of the garden."

"Why is it so hard? To get vegetables."

"The distribution system," Frank said, not really paying attention. "It's better than it used to be."

Simon, up front with Boris, looked at Frank in the rearview mirror, a doubling effect, their features so similar at this distance. His
jaw, Frank's. The same high forehead, wrinkled, preoccupied, neither of them looking forward to the weekend. Simon kept seeing
the groundskeeper stacking rakes in the utility shed, smelling something. How long? Frank was sitting forward, hands on his knees.
Square, long-fingered, like Simon's. Did it matter whose had been
on Gareth's throat? The same hands.

"You'll like the Rubins," Joanna was saying. "He's nice." As if
they were simply neighbors, not on Hoover's wish list.

"When are they coming?"

"Tomorrow lunch. I couldn't face it tonight, all that work and
everyone stays so late. So, just us."

"I have some people coming before dinner," Frank said.

"Who?" Joanna said, annoyed.

"Some people from the office."

"You might have said."

"I just found out. Boris got a call." He nodded toward the front.

"They're coming to the dacha? What's so urgent? Oh, don't tell
me. Why start now?"

"I'm planning a trip," Frank said pleasantly. "I thought we'd
take Simon to Leningrad. See the Hermitage. Then Tallinn, Riga.
Doesn't that sound—?"

"Riga?" Joanna said.

"It's supposed to be very attractive. Lots of Art Nouveau. We hav-
en't been away in so long. I thought you'd enjoy it, with Simon here."

"You're full of surprises." She looked forward to Simon. "Did
you know about this?"

He half-turned, facing them. "Frank said maybe after the book—

I'd hate to leave without seeing some of the country." What he thought Frank wanted him to say. Just a trip. He glanced back to see his reaction, but Frank was facing Jo, juggling again.

"And when is all this happening?" Jo said. "Do I get time to pack?"

"This week, if I can get the go-ahead from the office. Don't you want to go? I thought you'd be—"

She waved this away and started rummaging in her purse for a cigarette. "Wonderful, isn't it, to have a travel agent who comes to the house."

"We have some other work," Frank said blandly.

She lit the cigarette and rolled down her window to let the smoke out.

"I wish you'd stop," she said, not looking at him. "Retire."

Frank smiled, not biting. "And do what, crossword puzzles?"

"How many? Tonight."

"Two."

"It's only soup. There's plenty if they want to stay."

"I'm sure they'll want to get back."

"To wherever it is they go."

"Jo."

But the air had settled, the friction seeping out with the smoke. Simon looked at Frank. They were going to Leningrad, the little back-and-forth not even a quarrel, just making it more ordinary for Boris. Putting the pieces into place. No one knew.

Frank caught his glance. "How are you doing up there? You know what this reminds me of? When we used to drive to Maine with Pa." He looked at Jo, including her. "Simon always got the front seat, because he got carsick. Always in the front," he said, warm, reminiscent. "So nothing changes."

Simon looked back at him quickly, surprised, then turned to face the windshield again, the boy in the front seat. Nothing changes.

They had left the inner city and were passing the sprawling fields of garden allotments, each with its own hut, the dachas of the people.

"I thought the photographer was supposed to come next week," Jo said.

"Monday," Simon said.

"Monday?"

Simon turned. "I ran into him at the bar last night. At the National."

"At the National," Frank repeated, looking steadily at him.

"Mm. You know, the way you run into people." Talking in code now, eyes on each other, the doubling effect complete. One person. "He'd like to get it done while we can."

Frank nodded, accepting this.

"There's no hurry," Jo said. "I'd like Ludmilla to give it a good clean before—"

"Nobody'll know the difference," Frank said. "We're not supposed to be grand. Like anybody else."

"I told him ten," Simon said to Jo. "Sorry, I should have checked. But he was so anxious—"

But Joanna had already moved on, bowing to the inevitable.

"So it's the stringer for *Look*," Frank said, asking something else. "Interesting."

"What is?" Joanna said.

"Nothing. The foreign press. How many there are."

"My hair will be a mess."

Frank smiled at this. "No it won't."

They stopped at a farm stand in the village, a piece of tolerated capitalism since the farms were near the Service compound. At a signal from Frank, Simon got out to stretch his legs, leaving Boris sitting behind the wheel.

"Why the hurry?" Frank said quietly. "He's the Agency contact?"

"He says he has a package to deliver. Papers. Maybe exit visas. They didn't tell him what."

"Exit visas? That's not how we're leaving," Frank said, annoyed. "The last thing you want lying around. How do you explain that?"

"Maybe it's something else."

"I didn't ask for–" He caught himself. "Well, never mind. Careful around Boris on Monday. You don't think he notices, but he does."

"He say anything about yesterday?"

Frank shook his head. "Not yet. No idea." He looked up. "It's why I thought we'd hurry our trip along. They're bound to find him. Nothing to connect us, but you never know how people are going to react. You can plan everything, but there's always an X factor. So let's get ahead of it."

"Will you know Monday? Time. Place. *Look* will be there. Easy to pass the–"

"No. Only to DiAngelis. Use *Look* to get to him, that's all. I may know Monday. Depends on tonight."

It was real country now, stands of birch and pine, fields lined with windbreaks, dark, thick patches of old-growth forest. They passed through a security checkpoint at a manned gate.

"It's fenced," Simon said.

"The perimeter. You're not aware of it when you're inside. They patrol at night."

A weekend in the country.

The road split off in several directions, like veins, no signs, no visible houses, each dacha tucked away in the trees by itself, the fence and guards invisible. They followed the main compound road for a mile or so, then turned onto a dirt road that twisted through woods dense with undergrowth, a fairy tale track, then another turn onto a narrower road. Simon had expected a cottage, but the dacha was a substantial two-story house, surrounded by trees, with a broad open lawn in front and garden on the side. The step-up porch and gables were trimmed with gingerbread, like the houses he remembered on the Vineyard, Oak Bluffs, with their elaborate painted scrollwork.

"Smell the lilac," Joanna said. "The rain brings it out."

The bushes, some tall as trees, grew alongside the house, their heady perfume another memory of home. For a moment Simon felt that they had left Russia, even gone back in time, all of them who they had been.

They turned into the driveway to find another car already there, two men leaning against it, smoking.

"They're early," Frank said, recognizing them. "Well, so much the better."

They were stocky, their raincoats stretched across their shoulders, hair cropped as short as Boris's. They tossed their cigarettes when Frank's car pulled in, but didn't stand up, just watched sullenly, still slouching, like thugs. But what did DiAngelis look like in his raincoat? Not a gentleman's business. Frank greeted them and led them up to the house without introducing them. Joanna watched them go up, heavy military clomps.

"God help us. Thomas Cook," she said, a wry shrug to Simon.

Inside the house was country shabby, comfortable chairs that didn't match and a fraying carpet, bookshelves everywhere, like the flat in Moscow. An old woman, dressed out of Tolstoy, was in the kitchen already starting the soup. Joanna greeted her in Russian, more halting than Frank's but evidently understood since the old woman smiled back.

"You're in here," Joanna said, opening a door and switching on a light. "It's a little lumpy, but they all are. Furniture here— Why don't you unpack and then meet me outside. We'll have a walk while it's still light. They'll be hours." She nodded to a closed door. "With their timetables. And whatever else—" She stopped, hearing herself, and looked at Simon, then started down the hall. The way she'd always lived, not knowing.

When he came out she was picking lilacs, getting sprinkled by the wet overhead branches.

"Good. You found the boots."

"Where's the car?" he said.

"Boris took it. He has a place on the other side of the village. He'll drive us back Sunday."

"So we're on our own?"

"Unless they've wired the trees." She nodded. "On our own. Let me put these inside, then we can get some mushrooms."

"You really know the difference? Between the poisonous ones and—"

She smiled. "No. I just pick one kind—I know they're safe—and leave everything else. I don't even like mushrooms, but it's a good excuse to get out. They all do it. You'll see them in the woods with their Little Red Riding Hood baskets. Just let me put these—"

But before she could go up there was a barking, then a dog racing across the lawn.

"Pani," a voice called.

"Marzena," Jo said, her voice neutral.

"Who?"

"Perry Soames's wife. Polish. They met—well, I don't know how they met, actually. Marzena," she called out.

A woman in boots came around from the garden side, her blond hair protected from the damp by a headscarf.

"Pani, bad girl," she said to the dog, indulgent, then made a clicking sound which brought the dog over. "She gets excited. Oh, look at the lilacs. I love lilacs," she said, drawing out the l's, an exaggerated accent that reminded Simon of the Gabor sisters. "For tomorrow?"

"Yes. You're early," Jo said, looking at her wristwatch, a tease.

"I don't mean to bother—is Frank here?"

"He's meeting with some people. From the office."

"Oh," Marzena said, the code for off-limits. "It's my icebox. That's right, icebox? Kaput. I don't know why. And you know how handy he is."

"Shall I tell him to walk over when he's through?"

Simon looked up, hearing something new in her voice.

"If it's not too late. I don't mean to bother—" She glanced toward Simon, curious, waiting to be introduced.

"I'm sorry," Joanna said. "Frank's brother. Simon."

"His brother," she said, a theatrical delight. "Yes, I see it. Now that I look." And then, to Simon's surprise, she took off her scarf, shaking out her yellow hair, a kind of flirtation, as if she wanted him to notice her as a woman.

"Marzena, you knew he was coming," Joanna said, a gentle poke.

"Yes, but you know how I forget things." A habit meant to be charming. "So. I'm happy to meet you, Frank's brother." She dipped her head. "I want to hear everything. How he was, as a little boy. But tomorrow—you must have so much to do," she said to Joanna. "I didn't mean—it was just the icebox."

"I'll send the handyman over," Joanna said.

"Can I bring anything to lunch?"

"No, I've got Eva to help. Just come."

"It's always so well organized here," Marzena said to Simon, who was looking at her more carefully now. A pretty woman who thought herself a beauty, her face always tilted toward the light, a harmless vanity. Her eyes were lively, the way Joanna's had been when she danced, and he saw that for Marzena the world was still a ballroom, filled with partners to please. "Were you good friends as boys?" she said. Small talk, just to get a response.

"Yes," he said. "Best friends."

"So you know all his secrets," she said.

"Not anymore."

"No," she said, an awkward moment.

Simon bent down to pat the dog, the first he could remember seeing in Russia. But there must be dogs everywhere. Were there breeders? Kennel clubs? The whole pet world that had grown up around them at home? Or had they barely survived the war, a time too hungry for pets. Just a small moment, petting a dog, and he realized again how little he knew.

"Look how she is with you. You can tell a lot about a man from the dogs, how they are with you." Her eyes on Simon, actively flirting now.

"She must miss Perry," Joanna said.

Marzena nodded, suddenly fighting back tears, her voice shifting down. "It's so sad to see. She sits by his chair. Waiting. But of course he doesn't come."

"Marzena's husband," Joanna said, explaining. "He died a few weeks—"

"I can't believe it either. I'm like Pani. I look at his chair. Waiting."

"I'm sorry," Simon said automatically.

"It's one thing if you're old. You expect such things. But so young— At first you can't stand it," Marzena said. "But do you know what helps? The dog. After it happened, I didn't want to get out of bed. But Pani has to be fed. Go for walks. So you get up and you go on. And time passes. Well, you have things to do. You'll mention it to Frank? The icebox? But only if it's not too late. He's always such a good friend to us," she said to Simon. "Anything to help. Come, Pani." She made a clicking sound.

Joanna, hands still full of lilacs, watched her go. "Always such a good friend," she said in Marzena's accent. "God." She glanced at her wristwatch. "How about a drink? It's not too early."

"What about the mushrooms?"

"They'll keep." She looked over at him. "Just one."

She came back with two small glasses of vodka, giving one to him.

"You know how handy he is." Marzena's voice again. "She

probably pulled the plug out." She tossed back the drink. "Bottle blonde."

"You don't like her?"

"Ha," she said, swallowing the drink.

"Then why ask her for lunch?"

"They live in the next dacha over. We're friends. We're supposed to be friends," she corrected herself. "Well, Frank is." She looked at the Service car in the driveway, then took the glasses and left them on the steps. "Come on."

They started across the lawn toward the trees, opposite the way Marzena had gone.

"He shot himself, didn't he? The husband," Simon said.

"Unless she shot him. Or Frank shot him."

"What?"

"Not that he had to shoot him. Maybe it was just enough, if he knew."

"Knew what?"

Joanna waved a hand in front of her face, shooing this away. "Nothing," she said quietly. "Nothing."

They had passed into a grove of birches, the ground still wet from the rain.

"Knew what?"

"Nothing," she said again and then her shoulders were shaking, head down, hiding tears.

"Jo," he said, his hand on her arm. "For God's sake—"

"Sorry," she said, taking a breath, controlling her shaking. "Do you have—?" She reached out for a handkerchief.

He handed her one, then watched her wipe her eyes, blow her nose. "So stupid," she said, then started shaking again.

He put his arms around her, drawing her head against his shoulder. "*Shh,*" he said, smelling her, the damp leaves, feeling her against him. "It's all right."

She stayed there for a second, then slowly pulled away, blowing her nose again. "Is it? I thought it wasn't."

"What's wrong?"

She looked up at him. "Well, why shouldn't you know? You know everything else." Her voice steadier, over it. "You don't want to watch the show tomorrow without a playbill. The little glances that nobody else is supposed to see. The way she looks at him. Then his jokes so everything seems normal. Send him over to fix my fridge. Send him over. Just like that. Get one in before dinner. It's quite a show. And me? Blind, not a clue. Why would I suspect a thing? Everyone being so clever. But that's what he's good at, isn't it?" She stopped, then looked down. "But you never think he'd do it to you. You think it's different."

"I don't believe it."

She smiled, a halfhearted curve of her mouth. "Still the good angel."

"How do you know?"

"Because I do. Give me some credit."

"He loves you. He'd do anything for you." Risk everything, live in hiding.

She brushed her hair back. "Never mind. Nothing like a good cry once in a while. I suppose I look a mess," she said, pushing at her cheeks. "The funny thing is, I think it's over. After Perry died—a little unseemly. Even for Frank. Not that it stops her. Come fix my fridge. When all she has to do is pick up the phone. Anything to get him over there. Like before."

"What do you mean?"

"He was always over there."

"Maybe he went to see the husband."

"Why? To talk physics? What would Perry have to say to Frank?"

He heard Frank's voice at Novodevichy. He drank, he talked. I made notes.

"Of course, you can't help but wonder. Why he did it. Maybe he found out. Then how do you live with that? So Frank's not running over anymore."

"Maybe you're imagining things."

She shrugged. "Watch tomorrow. Then you tell me."

"It doesn't matter. It doesn't mean anything."

"What's that like? When it doesn't mean anything?" She wiped her eyes again, then cheeks. "So unfair. Men just look the way they look. We have to—" She glanced up. "You know that song? Pick yourself up. Dust yourself off. I used to think that was me. But it keeps getting harder. Each time—knocks something out of you. I thought after Richie—" She gave back the handkerchief. "Thanks. I shouldn't have— You won't say anything to Frank. Promise?"

"He doesn't know?"

"That I know?" She shook her head. "My secret, for a change. Everybody else has one, why not me? Watch me tomorrow. Not a clue. What would be the point? We'd just argue and how would that end? I don't have a lot of options here. Or haven't you noticed."

But you will, he wanted to say. A fresh start, a whole new life. With Frank? In hiding too? What Frank assumed. But the Service wouldn't care about her. Just Frank, the defector. What would happen if she did have options? Why hadn't he told her?

"There, how do I look?" she said. "Let's go give the comrades a drink. Funny, coming all this way just to go over timetables."

"Jo—"

She put her hand on his arm. "I'm okay. Really. Sometimes it's nice to have a shoulder, though."

He smiled, not knowing what else to say. "Any time."

"But nothing to Frank. I know how you are. But not this. My secret."

"What if you're wrong?"

She raised an eyebrow, dismissing this. "Yes, what if."

As they walked across the lawn, they could see Frank saying good-bye to the visitors, leaning into the car window for a final word, then waving them off.

"I thought you'd be hours," Joanna said.

"No, we're all set. I told them the Astoria in Leningrad. You liked it the last time."

"Marzena was here," Joanna said, her voice flat.

"Already?"

"Her fridge is on the blink or something. And would you take a look."

"Why doesn't she just call the gate? Send a maintenance—"

"But you're right here. I said you might be tied up, so you have an out."

"No, she'll just come back. Want to take a walk?" he said to Simon. "It's not far. Have a cigar before dinner." He pulled one out of his breast pocket. "Cuban." An enticement. "The boys brought some."

Simon had been watching them, an innocent volley, neither giving anything away, but now Frank's eyes were more insistent. Come with me.

"You'd better put on some boots. It's wet," Joanna said, turning to go, done with it.

They took the path past the garden, through trees and then a small clearing, no other houses in sight.

"We have the go-ahead for Wednesday. That give you enough time to wrap up the book?"

"Wednesday," Simon said.

"I moved the time up. Just in case," he said, looking at Simon, not saying more. "We're on the night train. The *Red Arrow*." He took a puff on the cigar. "Always popular with foreign visitors. They like the cover, by the way. I knew they would. What would I be doing poking around the Baltics by myself? Now the Agency won't suspect—"

"But they know."

"Stay on our side of the board. The Service operation."

"Which is what, exactly? You never say."

"It's better to—" He stopped, catching Simon's look.

"I think I'm entitled to know. Now."

Frank nodded. "The Agency's been in touch with a dissident group. Now they're coming to make contact. And we'll be there."

"Are they?"

"Of course not. They're coming to get me," he said, explaining something to a child. "There is no Agency operation. Except the one I planned. A typical operation, like the ones I used to run, the same details, so it's plausible. Everything has to be plausible. We round up the group, then we intercept the boat. And something else happens. The last minute, when it's too late."

"On the boat."

"Right."

"From Leningrad."

"No, we're tourists in Leningrad. What we want the Agency to think." He looked at Simon. "If they were watching. Which we want the Service to think. Keep the board straight. Then Tallinn, next stop, then Riga. But we never get to Riga. Just the boat in Tallinn."

"Why Tallinn?"

"I know the Service chief there. He's like Pirie, thinks he's God's gift and doesn't know his ass from his elbow. He'll go along with anything he thinks the Service wants. The station chief in Leningrad is good. He might have a question or two. We can't risk that. And it's further away from international waters. The Agency wouldn't dream of trying to make contact near Leningrad. But Estonia—"

"It's still the Soviet Union."

"But they don't think so, bless them. You know how the Agency is about that. Still fighting the good fight."

Simon glanced over at him. Almost a hum in his voice.

"Besides, there really is a group of dissidents in Tallinn. Estonian nationalists. Everything plausible, remember?"

"Like the Latvians," Simon said, half to himself. He looked up. "What happens to them?"

"What's going to happen to them anyway. But this way it works for us."

"Jesus, Frank–" Simon said, his stomach turning.

"If it's not me, it'll be someone else. The Service knows about them. They really are enemies of the state."

"This state."

"That's right. My last job for the Service." He turned. "It buys us out, Jimbo. We're in this. They're going to find Gareth. We don't have time to change plans now. Just get out. Don't worry, you won't have anything to do with the Estonians. Your hands are clean."

Simon looked down at them, not just hands in a metaphor. Pushing against his windpipe.

"Why don't I leave now then? Tomorrow. Just go. You don't need me anymore."

Frank stopped, alarmed. "You try to leave now, it throws a red flag before the play starts. The Service already approved the trip. Any change– You're the cover. For the Agency."

"But the Agency–"

"Stay on our side of the board. You make everything plausible. Besides, I need you to take Jo out."

"What?"

"The boat's a Service operation. Armed. I'm supposed to be bringing the Agency *in*. So how would I explain either of you? You're going to take the ferry to Helsinki. I have it all timed. All planned."

He dropped the cigar and put his hand on Simon's shoulder. "One more meeting with DiAngelis. We're almost there."

Marzena's dacha was more modest than Frank's, a three-room cottage with only tarred shingles for insulation, a summer place. The problem with the refrigerator turned out to be a blown fuse, easily fixed. Simon looked for some trace of guile, the fridge an excuse to see Frank, but there was nothing but wide-eyed gratitude, electrical switches a genuine mystery. They were familiar with each other, neighbors, no more. Or maybe it was because he was there, a chaperone. Frank's idea.

The talk over the thank-you drink was idle, about nothing, so Simon watched the conversation in their faces, the way he used to watch Diana and her men, waiting for the second he wasn't supposed to see. A chance encounter at a restaurant, a party, and then a look between them and Simon would know. He used to wonder how it had started, what signal. A glance? A shift in the air? What had they said? A kind of sexual recruitment, maybe the way Frank had been recruited to the Party, with promises.

But he saw none of that here, not even the studied politeness Diana used to cover things, giving herself away by not looking at all. Instead Frank seemed amused by her, by the charm in her vanity, but also wary, someone unpredictable. Then what had Jo seen? Her own fears, maybe. A look misinterpreted. Or something real, now part of the past. He looked over at Marzena, suddenly feeling an odd sympathy for the left behind. Whatever she had been, she wasn't part of the plan. Not even a good-bye.

"You see how she is," she said to Simon, looking at the dog, curled up next to the chair by the stove. "Always waiting. It makes me so sad to see it."

"What about you? How are you doing?" Frank said.

"Ouf. How would I be? Sometimes like Pani, sometimes— It's

something new, to be alone like this. You hear sounds at night and then, no sleep."

"You're safe here. It's a Service compound."

"And he was safe? Perry?"

"Marzena—"

"Yes, I know, you already told me. Foolish. But maybe not so foolish. I don't believe he would do that to himself. To me. They sent him into exile. So why not—"

"Exile. Half of Russia wants a residence permit for Moscow. A dacha."

"Where he can't work. For him, exile. They didn't trust him. And you know, when they don't trust you— So why not? Why foolish?"

"He should never have signed the letter."

"Oh, a letter," she said, waving her hand, dismissive. "Such a serious thing. To ask for world peace. Don't you want world peace?" she said to Simon.

"Everybody does," Frank said. "But they don't send letters to international congresses. I know he meant well but it was—awkward. For the Party."

"So he has to leave Arzamas. Why not just shoot him there?"

"Marzena."

"And now what? Do they take back the flat? This house? How do I live? I'm afraid."

"You're Perry's widow. The Service always looks after its own. Especially if—"

"He's famous. Yes, you told me." She turned to Simon. "You know, when we met, I had no idea he was famous. A nice man. Quiet. How would I know? Then I saw the photographs. When he arrived, the reception. Like a hero. The meeting with Fuchs. You know, they were both at Los Alamos and they never knew each other? So there was a laugh about that, how careful the Service was, they didn't even know each other. And then what? The letter. Other scientists too, not just him. End the arms race. Not disloyal, a good Communist. Always. And poof." She waved her arm again. "No clearance. No work. Politically unreliable. Perry, who gave them everything. And no one talks to us. Just you," she said to Frank. "The others run away, like mice. So he sits here. No more letters. No more anything. And then, when everybody forgets—no one looking—they do it. Tell me I'm wrong," she said to Frank, suddenly fierce.

"You're wrong," he said calmly. "The Service doesn't work that way. Stop. You'll make yourself—"

"Crazy. Yes, I feel crazy sometimes. What if I'm right? Then I'm next?"

"You're not right," Frank said, still calm.

"Then what was it?" she said, a catch in her voice, real pain. "How could he do it?"

Frank said nothing, letting the air settle, then put his empty glass on the table. "We have to be going," he said. "You'll be all right? No more appliances to fix?"

An involuntary smile. "How can you laugh?"

"I'm not laughing. It's hard. I know."

She nodded, her face softer, as if she had been stroked. "Oh, and now you're worried, how will she be tomorrow? With people. The first time since—"

"I'm not worried."

"No? I think Joanna is. If I ruin her party." She looked up. "But I won't." She put her hand on Simon. "You'll talk to me, won't you? Tell me about America. You know, Perry always liked it there. He said he wished I could see it."

Simon looked at her, at a loss.

"Of course, not possible." She glanced over at Frank. "You really think it will be all right, about the flat?"

"Yes."

She nodded. "Don't worry, tomorrow. I won't say anything in front of the others. My foolishness. It's different with you. Who's coming?"

"The Rubins."

She smiled, the hint of a giggle.

"What?"

"All spies." She touched Simon's arm. "Except you. Yes? Everybody but you."

They went back a different way, through woods so thick they had to walk single file.

"She liked you," Frank said, his teasing voice. "Better watch out. She's already buried two."

Simon looked up at the back of Frank's head, surprised at his tone.

"She was married before?"

"That's why she was at Arzamas. A Polish physicist. Radiation poisoning. And there was Perry. He never had a chance."

"Is it true what she said? They fired him for signing a letter?"

"It wasn't just any letter. Scientists everywhere. Put an end to weapon research. As if it was up to them. He was lucky. In the old days he would have been shot."

"But he wasn't," Simon said, a question.

Frank shook his head. "That's just Marzena's way of explaining it to herself. If the Service did it, then he didn't."

"Why did he?"

Frank was silent for a minute. "I don't know," he said finally. "Do we ever? But it wasn't the Service. He had no access, not after he left. He wasn't going to make any trouble. Besides, the atomic spies—there's a certain obligation. They're heroes here. Look at the Rubins. She was just a courier and they get a big apartment on Gorky Street. Watch this branch."

Simon ducked.

"If I had to guess," Frank said, "I'd say when he stopped working—that was the end of things for him. That's where he lived, not the real world. Signing letters, for Christ's sake. What did he think would happen?"

"You liked him."

Frank turned. "They're just down the road, so we saw a lot of them. He had the time and nobody to talk to. Except Marzena, but that gets to be a little one-note."

Simon looked at him. He talked. I made notes.

"And what does she do now?" Simon said. Frightened by night sounds.

"Oh, the Service will take care of her. She won't have to worry. Now what?" he said, stopping at the edge of the woods, Boris's car back in the driveway.

Joanna, picking something in the garden, spotted them and ran over.

"Boris is here. He's staying the night," she said, visibly upset.

"What?"

"He's worried that something might—"

"Might what? What's wrong?"

"Gareth. He's been killed. It's awful. Another one, so soon after Perry, so they're worried—"

"Gareth?" Frank said, his tone flawless, shocked.

Simon blinked, saying nothing.

"He's been killed," Joanna said again. "Murdered."

"What? How?"

"I don't know. Boris will tell you. He just said murdered. He wants to make sure you're—you don't think it's true, do you, that it has anything to do with Perry? That somebody—"

"No. I don't know. Where is he?"

"Inside. I didn't know what to say. About his staying."

"Let me talk to him. Gareth?" he said again, trying to absorb it.

"I know and we just saw him a few days ago," Jo said. "Oh, there's Eva. I'd better say good-bye."

Boris had come out on the porch and waved in their direction.

"Careful," Frank said, his voice low. "He'll say he's here to protect me."

"Isn't he?"

"Mm. Just be careful."

"Too bad Perry didn't—" Simon stopped. "Why didn't he have a Boris?"

"He did, for a while," Frank said, turning toward the porch.

Simon looked up at Boris again, feeling a click in his head, a camera shutter opening. No need when Perry had Frank, a friend, not a babysitter. Much more effective. Someone he could talk to. Did he suspect? He talked. I made notes. And how many of them now would go to DiAngelis? The full Service file? Or just enough to clinch the deal, a few names, the file a protected asset. Assuming there was anything in it. Years since Arzamas, his science out of date, his letter writing behind him. And talking to his wife, even better, something a Boris couldn't have done. The family friend. Unless she was listening too, provided by the Service, another Sergei. Everybody listening. Careful what you say. Boris was coming down the stairs, relieved to see them.

"What's this about your staying the night?" Frank said. "Gareth's dead?" Still pitch-perfect.

"The office thinks it's safer, until they know. Two Western agents, so soon. So maybe another."

"They think they're connected? How?"

"I don't know. A precaution only."

"Do you think they are?"

"Me? No. The Englishman—" He glanced quickly at Simon, flustered. "A crime of sex."

"God," Frank said. "Gareth. What did he do? Pick up someone behind the Metropol? It wasn't Sergei, was it?"

"They don't know," Boris said, embarrassed again. "Maybe a quarrel. Maybe a stranger. Not the Metropol. You know where?"

Frank grunted no.

"Novodevichy Cemetery."

"Novodevichy?" Frank said, jarred. "When was this?"

"The time is uncertain. Maybe yesterday. Maybe before."

"You mean he could have been lying there dead while we were—? What in God's name was he doing there?"

"He lives nearby. It would be a convenient place to meet somebody."

"What if we'd seen him?" Frank said, still unsettled. "Was he just—lying there? On some grave?"

"The caretaker's shed."

"God. To go like that," Frank said. "So—sordid."

"Unless arranged. To give that appearance."

"Is that what they think?"

Boris shrugged. "They're investigating."

"Well, of course you're always welcome to stay," Frank said, as if it were simply a weekend invitation. "We've put Simon in the guest room, but there's the back bedroom. Would that be okay? Jo, can we fix that up for Boris?"

"Of course," she said, joining them. "Poor Gareth. We just saw him."

"Yes?" Boris said.

"At the Aragvi. You were there. In his cups. As usual. Why would anyone want to kill Gareth. He wouldn't hurt a fly."

Simon glanced at her, saying nothing.

"It's crazy," she said. "Someone going around killing— What for? I mean, they're not even agents anymore."

"Not for us. But maybe one for them," Boris said quietly.

"What do you mean?"

"A plant. All along."

Frank looked over at him. "Elizaveta," he said.

Boris nodded.

"She's back? Christ."

Another nod. "They brought her in. She always said—"

"Elizaveta?" Simon said, at sea.

Boris glanced over, waiting for Frank's lead to go on. Service business.

"She's our Torquemada. The foreign agents. She thinks we're all really double agents, or why else would we have come? She used to make life hell for everybody. Donald couldn't work for years. Guy— well, you can imagine. Files and more files. Until they pensioned her out. I thought." This to Boris.

"A special assignment. When she heard about the English—"

"But not Perry," Joanna said.

"No, but an English. She always said the English would do this."

"She thought the Americans were too dumb," Frank said, explaining. "New to the game. But the Brits. She thinks they think the way she does. So now what?" he said to Boris. "Gareth gets killed and who did it?"

"The double agent. Gareth found out."

"Gareth? She really is batty, you know."

Boris shrugged, noncommittal.

"And Perry knew too?"

"Maybe not connected," Boris said.

"So, theory one," Frank said, holding up a finger. "Somebody's bumping us all off, one by one. For reasons—well, we don't know. Maybe he just doesn't like us. Theory two, Gareth found out there was a double agent and threatened to expose him. Presumably another Brit. Elizaveta would be disappointed otherwise. All those years chasing MI6 and now, snap. If she gets him. And three, Perry—well a tragedy, but it happens. And Gareth got involved with a rough customer who beat him to death, or whatever he did. Which happened a few weeks later. So which makes the most sense? But instead we get old Elizaveta back, making trouble for everybody." He made an exaggerated sigh. "Let's hope we find out what happened before she makes a real mess. Come on, Boris, let's have some soup," he said, putting his arm around Boris's shoulder. "The Service will get through this too."

Simon watched them head for the stairs, Frank as smooth as a dancer, every step effortless. The way he'd always been, knowing what to do. For a second Simon felt a rush of the old admiration, following behind, Frank making everything all right. Boris's friend.

"And now Boris for dinner," Joanna said.

But Frank made that all right too, never mentioning Gareth, instead getting Boris to tell one of his stories about the war, when the Germans had Moscow practically in sight. Simon listened quietly, imagining the evenings with Perry and Marzena, the stories from Arzamas, how the letter started, names. I made notes. When Jo cleared the dishes, he went out on the porch for a smoke, just to get away, his chest tight. There were still a few streaks of light in the sky, the way it had looked that first night at the airport, before everything.

"You okay?" Frank said, coming out.

Simon nodded. "I keep thinking I'll say the wrong thing."

"You won't. Just keep your head. Nobody's looking at you."

"Or you."

"Yet. It's a bad break, Elizaveta. Now they won't bury it, they'll investigate. Most of them are like Boris—they don't want to know, just get him in the ground. But she'll want a hunt, every foreigner."

"You've been here twelve years. You're—"

"Foreign. It's something primal with them. And she's the worst. She held up my security clearance for two years."

"Yours?"

"And she's still not sure." He stopped, then smiled to himself. "God, I'd love to see her face. When she hears. Well, let's hope she has her hands full with the Brits. At least until Wednesday. And I'm senior. She'll have to work her way up to me. We should be all right."

"Should be."

"Should be. She prides herself on being thorough. About nothing. Ah, Boris." He turned toward the door. "Here, have one of these. Not those Dymoks. They'll kill you."

"Good Russian cigarette." He stepped onto the porch, taking a puff of his. "Still light. In Leningrad, the white nights. I have never seen, but everyone likes."

"Why don't you come too?"

"No. Is already arranged. With Service people there. Maybe I go to Sochi."

Frank laughed. "And get a tan? I can't see you just lying on the beach."

"I like the sun. Good for the health. Comrade Burgess goes there. Well, not now. I think Elizaveta will start with him, no?"

"I suppose he was the closest to Gareth."

"But not for sex," Boris said, uncomfortable.

"No, I don't think so. Anyway, not since Sergei."

Boris nodded. "Like a marriage. So why Novodevichy? To meet someone else? Sergei says no. He wouldn't." Sergei already questioned.

"Sergei wouldn't know."

"Possible," Boris said, thinking about it.

"And Gareth— We won't speak ill of the dead, but loyalty wasn't exactly his strong suit."

"He was loyal to the Party," Boris said simply, another puzzle piece.

"Well, that's a different kind of marriage."

Boris looked up. "For life." All that mattered.

They heard the phone ring and Joanna answering it. No one

said anything, listening, apprehensive, the hour late. A call from the Lubyanka? Marzena hearing night sounds? They all turned when Jo came to the porch.

"It was Hannah. They want to bring Ian. They have him for the weekend apparently. I could hardly say no. We'll just set another place."

"The more the merrier," Frank said, his shoulders relaxing.

Simon looked at him, a silent Who?

"Ian McAulife. You've probably never heard of him. No head-lines, like Guy and Donald. But probably a hell of a lot more useful. Right under their noses at Harwell. For years," he said, a trace of Service pride in his tone.

But Boris had turned rigid, alert to something in the air. "An English," he said, and Simon could see that it had already begun, the drawing away from each other, the Service turning on itself, not wanting to be caught in the conspiracy in Elizaveta's head. What would happen after Wednesday, a real crisis? The double agent no one suspected. He looked over at Boris, smoking his Russian ciga-rette. Maybe in Sochi when everything blew up, the defection still on his watch. Why hadn't he seen it? Had he been part of it? Ques-tions, while the Service tore itself apart. He'd be punished some-how, knee-jerk Service justice, the wheels as indifferent as he'd been, a political officer at the front, taking no prisoners. Simon looked away, another improbable moment, for a second on the other side of the board, worrying about an officer of the KGB.

He had laughed at Marzena, but in fact there were night sounds, sudden animal rustlings in the woods, a car engine in the distance. Going where at this hour? He looked at his watch, the barely visible dial. Two. Now a tinkling sound, ice in a glass. A thin strip of light under the door. Someone still up. Not Boris, who never used ice. Not Frank, who'd claimed exhaustion, the evening mostly spent on the phone to the office, more details.

Simon got out of bed and put on his robe, then opened the door a crack, gently, trying not to make noise. Joanna was on the couch, hunched forward over the coffee table, glass in one hand, turning pages with the other. Not a book, stiff paper, a photo album. Stopping for a minute, hand hovering over the page, staring, taking a drink without looking, the ice tinkling again, no louder than one of the insects outside. A cone of light from the small end table lamp, the rest of the room dark. Simon stood peering out, not moving. How long had she been out here—in her nightgown, unable to sleep, waiting for the house to quiet, to be alone. A girl surrounded by people, hair falling back. Now she put down the glass and folded her arms across her chest, pitching forward, rocking a little, her face turned so that he had to imagine tears, the sobs just twitches in her shoulders. Back and forth, holding herself, a silent keening. Then a loosening, a letting go, slumping back against the couch and lying on her side, still no sound. Simon waited, not wanting to intrude. Something he shouldn't have seen. Another few minutes, no movement on the couch. But then he noticed the smoke, a thin stream rising from the ashtray, the cigarette still going.

He tiptoed out into the room. Joanna's eyes were closed, her breathing even. Just put the cigarette out and go. On the table, next to the vodka bottle, the album was still open. Simon looked down. Family pictures, a couple with a child, the same front porch just outside. Smiles. A winter scene, Richie in a snowsuit on a sled, Frank in a fur hat pulling him. Blowing candles on a birthday cake. The life they used to have, not mentioned in the book, not talked about. He glanced at the couch, Joanna still sleeping, then reached down and turned a page. The dacha lawn, Richie just a toddler, the three of them together. Richie playing with her hair, pulling her head back, Joanna laughing.

He turned to the couch. She had pulled one arm up to her chest and now it moved with her breathing, her hair spread out behind her on the couch pillow. The way he remembered it. She hadn't known then either, that he'd watched her sleeping, unable to move, afraid to wake her, break the spell of their good luck. Outside the soft Virginia countryside, wet with early morning, open, not dark woods behind a patrolled fence. The memory of it so strong that he felt he was living it now, could reach down and brush the hair from the side of her face, kiss her ear, tell her it was time to get up. Then get back into bed to watch the light come through the window, head next to hers.

She stirred for a second, as if she could feel him looking, then turned her head on the pillow, her face drawn, not the girl in Virginia, a different sleep, tormented by old pictures. Not Joanna at all, lazy with sex, someone else, worn out, listened to and watched so that even grief had to be muffled by running taps, the only private thing left. He stood, rooted, seeing the different face, not the memory anymore, the face she had.

He almost jumped when he felt the movement behind him. Frank put a finger to his lips, *shh,* then leaned down and rubbed out the cigarette. He took the album and closed it, shoulders slumped, something he'd done before, then looked up at Simon, still not speaking. He raised a finger to his lips again, then picked up the afghan lying on the arm of the couch and spread it over her lightly, so the touch of the fabric wouldn't wake her. How many nights had he done this? Marriage was private. Frank had drawn a veil over theirs with an afghan. What were they to each other now? How could anyone know? People thought he and Diana were happy.

He looked down at the couch, the unhappy woman who cried

without making a sound. When he looked back up, Frank was moving toward the table lamp, motioning with his head for Simon to go to his room, a kind of dismissal. I'll take care of the lights. And my wife.

———————————

Joanna had sun for her party, a spring day warm enough for summer. A long wicker table and chairs had been set up on the lawn, something out of a tsarist era photograph, the family posed around an outdoor table with fields stretching behind, corsets and high collars, servants, a samovar bubbling on the table, the revolution just a thundercloud away. Now there were bottles of Georgian wine and Hannah Rubin in a dowdy sundress. Where had Joanna got the salmon? Gastronom 1 had been out for days. A friend had put her on to a plumber who did private work. "I know we're not supposed to, but I had to get it fixed." Did Joanna still get her hair done at the Pekin?

She was a slightly plump, friendly woman with curly hair and a New York accent, warm, the sort of woman who'd give treats to the kids in the neighborhood. Her husband was more recessive, happier behind a newspaper than talking, but willing to let her take the lead. Looking at them now, it was hard to believe they'd once been notorious, Hannah a courier with atomic plans in her purse, Saul the contact man for a small network of agents who'd favored, according to the *Mirror*, meetings at Chock full o'Nuts. The man they'd brought, more valuable than Burgess, was thin with receding hair and soft eyes, someone you wouldn't notice on a bus, any clerk. Today he was visibly nervous, more aware perhaps of the dread that hung over the table, the news everybody was ignoring, Gareth's name not yet mentioned. Marzena was late.

"How is she?" Hannah said. "It must be so hard for her. Such a terrible thing. Was she the one who found him?"

"No. Frank," Joanna said.

Simon looked up. The first time he'd heard this.

"How awful," Hannah said. "I can't imagine. You know what they're saying. Maybe it was like Gareth. One after the other."

"Who's saying?" Frank said.

Hannah looked at him, reprimanded. "You're right. Gossip. It's ridiculous. But what a thing for you," she said to Simon. "Your first trip. You'll think it's always like this. But really it's like anywhere else. You probably don't believe that, the way the papers are. When I read *Time*, I can't help it, I think, where are they talking about? But that's nothing new. Anything to undermine the Soviet Union. What did they think at home about the Gary Powers trial? Were people at least embarrassed?"

"I think they thought he was unlucky. And the trial—"

"Soviet theater," Frank said mischievously. "You can't blame them. They're so good at it and they don't get the chance much anymore. Not since Stalin."

Boris lifted his head at this.

"Frank," Hannah said, a mild scold, looking around to gauge the reaction at the table.

"It's just us," Frank said. "Nobody's listening."

"You'll give Simon the wrong impression." She turned to him again. "Eisenhower was embarrassed, you could see it. When Powers was captured. But the one you never saw was Dulles. You'd think— Nothing. Not even an apology."

"What about the pill? The poison?" Saul Rubin said. "I read somewhere people think he should have taken it."

"Some, I guess," Simon said.

"I don't see it. I mean, what the hell was he supposed to know? A pilot. Taking pictures."

"I guess the idea was to—avoid what happened. The trial."

"It's a lot to ask, no? I mean, I was doing a lot more than taking pictures and nobody ever gave me a pill. They give one to you?" he said to Ian.

"No," Ian said, sipping some wine.

"I thought all that went out with the OSS," Frank said. "Behind-enemy-lines stuff."

"Aren't we?" Joanna said, then caught Frank's expression. "I mean, it's not like a real war. But if you're spying—"

"It's the same," Boris said.

"Not that I think anybody should have to do that. A suicide capsule. What information could be worth that?"

"That depends on the times," Saul said. "When Hannah was carrying the plans for the bomb, for the design, talk about a matter of life and death. Of course, she didn't have to do anything like that, she was too clever for them." He looked at Simon. "You ever hear the story of what happened in Albuquerque?"

"Oh, Saul."

"Cool as a cucumber. She's got the papers in her purse, the most valuable piece of paper in the world right then, and she gets to the train station and they're inspecting bags. IDs, all that. Why then? Who knew? Maybe just routine. But she's got to get on the train. So she's wearing a sun hat and she takes it off and slips the paper in the hat, you know, behind that ribbon that goes around on top. And she gets to the MP and she says, here, would you hold this? While she opens her purse to find her ID. So he's holding the plans for the bomb while she's fishing around in there. So then thanks, here's your hat, and she's on the train. It's one for the books. She never broke a sweat."

"I sweated plenty later," she said, then looked down, thoughtful, twisting her ring. "I don't know. How can we know what we would have done? I think I would have taken the pill. It was a different time. We thought, they have the bomb, they could destroy the Soviet Union. The Party. Everything we worked for. For them to

have that power— So we did what we did. And that made us crimi-
nals. To somebody like Dulles. He should talk. But I'll tell you one
thing. Whatever I did, it never caused the death of a single American. Not one. That's important to me."

Simon looked at her, astonished, but the others at the table were
either nodding in agreement or indifferent, a self-deception they'd
agreed to accept.

"I still think of myself as American," Hannah said. "Not one
American life—"

"You can't possibly know that," Ian said abruptly, his voice so
English that the words seemed foreign.

The table was silent for a moment, as if some invisible trip wire
had been snapped and people were waiting for something to go off.
Hannah blinked, as still as the others.

Ian looked up, feeling the disturbance. "Sorry. I just meant—" he
said, then let it go.

"I understand that," Joanna said to Hannah, smoothing things
over. "I still feel American. Though I guess I'm not. What do you
think, Boris? Am I a Russian lady yet?"

"Good Soviet," Boris said, taking the question seriously. "Not
every Soviet is born in Russia. A question of choice."

"And we made it, didn't we?" Joanna said wryly, looking around,
as if the dacha, the bright day were visible proof of good judgment.
"Well, we'd better start or we'll be pie-eyed before we eat. Eva made
her cold borscht to start. Perfect day for it, isn't it?"

"Should we call Marzena?" Hannah said. "Maybe something's—"

"No, she'll swan in when she's good and ready. I'll just get the
soup. Ian, would you give me a hand?" she said, a polite rescue.

He stood up. "Elizaveta wants to see me Monday," he said,
blurting it. "First thing."

Another awkward silence.

Joanna put her hand on his arm. "Never mind. The old cow's

been trying to scare people for years. And nothing ever comes of it."

"It's like being summoned by the headmaster." He glanced down toward Boris. "It's not right. Treating us this way. After all we've—"

"Come on. Soup," Joanna said, still trying to deflate it.

But Ian was standing his ground, looking directly at Boris now, the responsible party, the only Russian.

"She is not the Service," Boris said, his voice tentative, trying to get it right. "Maybe the old days, not now. It's in your book." He waved his hand to include Frank. "It's like that, not her."

"Yes, I can't wait to read—" Hannah started.

"But why pick on me?" Ian said.

Boris smiled. "Me too. Pick, pick." He made a beaking gesture with his hand. "Everybody. Her way, that's all."

"Bloody awful, if you ask me," Ian said, but retreating now. "They shouldn't allow it. Sorry," he said to Joanna.

"Come on. You'll feel better with some food in you," she said, beginning to lead him away. "There she is." She waved to Marzena, coming out of the trees. "Just in time. Oh good, she's brought her dog." Simon glanced up. An edge no one could have missed.

"She never makes any trouble," Frank said. "The dog."

Hannah waited until Ian was in the house. "She probably wants to see him about Gareth. As if he'd have anything to do with something like that. She really does go too far. I know she's been loyal to the Service." A nod to Boris. "But sometimes—"

"What you said before," Simon interrupted, before Boris could answer. "About *Time*. Do you get it here?" Moving away from Gareth.

"At the Institute," Hannah said, slightly surprised. "They get all the Western publications. For analysis. Of course, it's a restricted list, but *Time*, a few others, I get to keep up pretty well. Although like I said, sometimes it makes me so darned mad, the way they—"

"We're going to be in *Look*," Frank said. "They're coming to take pictures. 'The author at home.'"

"Are they allowing that?" Hannah said, another glance to Boris.

"Oh yes, all approved. Part of the 'active measures.' Shame *Look*'s not here today. Get the whole gang. America's Most Wanted."

"Frank," Hannah said, disapproving.

"Shame who's not here?" Marzena said, finally at the table. "Pani, be quiet."

The men stood, everyone saying hello.

"A photographer. We're going to be in an American magazine, me and Jo. Simon too, if he's not too shy," he said, smiling at him.

"Do you really think that's a good idea?" Saul said. "They'll probably make you look—"

"I know. But Simon says it's good for the book. Publicity."

"Things have a way of changing," Saul said. "One day they think one thing, then—" He paused, a side glance to Boris. "Remember in the beginning? How they didn't want us photographed at all?"

"When we weren't really here," Hannah said. "Keep Hoover guessing."

"Well, he knows we're here now," Frank said.

"They would never allow Perry—" Marzena said, then stopped. "What kind of pictures?" She touched her hair, an absentminded primping.

"Oh, the usual, I guess. Me at the typewriter, banging out the magnum opus. Having coffee with Jo. Maybe out for a walk. Red Square probably, wouldn't you think?" This to Simon.

"Probably." Not the vodka bottles, Boris in the next room, the cage lined with books.

"You should wear your gray suit," Marzena said. "You look so handsome in that." A wife's comment. Simon glanced up. Maybe what Jo had heard, her antennae picking things out of the air.

"I thought the professional look. Cardigan and pipe. Something like that. Well, we'll let *Look* decide."

"They'll put you in a trench coat," Saul said. "Hat down over your eyes."

"How is an agent supposed to look these days?" Frank said, playing with it.

"Like everybody else," Hannah said. "So nobody notices." She smiled a little, as if she were offering herself up as an example. A woman who asked an MP to hold her hat while she rummaged through her purse.

"Ian," Marzena said, seeing him come out. "Nobody told me. Let me help you with that. Ouf, so heavy." She helped him set the tureen on the table, an unnecessary gesture. "But how nice. I was going to write you. Your letter—after Perry. I was so grateful." Looking at him, using grief.

Joanna had followed with a large tray, a spread of small dishes to go with the borscht, the usual lawn party finger sandwiches and strawberries replaced with whitefish and pickled mushrooms.

"You know who wrote me?" Marzena said to Ian. "His sister. She wants him to be buried there. His ashes. In America. What do I say to her? I thought, maybe he would like this. Not here. What do you think?"

"I don't think he cares one way or the other," Ian said. "He's dead."

Another awkward silence.

"I suppose there'll be a funeral," Hannah said, making polite conversation.

"There was a funeral," Marzena said.

"No, I meant for Gareth."

"Gareth?"

"Oh, you haven't heard. I'm sorry." She put a hand on Marzena's. "He was killed."

"Killed? Like Perry?"

"No, not like Perry," Hannah said, comforting. "I don't know the details. Do you?" she said to Frank.

"No. They're investigating," Frank said, his voice even, glancing at Boris.

"Killed. Murdered," Marzena said, folding her arms across her chest now, a sudden chill. "Now another one."

"I don't see how the one has anything to do with the other," Ian said, blunt again.

"Nobody said they did," Hannah said, moving Marzena toward a seat. "Here, have a drink, dear. It's a shock, isn't it? I know. So young too."

"Well, you have to admit," Saul said. "Two. One right after the other."

"Saul."

"It's not connected," Boris said.

Everyone looked up at this, waiting for more, but Boris said nothing, an end to it.

"This looks delicious," Hannah said to Joanna. "So much trouble."

"No, all easy. Ian, why don't you pass these?" Putting him to work.

"Shall we have a toast?" Saul said. "To Gareth. I have to say, I always wondered what he was like as an agent. I'm glad I didn't have to run him. But I guess he never meant any harm. Anyway, nobody deserves this."

Simon raised his glass, staring at his hand, hearing Gareth's voice in the church. Sneering, ready to inform. No proof. He looked over at Frank, his hand also raised in the toast, and saw the blur again as it smashed down.

There was sour cream to swirl in the borscht and heavy, dark bread and a tub of ice to keep the wine and vodka chilled, and they fell on the lunch with a kind of relief, wanting to move on and yet helplessly drawn back, as if not talking about the dead was a form of disrespect.

"I wonder who'll speak. At the funeral," Hannah said.

"Guy, I should think," Ian said. "He knew him better than anyone."

"Is there family? Do you think they'll come over?" As simple as getting the 6:04 from Waterloo.

"Maybe they'll ask you," Marzena said to Frank, then turned to Simon. "He was so good at Perry's, so—I don't know the word. Something that comes from the soul."

"Marzena."

"Yes, it's true. The soul."

"He was my friend," Frank said. He talked. I made notes.

Joanna, who'd been watching this, said, "So modest. You are a good speaker. I never knew about the Shakespeare. That his name was really Prospero. How did you? Know, I mean."

"He told me."

Simon looked up, seeing him turn the pages of a file.

"Not me," Marzena said, almost pouting.

"They might ask you," Joanna said. "To speak. Who else is there? God knows Gareth would love it. He was always after you, to be friends. Talk about the last laugh."

"I doubt it."

"They might," Saul said. "They don't like to see the rest of us in public. But you—you're in magazines. God. What would you say?"

"What I'd say about any of us. That he gave his life to the Service."

Simon looked over, appalled, but Frank met his eye without blinking and Simon saw that he could do it, use the same hands that had been on Gareth's throat to hold the lectern, that it was how he lived, safe in a lie, another underneath. But didn't they all? He took off his glasses, rubbing them with his napkin, and looked at the indistinct faces around him. All spies, Marzena had said. Ordinary.

Like anyone else. Would you mind holding my hat, please? Not just white lies, little lubricants to make the wheels turn. Treason. Lies that betrayed everyone. All of them, all these ordinary people, sipping wine and eating soup. Hannah, everybody's aunt, delivering the bomb. Frank delivering a eulogy. Simon listening to it all, one of them now, making plans to betray them. Just a few days.

"Do you want a hat?" Joanna said to him. "It's hot in the sun. You look all funny."

"No, no. Probably just the wine. At lunch."

"I thought that's what publishing was," Frank said. "Boozy lunches."

"Sometimes."

"God, like State. Try getting an answer to anything after three. Remember?"

Simon didn't answer, still wiping his glasses. What if he put them on and suddenly could see everybody clearly, who they really were, some magical power? But then he couldn't hide behind them either, everybody exposed.

"I don't think we have to go," Saul was saying. "To the funeral. I mean, we scarcely knew him. If I met him twice in my life—"

"It must be so nice for you," Hannah said to Simon, taking them somewhere else. "Seeing each other again. All these years. Who's older? You, Frank?"

Frank dipped his head. "But Simon's the smart one. That's what our mother used to say anyway."

"She never said that."

"She didn't have to. You *were* the smart one." He turned to Hannah. "I was the bad influence."

"I can believe that," Hannah said.

"They packed him off to another school to get him away from me."

"That's not—"

"And the next thing you know, he's valedictorian. The smart one," he said, nodding, case closed.

"And I always thought that was you," Joanna said drily.

Frank raised his glass to her. "Once in a while. Lucky mostly, though. But weren't we all?" he said, including the Rubins. "Nobody suspected anything in those days. You could waltz out of the Agency at lunch with a bunch of papers and nobody thought twice. Quick copy and back in the file the same afternoon. Imagine trying that now."

"It was different in the field," Saul said. "The Bureau had guys everywhere. And if you were caught, you were caught. They gave the Rosenbergs the chair. You don't want to forget that."

"You couldn't take anything out of Harwell," Ian said suddenly. "Not a scrap."

"So how did you—?" Frank said.

"I memorized it."

"Arzamas was like that," Marzena said. "Someone always watching. But they couldn't watch up here." She tapped the side of her head.

"But it wouldn't matter," Ian said. "Nobody's trying to get anything out here."

"No, that's right," Marzena said quickly, a confused backpedaling.

"There's never been a leak. Not from there. Harwell either, except for me. You know, you do something for years, you'd think you'd build up a little credit. Like something in the bank. But they never trust you. Not just Elizaveta. How can they not trust us? After everything?"

No one answered, fidgeting, uncomfortable.

"It's important to be careful," Boris said finally. "All loyal Soviets." He spread his hand to take in the table. "But it's always possible—just one. Think how serious that would be."

"You think any of us would betray the Party?" Ian said.

Why not? Simon wanted to say. You've already betrayed once, everything you knew.

"Not you," Marzena said, patting his hand, a side glance to Frank. "No one would think that."

"It's important to be careful," Boris said again.

Everyone looked away, not wanting to meet his eye, used to it now, being suspect, watched. Would Boris file a report? Someone else? Simon looked around the table, trying to remember what he'd said, how it would look on a typed page. But he hadn't said anything. Everything was still safe inside, like Ian's memorized secrets, the sound of Gareth gasping for air.

"Fine talk for a party," Joanna said. "Who wants some more wine?" Filling her own glass.

"Are your parents still living?" Hannah said to Simon, a polite afternoon tea question.

"My father."

"Ah. Well, maybe he'll come too now. After you tell him it's not so terrible."

"No. I'm afraid—"

Frank looked up, a flicker of shadow on his face, some stray internal cloud.

"He's too old to make the trip now. He's very frail."

"Oh, that's a shame. But you two must have so much to talk about. Catching up. How much longer will you be here?"

"Just a few days. We're almost finished with the book."

"The book. I'd forgotten. That's why you came." She turned to Frank. "They're really letting you—?"

Frank nodded. "Their idea. Not mine. Of course, they can always change their minds. But so far they seem to like it. Right, Boris?"

"Is excellent."

"Am I in it?" Marzena said.

"No. No one here. Just in America, before I came."

"But you must be," Hannah said to Simon.

"Just in passing. I wasn't part– Frank used other sources." When he wasn't using me. Lunch at Harvey's. How's everything at State?

"He's lucky to have you. A publisher in the family."

"We're all lucky," Joanna said, sipping her drink. "And now you'll go and we won't see you again, will we? I hadn't thought about it before. Leningrad. And then–poof."

"You're going to Leningrad?" Hannah said, interested.

"And Tallinn," Joanna said. "And Riga. See Riga and die." She giggled. "One of Frank's trips. And then he's gone. No more Simon." Looking at him.

But it was the trip the table wanted to know about. When? Where were they staying? Had it been difficult to get permission? They leaned forward, eager for details. Any travel. Somewhere away from the compound, the pine woods, the men at the gate. Away.

"You have to see the Hermitage," Hannah said. "And the Peterhof. The fountains. Such a nice time of year too. I remember I couldn't sleep, it was still so light."

"Shall I come too?" Marzena said. "I've never been to Riga. Is it nice? I could meet you there." Playing with it, not meaning it, all of them packing imaginary bags.

"Oh, just like that," Hannah said. "Just get on a train."

"Yes, why not?"

"And your travel documents, please?" A conductor's voice.

"I don't need any. A Polish passport. That's why I kept it. You can come and go with a Polish passport. One good thing about Comecon, yes? Soviets, you have to have this and that, but Poles– we can leave anytime we want. No exit visas. Just the passport. That's all I need."

Simon looked up. But everyone else would need a visa, Soviet citizens now. He glanced over at Frank, only half paying attention to this, one of Marzena's whims. Everything planned, the times, the ferry. Jo would have to have an exit visa there. The first thing DiAngelis arranged. But Frank had been surprised, dismissive, something she wouldn't need.

Simon took off his glasses, wiping them again, trying to think. Why not? Everything else planned, the whole trip arranged through the Service. Why not? He looked up again, the table a blur in the bright light.

"You'll have to bunk in with Simon," Joanna was saying, teasing Marzena, happy with drink. "No room at the inn."

Marzena laughed, flirtatious. "So, and then what would people say? To go all the way to Riga to—"

Simon stopped listening, looking through the blur at Joanna. Who had never been told the plan, everything too risky. Who needed a new life. Just a short ferry ride from Tallinn. Where she'd need an exit visa. Which Frank hadn't arranged, said they wouldn't need. Why not? He looked down the table, Frank's features coming into focus, and Simon felt himself begin to flush, the moment sweeping through him like blood. Because she wasn't going, had never been going. He stared at Frank, then lowered his head, fiddling with the glasses, hiding his face. The smart one. Think it through. The plan from the beginning. But everything had been about her. The one hook Simon would never refuse. He looked sideways at Marzena, still having fun with her fantasy trip. Or maybe Frank had meant for her to go. Hadn't he already left a country behind? New life, new woman, something Joanna had known just sniffing the air.

"Oh, but what about Pani?" she was saying. "Can we take Pani?"

Frank was looking away, his mind somewhere else. No. Not Marzena. But not anyone else either. Simon looked down again, his arms tight against his body. Joanna wasn't going. Nobody was going. But DiAngelis was coming to get them, streaming into the trap Simon had helped build. Killed for. Following Frank again. Who always knew what to do. But this, would he do this? Simon saw his face at Harvey's, casual, intimate. How's everything at State? Drawn in again. I can't do this without you. The smart one. Think what to do. He looked over at Frank, feeling him slide away, a second skin sloughed off, leaving Simon bare and wriggling. On his own.

6

TOM MCPHERSON ARRIVED WITH two heavy cases of equipment—lamps and filters and folding reflector discs for backlighting, all of it nestled in loops of wires that took half an hour to untangle and set up.

"I thought it was going to be just you and a Brownie," Frank said, amused.

"Not for *Look*."

"Is all this supposed to make me look better?"

He was wearing the cardigan, as promised, and waiting placidly behind the typewriter while McPherson adjusted the lights, the study now an obstacle course of tripods and cables. Joanna had made them tea and then retreated.

"How about you and your brother," McPherson said to Simon. "Working on the manuscript."

"Come on, Jimbo," Frank said. "Are we supposed to look at the pages or up at you?"

Simon stood by the desk, reluctant to sit down.

"Come on. This was all your idea in the first place," Frank said smiling.

Act as if nothing had changed. Simon took the chair next to him.

"A little closer," the photographer said.

"I won't bite," Frank said, slightly puzzled, Simon still holding back, at the edge of the picture.

"Okay, this way," McPherson said, and in the flash that momentarily blinded him, Simon saw his father looking at the magazine, head down, shamed by a notoriety that now included both boys, not just one. Making a profit on treason.

"How about one by the radio?" McPherson said. "Where you listen to the news."

Frank turned toward the old console with its mesh speaker and Bakelite knobs and leaned in, concentrating on the news.

Boris, usually in the other room, stayed with them in the study, fascinated by it all, the screen test prompting and the paraphernalia, examining McPherson's case as if he were looking for contraband. When he finally got bored and went out to get more tea, McPherson took an envelope from his breast pocket and slipped it to Simon. Documents, presumably the exit visas for Frank and Joanna. What DiAngelis knew they needed. What Frank hadn't asked for.

"They said to check the—" McPherson began, cut off by Frank's pointing up to the chandelier.

"One more by the radio?" Frank said, still in character, nodding to McPherson.

Simon shoved the envelope into his briefcase, evidence now, buried under manuscript pages, safe from Boris's snooping, but how could it be explained? Illegal documents. Prepared by the Americans. He looked at Frank, turning the radio knobs again. For a trip nobody was going to take.

Think it through. What he'd been doing since that night at the dacha, staring up at the ceiling, suddenly alone. Run to the embassy and tell DiAngelis? With some Service ear listening. There had to be one, maybe more, who'd ring alarm bells straight back to Frank. And what would Frank do? Wave him off fondly at Sheremetyevo? Shrug as DiAngelis got away? Explain it to the Service? A scheme that went wrong, Simon the X factor? They'd never listen, never forgive. Frank couldn't let him go, not yet. He'd never make it to the airport. Only to the Lubyanka. He saw Gareth's face in the church, stunned, Frank ready to accuse him, turn the truth inside out. Who do you think they'd believe, you? Not Simon either, the Agency tool, luring his brother back. Another Gary Powers, caught red-handed, the pieces of evidence right there in his briefcase. Would Frank actually do it? He'd have to. He couldn't just run away this time, leaving a mess. He'd have to save himself. And if they didn't believe him? Simon thought of the Rubins, all of them at the lunch, tentative, nervous, the Service like a scythe hanging over them. And if it struck, or didn't, Joanna was trapped forever, would die here, lost in a haze, even her privileges gone. Some plan, one that let Frank's play out to the last minute, both sides of the board unaware that they were now part of a different game. Too late to stop now, not this close. Be the smart one. Work out the details. Back at his desk at the OSS, planning operations. There was still time, a few days. Enough to think it through.

"The telephone," Boris said, coming back with a tea mug. "The office."

"Now what," Frank said, but getting up eagerly, summoned. "Why don't you get a few shots of Boris?"

"It's not permitted."

"Oh, I'll get it cleared," Frank said, waving his hand.

"Not for the magazine," Simon said. "The book. We're going to use some of the pictures for an insert. Don't you want to be in the book?"

Boris had only half-followed this but got the end and smiled, pleased. "Yes, in the book," he said, then went over to stand against a bookcase, shoulders back.

"And Mrs. Weeks?" McPherson said, still shooting Boris.

"She'd rather not. She's not in the excerpt, so—"

"But you'll want her in the book."

What could Simon say? Plenty of time for that later?

"We'll use some old pictures. From when she actually appears in the story." There must be some, not just the ones in his head.

"Boris, you look like a commissar," Frank said, coming back, breezy, in good spirits. "Take a few, so we have a choice. How much longer, do you think?" he said to McPherson. "I've only got the morning now. Have to go to the office this afternoon."

"The office?" Simon said.

"Don't worry about the book. We can finish it on the train or something. Anyway, you'll need to pack. Good news. We leave tonight. The *Red Arrow*. I was afraid the train would be—but it's all right. All fixed. We'll have to skip Riga, though. They want me back by the weekend. Lucky I could get away at all. What's wrong?"

"Nothing. Tonight?" Too soon. What about the meeting with DiAngelis? He couldn't just pick up the phone. DiAngelis would have things to arrange on his end. Too soon.

"Well, pack light. It's Jo I'm worried about. Where else would you like me?" he said to McPherson, professional again.

"We've got plenty of books. How about outside, in front of the building?"

"Can't. Believe it or not, it's supposed to be a secret. Where I live. In case the CIA wants to kidnap me. Or worse. I know, but back then— Anyway we never changed it, the rule. What about Patriarch's Pond? I walk there a lot, and you've got the water. Just down the block. Maybe Jo would like to come too. Some fresh air."

"So we leave midnight?" Simon said, trying to form a timeline in his head, Frank ahead of him again. Ahead of everybody, taking the board back, not giving anyone time. Did he know? Had he seen it in Simon's face, the eyes opening behind the blur?

Frank nodded. "That's right. The overnight train. You keep saying you've got to get back, so the sooner the better, no?" Simon's idea now. "I thought we'd do something special this evening. You know, your last— And the Service came through." He opened his hand, voilà. "Seats at the Bolshoi. You can't leave Moscow and not see the Bolshoi. Fyodorovna doing *Swan Lake*." He turned to McPherson. "They tell me the embassy's got a bunch of season tickets. Diplomatic perk. You have any friends there, tell them this is the night they want to use them." Said casually, but his eyes steady on McPherson. "You don't want to miss Fyodorovna. They should definitely go tonight. Everybody'll be there. Even us," he said, amusing himself, with a quick glance to Boris to see if he'd been too direct, insistent.

"I'll do that," McPherson said, message received.

Simon looked at Frank. Another feint, in plain sight, as clever as a card trick. Ahead of them.

"My last night," Simon said to himself, thinking.

"Yes," Frank said. "Doesn't seem possible, does it? The time just—went." His voice affectionate, no longer breezy, as if the idea of Simon's leaving had just hit home. Even the tone right, how a brother would feel. And for a second Simon wanted it to be true, not something for Boris and McPherson, for him, the old voice.

"Whose last night?" Joanna said at the door.

"Simon's. Well, not last. You'll have to come back to Moscow to fly home. We're moving up the trip," Frank said to Jo. "The *Red Arrow* tonight."

"Tonight? Why the change?"

"I have to be back this week. And we don't want to rush Leningrad. I know it's last-minute—"

"Everything is these days," she said, disconcerted, trying to read his face. She turned to Simon. "Usually it takes months to arrange anything. See what a VIP you are. Oh, but Simon, you're going?" A crack in her voice.

"Not yet."

"I mean, I knew you would, but not so—"

"All the more reason to make the most of it now," Frank said. "We've got the Bolshoi tonight."

"We do? You hate the ballet."

"Maybe the Metropol first?"

"To celebrate," Jo said vaguely, still looking at Frank, trying to work something out.

McPherson moved a standing lamp. "Now that you're here," he said to Jo, "would you mind? How about the two of you sitting over there?" A quiet evening at home.

"With my knitting," Jo said, sarcastic.

"We were going down to the Pond," Frank said, conciliatory. "Maybe something there?" He paused. "For the book."

She glanced at Simon, then nodded. "Let me put on some lipstick. I'll catch up."

"Better bring that with you," Frank said to Simon, indicating the briefcase. "Ludmilla tidies up—she means well but then you can't find anything. You don't want her near the book."

Or the exit visas. Left behind for anyone to find. An amateur's mistake, the kind Frank didn't make. Think.

They walked to Patriarch's Pond in pairs, Boris trailing.

"What's going on?" Jo said to Simon.

"What do you mean?"

"He's scarcely been into the office for months and now all of a sudden he has to be back? Nobody makes travel plans at the last minute. This is Russia. There are channels."

"The Service—"

"Oh, the Service. I know. Always pulling rabbits out of hats. But why now? I know him. He's got that voice that goes over his voice. Has he said anything?"

"Honestly, I don't—" The words sticking in his throat, lying to her. But what was a lie now?

"He trusts you. He never tells me anything. I'm a drunk. I'm not reliable."

"You're not a drunk."

She looked at him, a small smile. "Not the way he thinks I am. Maybe that's why I do it. If I'm unreliable, he won't tell me things. So have a drink. But you noticed. How far it goes. He doesn't. You notice things." She laughed to herself. "You'd make a good spy."

"I doubt it," he said, uneasy. "My mother used to say my face was an open book."

She turned to him. "Not anymore. I watched you at lunch. You hated them all, but you never let on."

"I didn't hate—"

"Disapproved, then. You disapproved. But you kept it to yourself. You do that. I should be grateful. Imagine how I'd feel if I knew—you disapproved."

"Jo—"

But she was turning away. "Would you do something for me? A favor? Don't make a fuss about these pictures. I don't want to. So they can see what I look like now? Poor thing. But what can you expect? No, thanks."

"You look fine."

A half smile. "Well, you're supposed to be goofy about me. Were, anyway." She stopped, her mood shifting. "I can see. I know what I look like." She put a hand on his arm. "Don't make a fuss, okay? They'll listen to you. I really don't want to."

He imagined her stepping off a plane, surrounded by flashbulbs.

"You're part of the story, you know," he said gently. "I can't change that."

"The first part. Not now."

"So we use the same old pictures. The ones the papers ran after you left." He looked up, as if the idea had just occurred to him, not a detail on a checklist. "How about your passport? Do you still have it?"

"My passport?"

"Your American one. The one you used to get here. It's exactly when you leave the story. I'd get it back to you."

"That doesn't matter. It expired."

"But you still have it?"

She nodded. "I don't know why. Memento, I guess."

"But the picture—"

"Oh, Simon, it's a passport picture."

"Which makes it authentic. Like a time capsule." He paused. "The way you looked at the time."

She stared at him for a second. "Now you're doing it too. What Frank does, the voice on top of the voice. The two of you—" She stopped. "All right, fine. Do you want Frank's too? Two mug shots. Like an FBI poster." She brushed his arm before he could speak. "But none today, promise? Just the old ones."

"Promise. Dig them out later, okay, so we don't forget?"

She hesitated. "Simon, you'd tell me, wouldn't you? If something were—I don't know, wrong, anything?"

"You're imagining—" he started, not trusting his voice. Deflect. "By the way, when I was noticing things? At lunch? I think you're wrong about Marzena."

Jo raised her eyebrows, waiting.

"She's not his type."

"Oh, his type," she said.

"You're his type."

She looked at him, stopped by this.

"Still," he said. Catching her, what she wanted to hear. What Frank would have done.

McPherson was fixing a camera on a tripod at the edge of the pond, framing the yellow pavilion across the water. Boris had found his bench near the bronze statue of Krylov and was lighting a cigarette just as he had that first day—how long ago now? Days. Everything different except the pond.

"How about you and Mrs. Weeks walking toward me?" McPherson said.

"We'll do Jo another time," Simon said, taking her place with Frank. "One more of us? How far away do you want us?"

"Go up halfway and start walking back. When I signal," McPherson said.

"What's wrong with Jo?" Frank said.

"Camera shy. Anyway, we need to talk. The Bolshoi?"

"It's plausible. For DiAngelis to be there. Everybody wants to see Fyodorovna. Then plausible to have a pee at intermission. You too. It's a long first act. McPherson will tell him to wait if you're not there, wash his hands again, something."

"Me."

"I can't be seen with him. Not even by accident. So it has to be you."

"And what do I say to him?"

"You give him the meeting time and coordinates."

"The coordinates."

"For the boat." He pointed to a toy sailboat idling in the middle of the pond. "Like an address on the water. Thirty-Fourth Street and Fifth, except coordinates. Nautical locations. You'll have to remember them, nothing in writing, but they're easy. Anyway, you have a steel-trap memory—you still do, don't you?"

"I'll remember."

"You don't want to get it wrong. If you're off by even—"

"I'll remember. Does this give him enough time?"

"He'll have to scramble," Frank said, smiling a little. "But he will. And now there's less chance of a leak. People hang around waiting, they talk. This way it's just him. The coordinates stay up here." He tapped his head. "No one else. He should know that, but it doesn't hurt to remind— No one else."

"Except me."

Frank nodded. "So any leak, it's from his side. Better remind him of that too. No leaks. If he wants me alive."

Weaving another strand, all of it real to him.

"But don't your people know? Somebody must. If you've organized this—a boat, all the rest of it."

"We don't have leaks. You don't think the Agency has anybody inside the Service, do you? The Service would never let that happen." Still proud, closing ranks.

"Unless he's one of their own."

Frank glanced at him, uncomfortable. "That's right. Now, what's wrong with Jo?"

Simon shrugged. "Vanity. She doesn't want anybody to see—"

"The little wrinkles. I know." He paused. "It's not that. She doesn't want to have anything to do with the book. With me."

Simon looked over, a crack, an opening. "When are you going to tell her?" he said, asking something else. When are you going to tell me? Tell me I'm wrong, it's all just as you say. Not a scheme, a real plan. There's still time to fix things. You can fix anything. Tell me I'm wrong.

"You can tell her. On the ferry."

"When we're safe and sound," he said, drawing a line.

"That's right," Frank said, not seeing it.

Simon felt something twist in his chest, a tightening. Save yourself.

"Okay, come back," McPherson shouted. "Straight toward me."

They started walking. Two men in a park. The photograph another lie, their real faces erased, like an old Stalinist picture.

They were another hour, Simon joining Boris on the bench to smoke, Jo gone home to fix lunch.

"Complicated. Photography," Boris said, watching McPherson change lenses.

"Why don't you come with us to Leningrad?" Simon said. The devil you know.

"Thank you," Boris said, pleased, taking this for a compliment. "It's important to you, this trip? To see the art? It would be better to stay in Moscow."

"Better?"

"For Colonel Weeks. Better to stay close to the office."

The medieval fortress, Moscow's mental geography.

Simon looked at him. What had Frank told him? Anything? Off in the Sochi sunshine while Frank made his play. Or was he part of it, another sleight of hand. But part of what? Which side of the board?

"Why?"

"Busy time. It's good for Colonel Weeks to be busy again."

"Hasn't he been?"

But now Boris said nothing, closing down, the Lubyanka a protected world.

"Anyway, it's too late now," Simon said. "He's gone to so much trouble—"

"For you. To show you Russia. Good things here. But sometimes you need to—what's the English? Protect—no, watch your back." Easy and idiomatic, not his usual halting phrases.

"Does he need to do that?" Imagining a maze of office corridors, shadows.

Boris smiled a little. "A precaution. Many changes now at the Service."

Like the old days at Navy Hill, then down at State, glancing over your shoulder. Not sure of anyone, except Frank.

"Then I'll get him back as soon as I can," Simon said easily. "Not that he listens to me."

"To you, yes. Think of the book, the episode with the Latvians."

Simon glanced over. Hearing everything, not just reading *Izvestia*.

"Well, sometimes. Maybe we can just do Leningrad and back. Skip Tallinn," he said, trying it. What did he know? "What's there anyway?"

But Boris didn't bite. "Yes, maybe just Leningrad. It's better, I think." Not playing on either side.

He sat back, as if somehow this had settled things, and drew on his cigarette, squinting at the water. "Maybe he will have to swim for it," he said.

"What?"

"The boy," Boris said, pointing to a child squatting at the edge of the pond. "His boat. No air to move it."

Simon looked at the boat, lying still in the water, the boy trying to make waves by splashing. No way to reach it until a breeze came up again. Trapped on the water, rocking gently in its coordinates. Boats were unreliable that way, sometimes a trap, impossible to maneuver quickly. Thinking. Now a leap, not plodding anymore, an idea that pulled its own details behind it. Too late once you were on the water, vulnerable. Better to be off the board, an unexpected move. In plain sight.

He got up and walked toward the pond. McPherson, finally done, was packing up his equipment.

"Let me give you a hand," Simon said, grabbing a tripod. Then, to Frank, "Are you really gone all afternoon?"

Frank looked at him, surprised at the question.

"I was just wondering if I could borrow Boris. I mean, if he's not going—"

"Borrow?"

"To take me to Tolstoy's house. It's the one thing I wanted to see, and if we're leaving tonight—"

"Tolstoy's house?" Frank said, a tolerant smile. "The book man. I forgot."

"If I go by myself, he'll just have to get somebody else to tail me, so it's easier—"

"Yes," Frank said, a glance at McPherson, embarrassed by this. "Let me ask. Strictly speaking, it's his time off. When I'm at the office." The office, neutral, as if it were still an insurance company. Simon watched him head for Boris's bench.

"Would you take another message," Simon said.

"To DiAngelis."

"No. Remember Spaso House? The guy who introduced us?"

"Hal Lehman."

"You know how to reach him?"

"We're in the same building. Press ghetto. They put us all together. Saves tails," he said, a quick nod in Boris's direction.

"Tell him I want to see him. Tolstoy's house. After lunch."

McPherson waited.

"I promised him a story. And now we're leaving."

"So you want to meet him at Tolstoy's house."

"Two birds with one stone."

McPherson just looked.

"Can you do it? Get the message to him? I don't want to call."

McPherson nodded. "If he's around. What's the story?"

"Family stuff. How did it feel seeing Frank again—all these years."

"How did it?"

"This one's for UPI. Not *Look*. After the pictures run, don't worry."

"Doesn't matter to me. I'm freelance." He turned, looking back at Frank. "He doesn't seem to have many regrets, does he?"

"No," Simon said, "not many."

———————

Tolstoy's house, hidden from the street behind a long wooden fence, was a country house in the city, solid and plain rather than grand, set on grounds that seemed to be outgrowing their keepers, scraggly and wild in patches, even the grass along the gravel walkways needing a trim. There was a white-haired woman in a kiosk at the entrance who, surprisingly, spoke to them in French, like a governess in one of the novels.

"Deux? Voilà, un plan de niveau de la maison." She handed him a worn sheet of plastic, protecting a faded floor plan.

Boris frowned, the French like some Romanov ghost, a reproach, then saw that Simon was charmed and let it pass. The place itself seemed another ghost, deserted in mid-afternoon, only a gardener clipping away at the side of the house, the same stillness he remembered at the Novodevichy. Boris found a shaded chair near the entrance and settled in as watchdog.

The quiet followed Simon inside, through the big dining room, settings in place for a family dinner, then up the stairs to the large salon, where Tolstoy had read to Chekhov and Gorky, and Sofia offered supper. Where was everybody? The meeting should look like an accidental encounter in a public place, not something arranged. Finally he saw two women in the next room, heads together, admiring Sofia's knickknacks. He glanced at his watch. Lehman was supposed to be here first. A Spartan bedroom, the daughter's. Then Tolstoy's study, the desk where he wrote, and Lehman standing beside it. A pretense of surprise.

"Why here?" he said.

"Sort of place a publisher would go, don't you think? Look, his shoemaking tools."

"He made his own shoes?"

"To make a point." He glanced behind him, the two women still inspecting Sofia's drawing room. "Thanks for coming. We have to be fast. I've got the KGB waiting downstairs."

Lehman looked up.

"Just part of the service. For my protection. But curious. You know. So we have to be—"

"You have a story for me? The interview?"

"Well, that too. But better. You may not want it. All I ask is that if you don't, you just say so and go away and you never saw me. Agreed?"

"What's going on?"

"Agreed?"

"Agreed. Why wouldn't I want it?"

"It comes with some strings attached. For one thing, you'd be chucked out. Maybe worse. Still interested?"

Lehman peered at him. "They're going to throw me out anyway."

"This would guarantee it."

"You trying to scare me?" Lehman said, not sure whether he should be amused.

"Warn you."

"So, what? This is the story on your brother?"

"Part of it."

"And this is coming from him or from you?"

"Me."

"With strings attached."

"And some incentive. You'll be out of a job here but the story will get you back to New York. With a book contract when you get there. Keating & Sons." He looked at Lehman. "There's some risk."

"A book contract," Lehman said. "With you dangling it. And

this is—what? You're the devil. And I'm being tempted?" he said, holding up his hand to mime a paper dangling.

"Something like that. No eternal life, though."

"Just a story."

Simon nodded. "Look, I need your help. It's worth a contract to me. But you have to decide if it's worth it to you. Like I said, there's some risk."

Lehman stared at him. "How about we start over? What story?"

"I have your word? If you're not interested, this never happened?"

Lehman waved this away.

Simon looked around the study, like standing at the end of a dock. Jump.

"Frank is going to defect."

"What?" Lehman said, just to make a sound.

"It'll be your story. Exclusive."

"Defect," Hal said flatly.

"He wants to go home."

"Home." Another echo effect.

"And you're going to help. So, your story."

Lehman said nothing.

"Want to hear more or do you want to go?" He lifted his fingers. "No strings yet. Your choice."

"He can't. He can't do it."

"No, but I can. That's why I came."

Another long stare, Hal's mind trying to catch up, not even aware of the sound of Russian coming into the room. The two women. Simon pointed to the adjoining washroom where the shoe-making tools had been.

"See the bicycle? He didn't take it up until he was in his six-ties. Physical fitness kick. Come this way." Nodding to the women and putting his hand on the small of Lehman's back to steer him down the stairs, an English-speaking guide, perhaps, or two foreign Tolstoy enthusiasts.

Still, English, something suspect. The women stopped. And then luckily there was the sound of more Russian, a tour group clomping through the dining room.

"What do you think this is?" Simon said, pointing to the small room off the back stairs. "Pantry? Can you read the Cyrillic?"

Lehman said nothing, still slightly dazed, then leaned forward to read the card next to the doorjamb. "Pickling room," he said.

"That explains the barrels. Imagine a whole room just for pickles." Chatty, turning his head slightly to see if the women were listening. But they now seemed to be fascinated by the writing desk.

"Boris is outside. We have to talk here. You have to decide today—you'll see why in a minute. If it's no, just leave some kind of message for me at the National. Anything, it doesn't matter what. Otherwise, I'll assume we're in business, okay?"

Lehman nodded.

"I'll tell you how this is going to work. Then you figure out the odds yourself. No contract is worth the wrong odds. So you decide. All right?"

Lehman said nothing, still calculating.

"Hal?"

"Tell me."

A large, noisy Intourist group had taken over the Metropol's dining room, but the maître d' said he'd arrange for some food in the bar.

"We won't make the ballet if we wait for a table," Frank said. "Anyway the point is just to see this." He pointed to the vast room, a tsarist relic of tables grouped around a central fountain, potted palms, and lamps on tall gold standards, all dwarfed by a vaulting stained glass ceiling, bright blue, a glass sky. "Paris had the Ritz and Vienna had the Imperial, so Moscow had to have one too. To keep up."

"Hard to imagine now," Simon said, taking it in, the worn red velvet, the usual Soviet dinginess. "That must have been the string quartet." He nodded to a raised platform at the end of the room.

"While they stuffed themselves with caviar. And outside people were starving," Frank said. "The good old days." He looked over at Simon. "Nobody starves now. So there's that. Let's have a drink. Jo won't be here until the last minute. Hairdresser," he said, touching his own hair. "To look nice for the trip. All packed?"

Simon nodded.

"Almost there," Frank said, putting a hand on Simon's shoulder to lead him to the bar. "Got the coordinates?"

Simon repeated them.

"Let's hope old Pete's memory's as good as yours."

"We'll only have a minute in the men's room."

"Say something twice and it's yours. So make him say it twice."

They were on the second glass of Georgian wine when the waiter came with small plates of food.

"Will I be followed? At the Bolshoi?" Simon said.

"No, you're with me. He will be, though. So make it quick. Just what you'd do in a men's room. Wash your hands. Get a towel. Excuse me. Beg pardon. Like that. In and out."

"Like that."

"Don't worry, it will be."

"And if he has a question? Wants to change the meeting spot—something."

"He won't. It's like I showed you on the map. They'll still be in international waters. They'd never cross into Soviet territory. Agency rule. I know, I wrote it. They'd never risk that. So we go to them."

"Outside Soviet waters. And the Service has no problem—"

Frank brushed this away. "It's not like a fence. Just water. Sometimes it's hard to know which side of the line you're on. And he'll be close enough to make them think he's over. If he follows the coordinates."

"So your people intercept—outside Soviet territory."

"They don't have to know that. They just know there's an American boat out there up to no good. And coming in. Better to act and figure out your location later. For the record."

"When it's your word against DiAngelis's."

Frank looked at him. "Except I won't be here."

Simon sipped his wine. "What if DiAngelis says he can't make that time. For whatever reason."

"Then he'll miss the high point of his career," Frank said smiling. "Don't worry, Jimbo, he'll make it. The leverage is on our side. They want me. It would be a coup for them."

"And vice-versa."

Frank looked up.

"DiAngelis would be a coup for you. If it worked the other way."

Frank said nothing, not sure how to respond. "But it's not the other way," he said finally.

"No. So what could go wrong? Just in case."

"Come on, Simon. You see somebody in the men's room, that's all. Say a few words and out you go. Mission over." He looked down at his watch. "She's cutting it close." He raised his head, taking in the other end of the bar. "Well, look who's here. Back at the old watering hole."

Simon half-turned. Sergei, nursing a drink.

"How does he afford it?" Frank said.

"Doesn't he get Gareth's—?"

"No. Next of kin. Except there is no next of kin."

"So what happens to him now?"

Frank shrugged. "He finds somebody else."

"Or the Service does," Simon said, curious to see Frank's response. "A new friend."

"That's not how it works. Gareth picks somebody up, we have to vet him. Make sure he's not—a plant. But we don't provide." Still we.

"Let's go before he sees us."

"We just sat down."

"I'd rather not, that's all. Considering." Glancing down at his hands, seeing them squeezing.

"Considering what?" Frank said blandly. "Nothing happened." Each word emphasized. Simon looked up at him. And nothing had, Novodevichy not even a bad memory. "Anyway, he's seen us. He's coming over. Sergei," he said, raising his voice, public. "I'm sorry we're going to miss the funeral. We'll be in Leningrad."

"No funeral. They don't want to attract attention."

"They?"

"The office. You know. They're afraid the foreign press—" He hesitated. "So, for the obituaries, he died after a long illness. And that's the end of Gareth. A long illness. I asked, could he be buried in Novodevichy—you know, so close to us and he liked to go there. But they said no. Somewhere out near Izmaylovo Park. So far. Who goes there? An hour on the Metro if you want to visit the grave."

"I'm sorry. But maybe it's for the best," Frank said, his voice steady, reassuring.

"Yes," Sergei said, polite, not believing it, then looked up at Frank, hesitant again. "I know we're not supposed to say, but I wanted to thank you. What you're doing for him." Simon looked up.

"Me? I don't—"

"I know. Everything's a secret there. But people talk. So I just wanted to say thank you, that's all. Now they'll find him."

"Find him?" Simon said, not following.

"The murderer. I thought at first, it's like the funeral. Sweep it away. Pretend it never happened. But now they have to do it. They'll listen to you. And to bring her in—it sends a message. Gareth used to say there was no one like her. A bloodhound. So now maybe we'll find out."

"Sergei," Frank said quickly. "You don't talk—office business. Not in front of—"

"No. I'm sorry. I'm sorry." Nervous now, guilty. "Excuse me. It's just—" He turned to Simon. "I wanted to say thank you, that's all. Your brother, he's a hero to me. Gareth, too. He always liked you. And now to do this for him. I know what the others think, how they laughed at him. But now something will happen. Justice."

"Let's hope so," Frank said smoothly, a kind of dismissal.

"So please go on with your drink," Sergei said, about to move away, and then grasped Frank's hand and shook it. "They said today, nothing so far, but maybe soon. Justice. How pleased he would be, Gareth, to know it was you. Excuse me."

Simon watched him go, heading toward the ornate lobby and out into the Moscow night. He pressed his fingers to the bar, holding himself in, and looked at Frank.

"He talks too much," Frank said. "Everybody talks too much. Most secret organization in the world and everybody talks too much. What Pa used to call an irony. Come on, let's finish here." He tossed back the rest of the wine.

Simon kept looking at him, not sure how to begin. "Brought who in?" he said finally, already knowing.

"Elizaveta," Frank said, looking back.

"To investigate Gareth's murder."

Frank nodded. "Under me. Would you rather have someone else in charge? She'll look at everybody but me. It warms the heart to see it, how grateful she is. To be back at the office. The Service is like that—once it's in your blood. And now she owes it to me.

One of the foreigners. Another irony. All of them suspect now except one."

"Until there's no one else."

"But by then I'll be gone. We couldn't let this get in the way. It would have ruined everything."

"And if you don't go?"

"What do you mean?"

"Hypothetically. If you were still here. You couldn't call her off now. How would that look? What happens if she doesn't come up with anyone?"

"But she will. The Service always does. Someone will have to pay. But not me." He looked over. "Not you either. I told you I'd look out for you."

Simon turned back to his drink, stomach clenching again.

"What did he mean about today? Nothing so far today."

"There was an interrogation."

"Ian," Simon said quietly.

"Yes."

"That's why you were there today."

"Well, you have to show a certain amount of interest. Especially in the beginning. Before you let her off the leash."

"You interrogated him?"

"I was there."

"Did he know, on Saturday, that it would be you?"

"No, of course not. It's better this way."

"Better?"

"It throws them off balance. Even your friends suspect you. Why? What did you do? You think about everything you've ever said, how it might sound. You go over it and over it. You'd be amazed what comes up, all those things you thought you forgot. That might explain it. Why you're there."

"And then you get tired. Say things."

Frank nodded. "It's not my favorite part of the job—"

"But he didn't do it."

"We have to give Elizaveta somewhere to look." He paused. "I never said it was pretty. But neither's Norilsk. Freeze to death. Starve. Or a bullet. You pick."

"And when she doesn't find anything?"

"We'll be long gone. But she's very good, you know. And she needs a win. She just might pull it off."

With Frank still here, helping her.

"When were you going to tell me this?"

"I wasn't. If Sergei hadn't opened his—" He stopped. "You're not used to it, the business. I didn't want you to be—distracted."

"Distracted? Frank, we killed a man. And now we're making someone else—"

"Listen to me," Frank said, grasping his arm. "We didn't do it. That's right, isn't it? We didn't do it. So somebody else must have. Or do you have a better plan?"

Prince Siegfried had already celebrated his birthday and was off with his hunting bow to Swan Lake before Simon could pay any attention to what was happening on stage. Up to now it had just been part of the blur—the lines of black Zils with Party officials, the lamps in Theater Square, Jo all dressed up, turning heads, as if she had stepped out of the Metropol's fantasy of itself, how people used to look. They had crossed the square into another piece of tsarist Moscow, red velvet and gilt, the royal box still like a throne room at the center of the mezzanine.

"Stalin never used it," Frank said. "He used to sit there, on the side."

"Man of the people?"

"No. Afraid somebody would take a shot at him. In the tsar's box. Sitting target."

"But not in his box?"

"Well, he used to sit back, away from the railing. I didn't say it made sense. He was crazy. That's the way he thought." He smiled at Simon's expression. "My loyalty was to the Service, not him. I used to think, if we can survive this—and we did."

"At a cost."

"That's right. At any cost. First you have to survive. Right?"

Simon stared at the curtain for a second, then turned to him, his voice low. "Frank, promise me something."

Frank waited.

"Ian. Promise you won't let him be—I mean, it's bad enough, Gareth—" He stopped, glancing across to Jo, but she was looking around the theater, distracted.

"But you can somehow talk yourself into believing that was self-defense," Frank finished. "Is that it? But not Ian. Even though it comes to the same thing."

"No, it doesn't. It's not right."

Frank looked at him. "Not right. Still Mt. Vernon Street. One of Pa's dinner problems. Right. Wrong. You think it matters?"

Simon said nothing.

"Anyway, in a few days I'll be suspect number one, not Ian. Unless you forget the coordinates." Trying to be playful.

"Promise me anyway."

"What's this all about?"

"I don't know. Bad luck, maybe. We don't need another—"

"You'd rather they think it was me."

Simon looked at him. Turn the board. "You'll be gone. What difference does it make?"

Frank held his gaze for another second, caught off guard, then turned. "Fine. Ian didn't do it. Feel better?"

"You'll make sure?"

Another curious look.

"This is what you're worrying about? Tonight? Ian fucking McAulife?"

Simon shrugged. "Now it's one less thing." As if Frank would do it, his promises real.

"What a pain in the ass you are," Frank said, not able to let it go, then faced forward again. "It's all self-defense, Jimbo."

"What are you two whispering about?" Joanna said, leaning over.

"Stalin," Simon said.

Her eyes darted left, uncomfortable, as if he had made a bad joke.

"Where he used to sit."

"Up there," Frank said, pointing.

"How do you know? You never went to the ballet then. Or now. I can't think why you—oh look, the ambassador. They always stick out like sore thumbs, the Americans. It's the suits. And the haircuts." Glancing toward Mike Novikov's crew cut, heading down the center aisle. Next to him a tall, vaguely familiar man and his wife. No DiAngelis.

Simon looked back up the aisle. No stragglers, no one else in the party. But he had to be here. In the embassy seats.

"What's the matter?" Jo said.

"Nothing. I must stick out then too. The suit."

"Mm. Isn't it funny, you at the Bolshoi?" She looked away. "Any of us."

Novikov was settling in next to the ambassador. Still no DiAngelis. One intermission, only one chance before they left.

He felt the audience stirring behind them, heads craned, a line of gray suits entering the royal box. For a second he half-expected to see Khrushchev, the tsar, but the familiar bald head never appeared, just the gray suits with blank faces, presumably Politburo members everyone else recognized. A big night at the Bolshoi. Would this mean extra bodyguards, plainclothesmen, all of them alert to American suits? He glanced around the crowd. Who was anybody? No DiAngelis.

And then the lights were dimming and the music was starting and he felt his stomach jump, not just nerves, not butterflies, a falling, a sense that something was wrong. He stared straight ahead, past Prince Siegfried, running through a mental checklist. Tomorrow they'd be under the watchful eyes of the Service, new eyes, eager to impress. The meeting had to be tonight, only a minute, two, swallowed up in an impersonal crowd. DiAngelis would need the time to set things up. Maybe he was sitting somewhere else, the ambassador a blind, waiting for the intermission.

The stage got darker, the lake at night, Siegfried with his bow. Simon twisted in his seat, restless, but everyone else was still, expectant. He had always assumed *Swan Lake* was kitsch, a ballet for tourists, but here it meant something else. There was a fluttering of white, the entire stage suddenly swirling with white, darting, floating. A quiet gasp went through the audience, a collective pleasure, everything as it should be, the precise toe steps, the graceful leaps, inexplicably beautiful, the dreary city falling away, mad Stalin in his side box, the brutal prison stories, lives with years snatched away, betrayals, all of that gone now, out of sight, nothing visible but this twirling, what the world would be like if it were lovely. Nobody moved, drinking it in, an old ritual, maybe their way of reassuring themselves they were still capable of this. He turned to Frank, prepared to smile, an appreciation, and saw that he wasn't watching at all, his eyes fixed on the embassy seats, waiting for DiAngelis.

After the swans flew off, he lost the thread again. Odette would become Odile, or was it the reverse? In New York, there would have been a synopsis to follow in the playbill. Here it was already in the blood, the whole implausible story. Real stories, Frank's stories, were plausible. Simple. We intercept them coming in. But there were two stories, so the trick was keeping them both simple, both plausible, easier to juggle. Run through the details again. No surprises. Except there was always something you couldn't control, someone. You couldn't do it alone, you had to trust someone. The way Frank trusted him.

He glanced to his side, Frank still scanning the audience, then back to the stage. Any minute now and he'd have to get up, do it. During the war he'd never had to do anything, all the careful plans passed on to someone else. Now, finally, he had to act, like the boy in one of Pa's dinner problems. Right. Wrong. The question isn't what's right, his father would say, tracing lines on the tablecloth with his fork. The question is, what's the right thing to do? How do we act? They're not always the same. What's right is just an idea. But what we should do—there are other considerations. So it's not always clear. But if it's right, Frank had said, then it has to be the right thing to do. And then had done it, acted, and blown up all their lives. People were applauding, the curtain coming down. The jewel box room getting brighter. Now.

"I'll be right back," he said, standing.

"Meet us in the foyer," Jo said over the applause, putting an imaginary cigarette to her mouth.

Simon started out, only to be blocked by clapping people in the row. Impossible to step over them. He looked back, a few people trickling out, the aisles beginning to clot. At the embassy seats, the ambassador and his wife were following a path Novikov was making for them.

"Relax," Frank said. "It's a long intermission."

Some people were still clapping, but now the rush began. Out to the grand foyer, under the giant chandelier, then down the white marble stairs to the tiled vestibule, looking for a men's room. What was the word? *Muzhskoy*. But what would that be in Cyrillic? Finally a sign with stick figures, one with pants. Follow the arrow, the crowd now thick around him, the long room already filling with cigarette smoke, all the doors open to the outside.

"Simon?" A voice behind him, American. He turned. "I thought it was you." Hannah Rubin, all smiles. "Isn't it wonderful? I'm so glad you got to see it. I never miss the Bolshoi. Saul, he could care less. He falls asleep. I said, you could do that at home."

Which meant she was alone, eager to talk. Simon glanced past her head, searching the crowd for DiAngelis.

"But I thought you were going to Leningrad."

"Tonight. Later. Frank got tickets for this last minute."

"Well, he could. And lucky you. Fyodorovna—"

Settling in for a chat. Heads passing behind her. There'd be a crowd in the toilets soon.

"I was just heading for the men's room," he said, anxious, actually having to pee now.

"Men. I don't even bother. The line's always out the door. You've heard? About Ian? No wonder he was so nervous about Elizaveta." She stopped. "Well, I suppose I shouldn't say, but you were at the lunch, so you already know—"

"What?"

"They've kept him overnight. That's not a good sign. Something must be—"

Not now. Now he had to meet somebody. One chance.

"I thought they did that all the time," Simon said, looking over her shoulder again, then realized he had offended her.

"Not unless there's something wrong," she said, believing it, the sleep deprivation, the lights in your face, the isolation cell just bits of melodrama the West used to discredit the system.

"Well, let's hope not. He seemed a nice man. Hard to believe he'd—"

"It always is, isn't it? What interests me is why. Why would he—why would anybody—?"

More heads passing.

"Excuse me. I really have to go." A weak grin. "Call of nature."

"And here I am yakking away." She put her hand on his arm. "So nice to run into you. Is Joanna here?"

"In the foyer," he said, pointing up.

"Oh good, then maybe I'll see you again before we go in." She paused. "Did you say tonight? You must be going straight to the station. Me, I'd be a nervous wreck."

"Boris is meeting us with the bags."

"Oh," she said, filing this away, even stray information worth something. What? "I'm always hours early. Saul says it's a thing with me. But I don't miss the train either. Go, go," she said, shooing him off. "I'll see you upstairs."

He started through the crowd, taking in faces in glimpses, like snapshots. No one he knew. Late now, but DiAngelis had been told to wait. Near the men's room door, a man with a cigarette stared at him, then looked away. The Service? But so was Hannah. Who just happened to be here. Maybe he was being passed along, one observation post to the next. Why not Hannah? A woman who hid the atomic bomb design in her hat. And got on the train. Me, I'd be a nervous wreck.

DiAngelis wasn't in the men's room. Simon peed, then took his time washing his hands, looking at people in the mirror. A few looking back, at his suit. Everything noisy, toilets flushing and people talking in Russian, stall doors banging. DiAngelis wouldn't be in one of those. He needed to be seen. Simon wiped his hands on the towel, people passing on either side of him. He couldn't stay here much longer. Maybe DiAngelis had already come and gone, just outside in the vestibule, waiting. The line for the urinals inched forward. Novikov's crew cut, his head looming over the line. The last thing Simon wanted, somebody who'd recognize DiAngelis, see them meet. Leave. But Novikov had spotted him, made eye contact. When Simon passed, he nodded.

"How are you?" The English low but audible as something separate. "Enjoying it?"

The man behind Novikov was looking away, pretending not to listen. Novikov leaned toward Simon, his voice almost a whisper.

"Have a cigarette. Outside. Last pillar on the left." Then louder, pulling his head up again, "The second act is supposed to be even better."

Simon went out to the vestibule, packed now, the crowd spilling out to the portico, the sky still light. No one was supposed to know but DiAngelis, no leaks. Unless Novikov was literally just a messenger, repeating words. Last pillar on the left. A few people, but not so many as near the central columns. Simon went to the very edge of the portico, where it began to sweep down to the square, and stopped at the last pillar. He lit a cigarette.

"Over here." DiAngelis, leaning against the building. "Go around to the side." He motioned his head left. The Maly Theatre side, another long portico, not as grand as the main entrance, just somewhere to stay out of the rain.

"I thought you weren't coming."

"With the ambassador? Whose idea was that? Tell Frank he's getting rusty. Moscow rules. Two changes of cars. No tails. Usually takes the whole evening, just to shake them. So when?"

"Thursday. We go to Leningrad tonight. Tomorrow we see the sights. Wednesday, the Peterhof. Then Tallinn. Boat goes out at six. Memorize these." He gave him the coordinates. "Do it twice, make sure. That's the meet the Agency's expecting. And the Service. Now these. Lat 60.7095 by Longitude 28.734."

DiAngelis looked up. "That's in Russia."

Simon nodded. "You'd make a good sailor. Vyborg. You won't even need the coordinates. Just head for the port."

"What the fuck's going on?"

"Wednesday. An alternative boat. This one you arrange. Yourself. No leaks."

"The Agency doesn't have–"

"Just assume. Thursday is still the plan. But if anything happens, if we have to move faster, then Wednesday. Vyborg. Where nobody's expecting us. Except you."

"In the Soviet Union. I can't do that."

Simon nodded. "Send locals. A fishing boat. Finnish. Maybe they need some repairs. Wednesday, late morning. If we don't show, they go home."

"Why Vyborg?"

"Close to Finnish waters. If we have to make a run for it. The port's not far from the train station. An easy walk for us."

"How do you know?"

"I can read maps."

"You or Frank?"

"Get someone who's never heard of Frank, or the other plan. Keep them separate."

DiAngelis looked up, his face a question mark.

"The Lubyanka's been jumpy. They lost a man and that makes them crazy. Especially about the foreign agents. So we have to be careful. We're assuming it's still a go Thursday. But if anything happens, we need an escape hatch. In case."

"And I'm supposed to arrange all this in a day."

"You're the Agency. Start tonight."

DiAngelis started to say something, then stopped. He dropped his cigarette. "He'd better fucking be there."

"He will. One or the other. Let's hope it's Thursday. So you can haul him in yourself. Your big fish. You already have the boat?"

DiAngelis nodded.

"Then we're set. Oh, one more thing. I need a gun."

"A gun. Where do you think you are? This is the Soviet Union. You get caught with that—a foreigner—and you don't leave. Ever."

"That's something to keep in mind."

"Don't be a smart-ass. You even know how to use it?"

"It'll come back. I was in the OSS."

"In an office."

"After training. We're wasting time. I need the gun."

"What for?"

"Protection. What do you care? I'm delivering Frank. I don't want to get nervous."

"And where the fuck am I supposed to get it?" He glanced at his watch. "At this hour?"

"You're the Agency, aren't you? You can do anything." He put up his hand to cut off DiAngelis's reply. "Just get it to me. We're on the *Red Arrow* tonight. Compartment 62. Or the Astoria in Leningrad tomorrow. I don't care how you get it to me, just do it. Before Wednesday. Or the whole thing's off."

"Off?"

"One that works. I don't want to blow my hand off. Have Mata Hari leave it on the train. However you want to do it. You must have Moscow rules for this too. Or use your imagination." He looked over. "I don't move him without it."

DiAngelis said nothing for a second. "I thought he was moving himself."

Simon looked at him. "And I'll make sure he gets there. Anything else? I was just supposed to give you time and place and go."

"Then that covers it. Tell him I got the message." He paused. "You don't want to let all this go to your head. The cloak and dagger. People get hurt with guns."

"Want to give me the coordinates one more time?"

"Go fuck yourself."

He waded back through the crowd in the vestibule, feeling a little dizzy, as if he'd been holding his breath and could now exhale. He'd done it. And no one knew. The stares, the curious looks, were for his suit, not him. Nobody followed him in from behind the pillar, trailed him up the stairs, even thought him capable of espionage. In the heart of Moscow.

Frank and Jo were still in the main foyer, smoking near the open windows.

"I thought you got lost," Frank said.

"There was a line."

"You just missed Hannah," Jo said. "She said she ran into you downstairs."

"Everything okay?" Frank said, unable to resist.

"Yes, fine. Just crowded, that's all."

"Think what it's like for us," Jo said. "All the clothes. And back then. Those skirts. Oh, there's Melinda. And Donald. I'd better say hello. They get wounded if you don't."

"No Scrabble," Frank said, then when she'd moved away, "No Scrabble. So that's one thing to look forward to. Everything went all right?"

"He'll be there Thursday."

Frank breathed out. "Well, that's that, then." He looked around the bright room, as if he were saying good-bye, then turned to Simon. "Thanks, Jimbo."

Odette's lookalike came to seduce Prince Siegfried, the swans now in black, and the ballet went on and on, Simon trying to keep his eyes fixed on the stage, not be obviously restless. Would Frank sense something, guess what was happening? Used to reading people, the rhythms of an interrogation. But Frank just seemed bored, restless himself, his mind elsewhere, but not on Simon. Thanks, Jimbo. Odile twirled. What exactly would Ian's motive be? The simple, the plausible. Gareth had caught him making contact with MI6, the move Elizaveta had been expecting for years. But why would Frank suspect? Simple. Something Perry had said, no longer here to contradict, another scientist, a man willing to sign letters. Let's go over it again. He wouldn't have to plant evidence, just the suspicion. Hannah already believed it. Sitting somewhere behind them watching Siegfried betray Odette. The setup by Von Rothbart. The air they breathed here. One more day.

The applause lasted for several curtain calls and gifts of flowers, as endless as the ballet itself. Finally the row began to move toward the aisle, joining the stream out. Simon checked his watch. Plenty of time. Novikov's head again, behind him the ambassador and his wife. They paused to let people out into the aisle, then looked up and stopped, recognizing Frank. A flash of surprise, then embarrassment, Frank's being there something that couldn't be acknowledged. The ambassador looked away, as if he hadn't seen anyone, and took his wife's elbow. More than just a social snub, a turning away, afraid to make contact. What Frank was now, a pariah.

Simon glanced back to see if Joanna had noticed. A slight flush, biting her lower lip, following the ambassador's wife, her back like a closed door. What it would be like, a line of turned backs. But what was it like here? She looked down, shoulders dropping, and Simon saw her on the dacha couch, turning pages. The album. It hadn't occurred to him. She'd be leaving with the suitcase she'd brought to Leningrad, no pictures, no Richie. Impossible to get them now, a detail overlooked. What else hadn't he done? All planned, but he'd forgotten the pictures, something she'd miss for the rest of her life. Pointless to think they could be sent on later, with the Service hunting for Frank.

A car took them to Leningradsky Station, one of three railway terminals surrounding Komsomolskaya Square. After the Metropol and the Bolshoi, Simon somehow expected another piece of nineteenth-century extravagance, built for the Age of Steam, but Lenin-gradsky was gritty and functional, a hangar-like shed with scratchy loudspeakers and passengers looking for the right train. Boris was wait-ing for them on the platform, the bags already inside. The *Red Arrow*, Simon saw, really was red, a splotch of bright color in the gray station. Inside, the compartments were red too, swagging drapes with tassels, even the folded white bed linens, stacked neatly, trimmed in red.

"I hope you don't mind," Boris said to Simon. "We will have to share. The train—so crowded. I'll take the upper berth. So you won't be disturbed."

"You're coming? But I thought—what happened to Sochi?"

"Sochi later. It was decided I should go to Leningrad."

"Decided?"

"Just to be on the safe side," Frank said blandly. "You know, since Gareth. The office was a little nervous—traveling by ourselves."

"So. You don't mind, for the one night?"

"No, of course not," Simon said, an automatic response, cal-culating. He looked into the compartment. What if the gun had already been delivered? But there was nothing, just the stowed bag and his briefcase with the manuscript. And the visas. But Boris wouldn't have bothered with that. He knew the briefcase.

"Better get out your earplugs," Frank said, genial. "I've bunked with Boris. You get the full orchestra. Well, why don't we all have a nightcap?" He pointed to the fold-up table under the compartment window, laid out for tea and snacks. "I put a bottle in the small bag," he said to Boris. "Or are you on duty?"

Boris made a show of checking his watch. "On holiday."

Frank smiled. "So. Your place or ours?"

In the end they went to Frank and Jo's compartment, clinking glasses as the train pulled out, Simon's mind still on the briefcase next door. Locked, but that wouldn't stop anyone. Why leave the visas there? Then where? Carry them with him to the Bolshoi? He had expected to have the night to himself, to sort things out. Now Boris, a few feet away.

After another round, conversation stalled. At home Boris was part of the furniture, just there. Now, facing one another in the small compartment, they felt awkward, strangers thrown together.

"When does the porter make up the beds?" Simon said. "I need to get some sleep."

"No porter. Soviet train. I make beds," Boris said, standing up.

"No, no, you don't have to do—" Simon started, then was hushed by a wave of Boris's hand.

"Good night," Boris said, a formal nod to Frank. "So, I am next door." He turned to Simon. "A few minutes only for the beds."

"A Soviet butler," Frank said, amused, as Boris closed the door.

"Is he going to be with us all the time?" Simon said to Frank.

"Can't be helped. It's going to be like this—until they find who killed Gareth. A precaution."

"Am I allowed to go to the ladies' alone?" Jo said, picking up a cosmetic bag. "Take off the war paint. If I'm not back in twenty minutes, send the posse. Good night, Simon. Never mind about Boris. You get used to it. You think you do anyway."

"Was this your idea?" Simon said to Frank when she'd gone.

"In Leningrad the station chief would be worse. Very by the book. Easier to provide our own man. But in Tallinn we'll let the locals take over."

"He'll get in trouble. At least in Sochi he'd be—"

"Boris is a big boy. He can take care of himself." He finished his drink. "First Ian, now Boris. All these scruples. Jimbo, you can't. Not in this business. They'll trip you up."

"I'm not in this business."

Frank smiled. "So you keep saying." He looked up. "Don't worry about Boris. I have his back."

Simon's bed, made up on the pulled-out settee, was half again as wide as the upper berth.

"Are you sure–?" About to propose drawing matchsticks.

"I can sleep anywhere. You learn in the war."

He was sitting on the facing settee, smoking one of his strong Russian cigarettes, already undressed for bed. A thick old robe that looked as heavy as a carpet, pale, oddly thin legs sticking out, the top open to reveal an undershirt. The casual intimacy had taken Simon by surprise, but how could it be otherwise? Roommates. And now what? Change in the bathroom at the end of the car? That would only embarrass them both. He turned his back and started undressing. Boris, indifferent, gazed out the window at the flat, dark landscape.

"You have seen that film *Ballad of a Soldier*? Was very popular in America."

"Yes. Everywhere."

"They sleep in the hay. In the freight car. A luxury compared to how we had to sleep." He drew again on the cigarette, blowing smoke toward the open window vent. "A sentimental film. The soldier with the one leg? And the girl is happy to see him. You think it was like that?" He shook his head. "It was hard."

Simon turned, belting his robe. "Your wife died, you said."

Boris nodded. "An air raid. So at least quick. At the front people would lie there, waiting. Sometimes they would ask you to shoot them. To stop the pain." He poured himself another glass, settling in. "You were in the war?"

"Not like that. At a desk." He sat on his bed, lighting his own cigarette, shaking his head no to the offered bottle.

"Hm," Boris said, almost a grunt. "A desk."

"Like Frank. Operations planning," Simon said, as if that explained anything.

Boris looked up. "You worked together?"

"No. Frank got involved in the operations. I was strictly a desk man. An analyst."

"He likes that. The operations. The risk."

"Well, he didn't actually go on any. He was a desk man too."

"But think of the risk for him. Every day. At that desk." He put out his cigarette. "Passing documents. You know there were so many they would pile up here? So many to read. But for him each one could have been a death warrant. If he had been caught. So a man who took risks."

Simon said nothing for a minute, looking at him. "What's wrong, Boris?"

Boris raised his eyes, meeting Simon's.

"Why should anything be wrong?" Moving a man into place.

Simon shrugged his shoulders. "No reason."

"No," Boris said, lighting another cigarette. "No reason. A man who's a hero of the Soviet Union. Now a book. Thanks to the good brother." He dipped his head. "Soon famous everywhere. Such a man should retire. What's the English? On his laurels."

"I thought he had."

"That's what he tells you?"

"He doesn't tell me anything. First of all, he's not allowed. And second, I don't ask. I don't want to know. He's not a hero to every-body."

"But you're his brother."

"And?"

"You would want to protect him."

"From what?"

Boris shrugged, out of specifics. "From risks."

Simon waited. Another piece being moved.

"You know, the Service, it's an office of secrets, but if you listen, sometimes you hear things." He paused. "Something here, something there. An operation—there's an excitement. People talk. Maybe just a little, but they talk."

"What operation?"

Another shrug. "I asked myself, why Tallinn? Riga? Of course interesting, but the brother, he's a man of books. Why not Yasnaya Polyana? So I listened. About Tallinn, Riga. Then no more Riga, so Tallinn. And the office approves, they want him to go. At such a time, when all the foreign—"

"You think he's running an operation? Why not just ask him?"

"That's not possible. So I ask you."

"Me? He'd never tell me anything like that. Anyway, isn't he getting a little long in the tooth for that?"

A puzzled look.

"Old. Frank doesn't run operations anymore. Not according to the book anyway. That was years ago."

"Unless there's a special expertise he can bring. A familiarity."

"Familiarity?"

"To know the enemy so well, it's an advantage. To know the patterns, how they do things."

"Who's the enemy? Us?"

Boris smiled a little. "Always you. The Main Adversary. But this time closer to home. You remember in the book, the story of the Latvians? Like that, very similar. But now Estonians. It's always the same there. Nationalists. Sentimentalists. Even a few can make trouble. So of course the Main Adversary encourages them. But if we can stop them before they—" He let the thought finish itself.

"And you think Frank's involved with this?"

"I think he offers his expertise. But plans—that's one thing. What happens is another. Not so predictable." He looked over. "For a desk man."

"So that's why they sent you? To watch him?"

"No. They sent me to watch you."

He had raised his eyes so that for a second they seemed to be looking over a handful of cards, and Simon saw that it wasn't chess they were playing, but some elaborate game of poker, all of them playing, all of them cheating.

"Me," he said, his tone flat.

"The Agency allows you to publish this book. Perhaps you do a favor for them."

Simon shook his head. "It doesn't work that way. They don't 'allow' me. Anyway, what kind of favor?"

"The usual kind. Make confusion. Misdirect. So the operation doesn't succeed."

"Work against Frank, you mean. Do you think I'd do that?" All of them cheating.

"The Service is careful." He looked down. "Me? No."

"Then why–?"

"I'd like your help."

"What, watching Frank?" Rearranging the cards now, out of order.

"A shorter trip. Leningrad only. You can suggest it. He's making this trip for you."

"But I thought you said the Service wants him to go to Tallinn."

"Not everyone in the Service is his friend."

They looked at each other for a moment.

"You know that he won't listen to me if the Service has asked him to do something. He can't."

"Suggest anyway. Then we know. Then I know how to help him."

"What's wrong, Boris?" Meaning it this time.

"An instinct. You learn that in the war too. You feel it. Get quiet. Don't move. Why? Because something tells you."

"All right. I'll ask," he said, getting up. "But you know he won't." Another minute. "You look after him, don't you?"

"It's my job."

Later, when he lay in bed, nodding to the clicking of the wheels, he realized it was quiet enough to hear footsteps in the corridor, someone's late night visit to the bathroom. So Boris didn't snore after all. Unless he was lying awake too, listening.

7

A VOLGA WAS WAITING for them at Moskovsky Station, the driver holding an umbrella against the morning drizzle. They headed straight down Nevsky Prospekt, the city flashing by between sweeps of windshield wipers. Leningrad, at first glance, was a faded beauty that had stopped wearing makeup—all the buildings, the pastel façades, needed paint.

"Rain," the driver said. "Very unusual this time of year. The afternoon will be better."

More a hope than a forecast, Simon thought. The rain, the mist over the canals, seemed part of a deeper melancholy. The imperial scale of St. Petersburg, without the crowds, the old government ministries, made the city feel empty. Moscow, by contrast, hummed with purpose. This was more like a ballroom after a party, just streamers left, and half-filled glasses.

The Astoria, a grande dame hotel overlooking St. Isaac's Square, was busy with an Intourist group of Chinese, some wearing Mao tunics, all of them looking weary, sitting on suitcases while they waited for the one interpreter to sort out their rooms. Simon glanced around the lobby. An ornate cage elevator, marble floors, a tea salon with potted palms. A man in a suit reading a newspaper. No one else. But it was early. He wouldn't be here yet.

Boris jumped the line to get them checked in, the Chinese watching without expression.

"Are we bunking together again?" Simon asked.

"No, no, down the hall." He handed Simon a key. "A corner room, on the square." Then another to Frank. "This faces the cathedral."

"I don't know how you do it," Frank said.

"It was already arranged." He checked his watch. "The guide is here in one hour."

"Oh, good," Joanna said. "Time for a bath."

They started for the elevator, bellboys following with the bags, and waited for the cab to descend behind the grille of lacy metalwork. French doors, opening out.

"Oh." A woman's voice, breathy, as if she'd been caught at something.

"Marzena," Frank said, equally thrown.

"Oh, I wanted to surprise you at lunch."

"You've surprised us now," Joanna said, so drily that Frank flashed her a scolding look. "I mean, I thought you weren't—"

"No, but then I said to myself, why not? It's so hard to travel alone. But with friends— You don't mind?"

"Of course not. How nice," Frank said, a quick recovery, but still rattled, only Simon sensing the displeasure underneath. Club manners, like Pa's, real feelings tamped down. "We were just going up. Then off to the Hermitage."

"The guide comes in one hour," Boris said, unruffled, the only one taking her presence in stride.

"Oh, Joanna, you don't mind? I'm not a party crasher?"

"No party to crash," Joanna said, smiling a little, watching Marzena maneuver. "Always room for you."

"So. One hour. Here in the lobby?"

"Unless you'd rather—"

Marzena ignored this. "Now maybe a manicure," she said, looking at her hands.

"What made you change your mind?" Joanna said.

"I don't know. To see the art, I guess."

In the elevator, everyone was quiet, preoccupied. The kind of turn that changed everything, rain at a picnic. Simon's floor was first.

"One hour," Joanna said, using Marzena's voice. "In the lobby. Watch out for my nails."

Simon smiled. "I will."

"Well, I didn't ask her," Frank said.

"And yet here she is," Joanna said. "For the art."

Simon's room looked down on the street, then catty corner across the giant square to the Mariinsky Palace. There were a few parked Intourist buses and official Zils, but otherwise it seemed another of those empty Soviet spaces, designed for parades. The room itself was bigger than his room at the National, but with the same period furniture. A fruit basket and mineral water were waiting on the writing desk and, at the foot of the bed, a wicker shirt basket with some folded laundry. Except he hadn't sent out any laundry.

A pillowcase, ironed and folded. He reached underneath. The cool touch of metal. He pulled out the gun, then checked for bullets, a silent nod to DiAngelis. As ordered. But now what? You couldn't just leave a gun lying around a Russian hotel room. Not in the briefcase. Not on top of the armoire. He glanced out the window at the drizzle. A break after all. His raincoat with deep pockets, where a bulge wouldn't show. Still in his suitcase.

He jumped at the knock on the door, then put the gun back in the basket and covered it. The bellboy had trouble with the luggage rack, but finally opened it, then started to explain the room's features in Russian, Simon nodding as the boy pantomimed the use of the drape chords, the light switches. Simon glanced at the laundry basket. Would he wonder why it was there? A newly arrived guest with laundry? What were the rules about tipping? Not in restaurants, but a bellhop? He took out a bill and handed it to the boy. A second's hesitation, as if it might be some kind of test, then a quick blur as he slipped it into his pocket. A whispered *spasibo*. When he was gone, Simon sat on the bed with the gun again, his body still tense, and took a deep breath. No possible explanation for a gun, not here. Supplied by the CIA. He opened the suitcase to take out his raincoat. Maybe it would rain all day.

The guide, a serious young woman who wore her hair in a bun, was called Nina and had textbook English for which she kept apologizing. They walked down to the Admiralty in a huddle of umbrellas, then along the embankment of the Winter Palace, the broad Neva choppy and breezy, almost a seafront effect. Simon looked left. If you got in a boat here, the current would sweep you out to the Gulf of Finland, out of Russia. Get through the day.

At the Hermitage they were asked to check their coats. Simon had forgotten: a Russian fetish, no coats indoors. He draped it over his arm, but the woman insisted. He turned his back, making a pretense of shaking the wet out and switched the gun to his jacket, letting it hang open so the bulge wouldn't show. He looked over at Boris. He must have one, out of sight in a holster. His job. The sort of thing he'd be trained to notice, bigger than a pack of cigarettes.

Nina was knowledgeable, leading them briskly through a maze of galleries, then lingering in the Raphael Loggias. "You see here where the papal coat of arms is replaced with the Romanov eagle." More galleries of Italians, then Flemish and Dutch, Rubens and Rembrandts. After another hour even Nina began to flag and they stopped to rest on some strategically placed benches.

"But did they look at them?" Marzena said to no one in particular. "Did they enjoy them?"

"They enjoyed getting them," Joanna said. "Having them. I don't know that they ever looked at them."

"I would have," Marzena said, fanciful. "I'd come every night in a gown, like Catherine, and look at my pictures."

"By candlelight. Squinting," Joanna said, then stood up, out of sorts but trying to hide it, going over to look more closely at a small still life.

They were all on edge, in fact, Marzena's presence an unexpected irritant. Frank was quiet, preoccupied, so she'd turned her attention to Simon, harmless remarks about the paintings which he barely heard, thinking about tomorrow, the weight in his pocket. Only Boris seemed to be enjoying himself, seeing the tour as a kind of patriotic act.

"It's the greatest collection in the world."

"Well, the Louvre," Frank said.

"No. The greatest."

When they left the gallery, Frank hung back with Simon, just far enough behind not to be heard.

"We have to get rid of her. She'll ruin everything."

"How?"

"It's one thing here. But Tallinn—"

"How?" Simon said again.

"She has to go back. You'll have to take her."

"Me?"

"Make something up," Frank said, thinking out loud. "You have to be back to fly home. You just wanted to see the Hermitage." He looked at him. "Flirt with her. Make her think—"

"What? How far do you want me to go?" he said, sarcastic. "For the Service."

"I don't care. Just get her out of here. There's always some hitch, isn't there?"

"What about Jo? The ferry?" What he would logically say.

Frank shook his head. "I'll have to take her with me on the boat. I'll work it out."

"And I'm sitting in Moscow when you go missing? They'll think I—" Playing the story out.

"Fly back Thursday morning. The boat doesn't leave until six. Get somebody at the embassy to put you on a plane out." He looked over. "We said our good-byes here. I go to Tallinn, you go home. It's not ideal, but it's still plausible. The Service wants me to go to Tallinn. You'll still have your trip to Leningrad. We've got today, the Peterhof tomorrow. That should give you enough time."

"Time?"

"To talk her into going with you. Get her out of here."

Simon looked down, as if he were thinking this through. "This still puts her in a hell of a position. After you disappear. Just having been here."

"I didn't ask her to come." He touched Simon's arm. "She'll be all right." Knowing she would be. Everybody cheating.

They headed into the Winter Palace, stopping at Rastrelli's marble staircase, sweeping up on two sides.

"My God," Marzena said, dazzled. "To live like this."

Nina rattled off dates, some architectural history, while they stood gaping, then began moving them up to the state rooms. Simon saw him first, starting down the other side, a blond woman next to him. The wife. What was her name? Nancy. But why bring her? Another complication. It was then that Lehman noticed him, their eyes meeting across the open space between the staircase wings. Simon made an almost invisible nod, then looked away, turning to Marzena. But aware of him now, moving in the corner of his eye, the same rhythm, one going down, the other up, like figures in a mechanical clock. So he was here.

After lunch they went to the Church on Spilled Blood and walked along the canals and finally balked at a plan to cross the Neva to see the Peter and Paul Fortress, pleading exhaustion. Disappointed, Nina led them back to the hotel, stopping to point out the building where Dostoevsky had lived. "Interesting for book publisher."

Upstairs, finally rid of the weight of the gun, he lay on the bed with a sense of relief, his mind floating. Were they really listening through the chandelier, the phone? But there was nothing to hear. No slips. He wondered if this had been part of the attraction for Frank, to see if you could play the part perfectly, not just the words, the emotions, all the senses heightened, actually believing it. Hal had arrived on schedule. Marzena had been unexpected but didn't matter, not after tomorrow. He went over the map in his head. How long it took would depend on the roads, probably two-lane with crumbling shoulders, Russian roads, stuck behind a tractor. Plan more time.

They should have been in a holiday mood at dinner, but instead the evening felt strained, all of them somehow scratchy, tired of one another. Marzena had dressed for a party, full makeup and flashy earrings, but the effort seemed wasted. Frank was distant, Joanna almost scowling with irritation. She had already had a few vodkas before dinner and had kept pouring more, ignoring Frank's glances, and was now moody and thin-skinned. Boris had retreated into one of his watchful silences. Which left Simon, an audience of one.

Marzena was making the most of it, drawing him out with questions, leaning in, a kind of coquetry as dated as the hotel, something out of old St. Petersburg. Make a man talk about himself and he's yours. She was impossible to ignore, or discourage, but the private asides had the effect of making Frank think Simon was flirting with her, his plan in action.

"Simon's not a very good long-term investment," Joanna said, looking at Marzena. "Are you? Back to the States and–poof." She opened her hand. "Gone."

No one knew how to respond, Marzena bewildered by the sud-
denness of it, like a slap.

"So let's enjoy him while he's here," Frank said, bland as a greet-
ing card.

"But you've hardly seen anything," Marzena said. "You should
stay longer."

"I've got a business to run."

"A capitalist answer," Marzena said, making a joke.

"Maybe next time."

"But there isn't going to be a next time, is there?" Joanna said,
brooding.

"That depends on whoever's handing out the visas. Here, I
mean."

"They wouldn't give you one before." She looked up. "Or
maybe you never asked. "

"But the book—"

"Yes, they want the book," Joanna said. "So open the gates. And
here you are. Now you'll need another excuse. Maybe when we die.
A compassionate visa. Just long enough to attend the funeral."

"Such talk," Frank said.

"Would you come for that?"

"Jo," Simon said.

"Oh, all right," she said, leaving it, looking out at the dining
room, most of the tables filled with the Chinese group. "What do
you think they make of it all? The Romanovs."

"They had Romanovs of their own," Frank said.

"Malachite," Joanna said, not listening. "Gold on the walls. And
they were surprised when the revolution came."

"A backward society," Boris said quietly. "But not now."

"No, now we are in space," Marzena said, enthusiastic, a Young
Pioneer.

"Is it hard for the Chinese? To get visas?" Jo said, still looking at them. "What's it like for them? Always in a herd like that. They don't know Russian, do they? I mean the alphabet."

"Neither do we," Simon said.

"I can teach you," Marzena said. "It's not difficult."

"Language lessons," Jo said, drawing it out. "Hard to say no to that."

"They need to have an interpreter," Frank said, answering seriously. "Guides. So that limits how many. And it's an expensive trip to make. A hotel like this. Must be a special group."

"Chinese VIPs," Jo said, playing with it. "I never thought. Is there a Chinese Social Register?" Her old voice, finding the world amusing.

"It'll be the Cubans next," Frank said. "Friendship tours." He looked over at Simon. "The Agency made a real cock-up there, didn't they? Was Pirie involved? Just the sort of half-assed idea he'd go for."

Boris raised his head, interested.

"I wouldn't know," Simon said.

"I'll bet he was." Frank shook his head. "One fiasco after another. One more and there'd have to be a real shake-up."

"Just what the Service ordered," Simon said, then, catching Boris's glance, "I mean, they'd like that, wouldn't they? A little confusion on the other side."

"The way things are going, they won't have to do a thing. The Agency will do it for them."

"Oh, we're going to talk shop," Joanna said.

"Not much longer," Frank said. "I'm beat. What is it about museums—?"

Simon felt a second of panic. Not yet. They had to meet first tonight.

"But so beautiful," Marzena said. "What did you like the best?" This to Simon.

"There's so much—"

"But if you had to pick," she said, pressing, a coy smile.

"The Dutch, I guess. The portraits."

"Oh, Jimbo. So Boston. Good burghers in black and white?"

"But the faces. You know everything about them."

"Well, what they want you to know."

Simon looked away, before his own face would show too much. There was a roar of laughter from the next table, everyone in his cups.

"Chinese *jokes*," Joanna said. "God, what do you think they're saying?"

And then he was there, gliding past the Chinese tables with his wife, surprised to see Simon.

"Mr. Weeks," he said. "You probably don't remember—Hal Lehman." Offering his hand. "Imagine running into—"

"Of course," Simon said, standing. "Spaso House. Nancy, isn't it?" She blushed, pleased. "What are you doing here?"

"Just seeing the sights. You owe me a call."

"I know. I've been meaning to—"

Hal turned to the table. "I didn't mean to barge in—" Expecting to be introduced.

"Frank, this is Hal Lehman. UPI. He's been wanting to meet you and I promised him an interview, so be nice."

Frank dipped his head.

"The first interview. After *Look* took pictures. Did they?"

"And this is—" Simon began the introductions, going around the table.

"A great pleasure," Hal said, shaking Frank's hand.

"Really? I thought I was a bad hat to all of you."

"An interesting bad hat. I'd really like to talk to you. Your feelings about the book, Moscow, whatever you'd like to talk about. Nothing—well, nothing you don't want to talk about. I promised Mr. Weeks that."

"You did."

"It's UPI. That's over four hundred pickups. It would be great for the book."

"And not bad for you either, is that the idea?"

"You've never given an interview. So this would be a first, yes. Mr. Weeks said they'd given you permission to do it. For the book. And they look at everything we send out anyway, so there's no problem there."

"For you."

"You review the copy."

"Frank, I promised," Simon said. "We need to present this right."

"So I don't look like a complete shit," Frank said, a wry smile.

"The book's going to be out there. There's bound to be plenty of—so start with me."

Frank sighed. "All right. Since Simon promised. We're back in Moscow next week," he said smoothly.

"Mr. Weeks said I wasn't allowed to come to the flat. The address is still an official secret or something. What about tomorrow? Right here? We could do it in the lobby," he said, ignoring a new round of laughter from the Chinese. "Maybe lunch? Mr. Weeks could sit in, if that makes it easier."

"No, we're away tomorrow. The Peterhof. Tsarskoe Selo."

"But so are we. I mean, that's where we were planning to go—"

"Moscow," Frank said. "I don't want to traipse around the summer palace wondering if that's you behind the fountain."

"How about this," Simon said. "We go out in two cars and you ride with Hal. Do it on the way. What would that be, an hour? And then that's it. You're done." He looked at Frank, eyes signaling for him to go along with this. "It's important for the book, Frank. I told you we'd have to do some of this here. Since we won't have you in the States."

Frank met his eye, a private exchange.

"You understand I can't talk about the Service," he said to Hal. "There are rules about that. We're leaving at eight. And I don't answer anything I don't want to."

"I will ride with you," Boris said.

"Deal," Hal said. "You won't regret it."

"I'm regretting it already. But my publisher insists," he said, a smile to Simon. "He wants me to be famous."

Nancy, who hadn't said anything, now nodded to each of them as she left, lingering for a second on Frank, her eyes wide, fascinated. Francis Weeks, a man in a hotel dining room. Before Hal could follow, the Chinese at the next table got up and filed out, separating Hal and Simon from the table.

"You brought your wife," Simon said, his voice low.

"If anything goes wrong, she'd be a hostage in Moscow. She won't be in the way."

"It's a complication."

"Then make sure nothing goes wrong. Was that okay?"

"Perfect." Smiling now and shaking his hand good-bye.

"Is this really necessary?" Frank said as Simon sat down.

"We need to do something and he's harmless. And he's here. With four hundred outlets there." He looked across. "How many interviews are you going to be able to do here? Spend an hour and you're in four hundred papers."

"But why can't they all come to Moscow?" Marzena said.

Simon looked at her, at a loss. "It's a long trip," he said finally.

"Didn't you think he looked a tiny bit like Howard?" Joanna said to Frank. "Think of his arm in a sling."

"Who?" Simon said.

"Howard Cutler," Frank said. "One of Joanna's old flames."

"Oo, there were so many?" Marzena said.

"No, not many," Joanna said, not rising to this.

"Why was his arm in a sling?"

"He was shot. Here." She pointed to her elbow. "In Spain."

"Another one in Spain. You were there, no?" Marzena said to Frank. "It's a weakness for you." Now to Joanna. "Always a man in the brigades."

"Not always," Joanna said, glancing at Simon. "Howard went over first. Before anybody really. And then there he is, back from the front, wounded, you can't imagine how romantic. Everybody was—" She stopped, patting Frank's hand. "Long before you."

"What happened to him?"

"He went to work for Browder. In the Party. And then—I don't know. What happens to people?"

"Hard to keep track," Marzena said, still playful. "So many lovers. You forget."

"No you don't," Joanna said, her voice distant. "You don't forget anyone. Not a single one."

"Well, before you start remembering and telling us about them, let's go to bed," Frank said. "I have an interview in the morning. It turns out."

"You go up. I want to sit with Simon for a little while."

"Yes, a nightcap," Marzena said.

"No, you too. Just Simon. Talk about old times."

"Jo, I really think—"

"No, I mean it. Off you go. All of you. Oh, don't say it. I've had too much. No more, I promise. Off you go. Shoo."

Frank looked at Simon, a you-going-to-be-okay? raise of the eyebrows.

"I'll get her home. We'll be up soon."

"My escort. Always a gentleman. Even back when. A gentleman."

Frank made a gesture behind her, wagging his finger over a glass. Simon nodded. Marzena hesitated, not ready to leave.

"Come to the bar," Boris said to her.

"Good," Joanna said when they were alone. "Now we can talk. I keep feeling the hours ticking away. And then you're gone. Let me have some of yours," she said, pouring from his glass. "Looks funny sitting with an empty glass." More Chinese passed them, the room emptying. She took out a cigarette, quiet as he lit it for her. "There, that's nice. We can talk. What shall we talk about?"

Simon smiled. "Tell me about Howard."

"Oh, Howard. I thought he was John Reed, somebody like that. Man of action."

"And you were Louise Bryant?"

"For about ten minutes. I mean, there he was, back from the front, and all the other boys were playing tennis." She looked down at the ashtray. "Maybe he does too now. *Golf.* So I was flattered."

"What happened?"

She shrugged. "Turned out he really was a man of action. One minute here, one minute there. I couldn't keep up. And then I didn't want to." She drew on the cigarette. "He was like you."

"Me?"

"He couldn't decide if he was in love with me."

Simon looked at her. "Would it have made any difference?"

"With him?"

"With me."

"I don't know. It's nice, somebody in love with you."

"Maybe not so nice for him."

She looked up. "Wasn't it? I'm sorry."

"It wasn't your fault. Anyway, it's a long time ago."

"But you weren't, really, or you would have held on—"

"You were already gone. Let's not go over this again. Things worked out the way they did."

She nodded. "But here's the funny thing. Tonight, when I saw Marzena making eyes at you, I wanted to scratch her face." She raised her hand, making her fingers claws. "Leave him alone. Not him too. As if I had any right—but who cares about rights? I thought, not him. He's not yours. He's— So there still must be something."

Simon managed a smile. "Jealousy, anyway. I don't deserve it."

"I couldn't help it. Pure instinct. Take your hands off him."

"No, I meant there was nothing to be jealous of." He looked at her. "She wasn't even in the room."

Jo moved her hand, covering his.

"Careful. Boris might be watching from the bar."

"I don't care. It's just—seeing her made me think of that time. I didn't leave you. Things happened, that's all."

"I know. Other people."

"So I can still feel a little jealous. I don't want her— First Frank, now you."

"Not Frank either."

"You said. How do you know?"

"Male intuition."

"Ouf," she said, waving her hand. "It's not a joke. I know what she's like. And he was there all the time. What's he doing there?"

Simon moved his hand away. "Spying on her husband."

"What?"

"Getting him to talk. As a friend. Then reporting everything to the office. They keep files on people like Perry. Troublemakers. He'll talk to a friend. Stories about the other scientists. Who else should they worry about? Make a file for. Marzena was just—there."

Joanna had sat back, her face slack. "That's a terrible thing to say."

"Why? Frank's a spy. For the KGB. What do you think they do?"

"He made reports on Perry? How can you know that? It's not true."

"Why not? He made reports on me. Pumped me for information and made a report. How do you think it's done?"

"It's not like that."

"Yes it is."

"He's too highly placed for that."

Simon said nothing, the silence its own reply.

She took a drink, grimacing when she put down the glass. "And what did you do? When you found out?"

"Do? He was gone. He was here. With you. I don't think he ever thought of it as wrong. Me, Perry, any of us."

"You had to leave your job. He ruined your life."

"No. I made another one."

She looked up. "But I can't."

Another silence, staring. "Yes, you can. I'll help you."

"Help me? How?"

Too close. No more. "We'll talk tomorrow. Figure something out. It's late. We should go up."

"Why would you do that? After—"

He took her hand again. "Old times' sake."

She smiled. "Old times' sake."

"Come on," he said, pulling her to her feet. She leaned against him as they crossed the lobby and waited for the elevator. He slid the cage door open. Bronze, mahogany panels that needed polishing.

"My escort," she said. "Are you going to kiss me good night? Maybe now, so the old dragon with the keys can't see us."

He leaned to give her a kiss on the cheek, but she moved her hands to the back of his head, pulling him toward her, opening to him. He felt the rush of blood to his head, the smell of smoke and perfume, everything warm, his mouth on hers. "So nice," she said, whispering, hot against his skin, and then kissing his face, moving over it. He moved down to her neck, nuzzling her, and she arched back, letting him have more, something he remembered from the weekend, something only she did.

"It's so nice with you," she said, still kissing him. "I could come with you. To your room."

His face still in her neck, the elevator slowing, his head dizzy with her, and for a second he thought they could, that he could change the plan, even last minute, just the two of them.

"Jo," he said, out of breath.

"I would. I would come."

The elevator stopped. He pulled his face away, brushing her hair.

"We can't."

She looked at him, then backed against the elevator wall. "No, we can't. What am I doing?" She put her hand to her forehead, a child hiding herself.

"Come on. It's your floor."

He opened the metal door. The floor concierge glared at them, handing him her key. Another report, but what would she say?

"Now I feel embarrassed," Joanna said.

"No. We've just had too much to drink."

"Oh, drink."

"But thank you for the offer."

She stopped next to her door. "You still can't decide."

He shook his head slowly, then kissed her forehead. "I always knew."

"What am I going to do?" she said to no one, to the hall. "I can't leave him."

"I know."

"No, you don't know. You think it's a love affair. Maybe once. Now—"

"You'll never leave him. I know that. Better than anybody. You're—tied."

She looked up at him, her eyes darting, moist. "Nobody else remembers him. Richie. Nobody else can talk about him. Keep him alive for me. If I lose Frank, there'd be no one. You can't talk to yourself, it's not real. He'd be gone."

He looked at her, his stomach falling, a kind of physical sadness, flowing through him and out to the tired hallway, so that it was finally everywhere, all you could breathe. The air itself a gray punishment, the way she lived every day.

He called Boris a little before seven.

"I hope I didn't wake you. I just had breakfast with Frank. Joanna's not feeling well."

"She's sick?" Boris said, his voice groggy.

"Hungover. She's going to need a little time. Would you call the guide and have her come later? Frank said you'd have the number."

"Yes, I have," he said, disgruntled.

"Nine o'clock, then. In the lobby. I'll tell the others. Sorry to wake you."

An hour's start. Enough distance. He went over the room again to make sure he had everything he needed. Visas. Raincoat, just in case, a convenient pocket for the gun. He'd have to leave the manuscript, but his notes, folded, slipped easily into the other pocket. No luggage, just a day at the Peterhof, admiring the fountains.

He opened the door and froze. Down the hall a woman was slipping out of Boris's room, her back to Simon as she closed the door. Still in last night's dress, her hair tangled, holding her shoes. Marzena turned, looking up and down the hall, a cat burglar, and started for the elevator. Simon watched her through the crack of his doorway. Had he been the assignment? Stick to Simon. Tell me what he says. Do what you have to do. But when had it started? A woman suddenly alone, her privileges—the flat, the dacha—now at the whim of—? Or had she listened to Perry too? Listened to Frank. Boris keeping watch. Her protector now. Everybody cheating. She passed Simon's door, eyes focused on the end of the hall, raising her head and trying to ignore the woman with the keys, a last gasp of dignity. At least she wouldn't be going down to the lobby. A change, a bath, a new meeting time. Two down.

The breakfast buffet was at the far end of the lobby but screened off from it. The Lehmans were just finishing, Frank and Jo not yet down. Simon ignored the spread of food and gulped some coffee, chewing on a brick of dark bread.

"Car ready?" he said to Hal.

"Out front."

"It's going to be a squeeze." A glance toward Nancy.

"I thought there were two cars," she said.

"But we're going in one," Simon said, looking at Hal, a question mark.

"She knows," Hal said. "Honey, you could still take the train. Finland Station. Do a Lenin in reverse. Meet me in Helsinki."

Simon shook his head. "How do we explain it to Frank? We're all going to the summer palace. We'll have to manage somehow."

"I couldn't stay in Moscow," Nancy said. "Not without Hal. Besides, it would look funny. Wives always go on the Helsinki runs. We do the shopping."

"Ah, there you are," Frank said, coming in with Jo. "Bright and early."

"Not that early. Boris has already finished. Better hurry."

"God, how can they eat all that," Jo said, looking at the buffet, avoiding Simon. She poured coffee.

"Apparently Marzena had a rough night," Simon said. "It's going to take her a while. Boris said he'd wait. We should start and they'll catch up."

"He wants us to leave without him?" Frank said.

"But not alone. There's another car following. To make sure we get there."

"By the book. Didn't I tell you?" Frank said. "The station chief here—"

"I can go with them, if you like," Simon said, chancing it, keeping it plausible. "So we won't be so crowded."

"No, no, you have to be referee. Make sure he asks the right questions." He smiled at Hal, the full Frank charm.

"I'll go," Joanna said.

"It's only an hour, less," Frank said. "We'll be all right."

"We'll meet you out front then," Hal said, getting up. "It's the Volvo."

"Really?"

"We bought it in Helsinki. It was either that or a Saab."

"No, I mean, it's your car? You drove here?"

"We're going on to Helsinki after. Shopping run. It's cheaper to bring the stuff back with you than to have it shipped. And sometimes it gets—lost. Stockmann's will ship, but it doesn't always arrive."

"Stockmann's?"

Hal grinned. "The Macy's of the north."

"And what do you buy?" Frank said, curious.

"Whatever you can't get in Moscow. People make a list. The other correspondents, I mean, not Russians. You have to have foreign currency."

"I had no idea," Frank said.

"Well, you have your own stores. You don't need—" He stopped, a sense of overstepping. "That's what I've heard anyway."

"And thank God," Joanna said. "Otherwise you'd never see a vegetable in the winter."

Simon glanced at her. Service hospitals. Service food stores. Where they lived. A Russia inside the other one.

The Volvo was at the curb, next to the bus waiting for the Chinese. Frank got in front with Hal, so they could talk, Simon in the back, wedged between Jo and Nancy. "The rose between the thorns," Jo said, but halfheartedly, still not catching his eye. They drove out of the broad square, leaving St. Isaac's behind.

"Where do you want to start?" Frank said to Hal.

"Let's start with the book. As far as I know, you're the first KGB officer who's ever written one. Why'd you do it?"

"Am I the first? I hadn't realized," Frank said, his public voice. "I suppose I wanted to set the record straight. We all want to do that, don't we? We just—most of us—don't get the chance." Concentrating, finding the right word, oblivious to the city outside his window.

Simon took a breath. The first gamble, hoping that Frank didn't know Leningrad, wouldn't see its geography in his head, just streets and canals and bridges. He worried when they crossed the Neva, away from the route to the Peterhof, but Frank didn't seem to notice, deep in the interview now, one bridge like another. He was enjoying himself, the familiar anecdotes told like moves in some version of cat and mouse, a game. After the Tuchkov Bridge there were few landmarks and no directional signs, no way to tell they were heading up to the shore road. How did anyone find it unless they'd driven it before? But Hal had.

"Late night," Jo said to Simon, dipping a toe in.

"You all looked like you were having such a nice time," Nancy said, just to say something.

"Well, we've known each other forever," Jo said, deciding to be pleasant, make the best of it. "I hope I didn't keep you up," she said to Simon, some kind of apology.

"No, I enjoyed it," Simon said. "Feel all right?"

"You mean do I have–?"

"It's an early start. That's all I meant."

"Oh," she said quietly, a quick thank-you glance.

"Why won't they let the defectors talk to the press?" Hal was saying.

"What makes you think we want to? What good would that do? Getting misquoted. It's always trouble."

"Why misquoted?"

"Well, people do—get misquoted. Not by you, let's hope, but you have to admit it happens. Anyway, what would you want us to say? That we were wrong? You think that. We don't."

"None of you? No regrets?"

Frank lit a cigarette, taking a minute. "It's a funny word, defector. Latin, *defectus*. To desert. Lack something. Makes it sound as if we had to leave something behind. To change sides. But we were already on this side. We didn't leave anything."

"Your country."

"Countries don't matter. In a way, I was already here."

"But Mr. Weeks—"

"Frank."

"Frank. Then why—?" Catching Simon's frown in the mirror. Not yet.

Frank waited.

"I mean, you didn't want to come to Moscow, did you? If you hadn't been exposed?"

"I wanted to be wherever I'd be useful."

"And the Rubins? Perry Soames. Gareth. Burgess. Maclean. They all came because their cover was blown. Wouldn't you all have stayed right where you were if that hadn't happened? Not come to Moscow?"

"I don't think anybody thought about it. You don't think about—getting caught. You're too busy not getting caught."

"But you were."

"Professional hazard. And not my fault. For the record. None of us expected Malenko to turn. But then if you're lucky, you end up here. Where you can still be useful. Look at some of the others. Alger. Harry. Wouldn't they have been better off here?"

"The Rosenbergs."

"Well, yes. The Rosenbergs. You know, when you start, you don't think, can I get away with this for the rest of my life? You don't think. You just do it. It feels—urgent. People are depending on you. Right now. You don't think about later."

"Alger," Hal said. "That's never been confirmed."

"It's not being confirmed now either. Hypothetical."

"It would be a big story."

"You've already got one. My first interview."

Hal smiled. "And it'll be a lot bigger when—" Another look from Simon.

"When what?" Joanna said.

"When it runs," Simon said. "UPI's in four hundred papers."

"What did you think when you first got here?" Hal said, moving on. "Was it what you expected?"

"Oh, that's all in the book," Frank said, swatting this away.

"Okay, tell me something that isn't in the book."

"I can't," Frank said, fencing now. "If the Service is involved."

"That doesn't leave us with much." He paused. "Who do you think killed Gareth Jones?" A left jab, unexpected.

Frank was quiet for a minute. "I don't know."

Simon raised his head. Through the looking glass again.

"I don't think it was political," Frank said, "if that's what you're implying. MI6 didn't do it because they can't. Not here. And I don't think we did it. Why would we?"

"Then why the witch hunt at the Lubyanka? Bringing Elizaveta back."

"Have they?"

"I heard you were the one who—"

"You should check your sources then."

Hal let this pass. "We're on the same side here, aren't we?"

Frank sighed. "I don't know about Gareth. Really," he said, easy as breathing. "A guess? Off the record? I think he met someone he shouldn't have. These things happen."

"There is no crime in the Soviet Union."

"But there are accidents. We'll have to leave it at that." He turned to the window. "Where are we? More *Khrushchyovki*. Khrushchev slums," he translated for Simon.

Rows of concrete apartment blocks, already cracked and stained with damp. Then pine trees and allotments. The farther they got from Leningrad, the poorer the countryside, sagging wooden farmhouses and muddy ditches, the same land he'd seen from the plane, open to tanks. They must be more than halfway there now. Vyborg had been a Finnish port before the Soviets snatched it. Simon imagined pitched tiled roofs and cobbles. A train station with a park in front, a quayside with a boat waiting.

"What happened to our friends?" Frank said idly, turning around. "I thought they were following."

"Probably behind a truck," Simon said. Not yet.

Frank went back to Hal, a question about wartime Washington, batting it back and forth ("the drop was in Farragut Square"), something he could answer without thinking, old stories. Then he sat forward, looking out the window, one side, then the other, working something out.

"The water's on the left," he said.

"What?"

"The Gulf. It's on the left. It should be on the right. You're on the wrong road."

"No."

"We should be south of it. Going west. It should be on the right."

Hal looked up into the rearview mirror. Frank followed the look and turned in his seat to face Simon, puzzled, then alarmed.

"We're going the wrong way."

A moment, suddenly tense. Now.

"DiAngelis changed the plan," Simon said evenly.

"Who? What plan?" Jo said.

"He's sending a boat to Vyborg," Simon said, watching Frank's eyes, panicky, just for a second.

"He can't go to Vyborg. It's Russia."

"He's sending some Finns. They'll pick us up there."

"But no DiAngelis." Sorting this out. "When was this decided?" The eyes his own again, calculating.

"Too many people knew about Tallinn. It's safer."

"Simon, Simon, what are you doing?" Focused on him, trying to see through him. "Not like this. We can't."

"That's the way he wants it."

"So he tells you? But you don't tell me."

"I was his contact. It'll work. It's a better plan."

"It's not the plan."

"A backup. The one nobody expects."

"What?" Jo said, upset now. "What plan?"

Simon and Frank stared at each other. Whose move? Finally Simon turned to her. "We're leaving. We're going home."

"What do you mean, home? Will you please tell me what's going on?"

"We're going to Finland. Then home. The States."

"Are you crazy? We can't." She turned to face Frank. "What is he talking about? Did you know about this? Did you?" This to Hal. Finally, almost a squeal, to Nancy, "Did you?" Nancy turned her head away. "Who am I supposed to be, the crazy lady?"

"I didn't want to—" Frank began, and Simon saw that he wasn't going to tell her—say that he hadn't told her because it wasn't going to happen—because he was trapped in his own story now, the double lie.

"What?" Jo said. "Who's sending a boat?"

"The Agency," Simon said. "To get you out."

"The Agency," she said, her eyes moving, someone being chased, then looking up at Simon as this sunk in.

Suddenly, too fast to anticipate, her hand came up, then both hands, hitting him, his arm raised to protect his face, the slaps falling on his chest.

"The Agency? They sent *you*? That's why you came? To trap us? You?"

Simon grabbed her hands. "Stop it."

But she was shaking. "You."

Behind him, Nancy was taking quick nervous breaths, not expecting this.

"You'd do this to him? To me?"

"Stop it. I don't work for the Agency. I'm trying to help you."

"Kidnap us. Send us to prison."

He turned to Frank. "Tell her."

Another unguarded moment, a kind of pleading look, and for a second Simon thought he might do it, tell the truth, but then the eyes cleared, disciplined, back in his story. Not even to her.

"He's not with them. I asked him to help us."

"Help us."

"It's time. You need to go home."

"I need?"

"I couldn't tell anybody. It's too dangerous."

"But they knew," she said, spreading her hand to take in the rest of the car. "And now what? We get in a boat? Sail away?" She nodded to Hal. "Are you going to take pictures? For UPI? And what happens to us?"

"We'll be protected," Frank said.

"Protected. Who arranged that?"

"I arranged it."

"And what's the price?" She turned, swatting Simon's hand away. "Well, what else could it be? And you'd do that."

"But you'll be out," Simon said.

"No we won't. You can't. Not here. We'll be killed."

"Killed?" Nancy said.

"Not if we do it right," Simon said.

"And that's your job?" Frank said, still trying to make sense of things. "Stop. Go back before it's too late. This isn't the arrangement. I go with DiAngelis. Only him."

"You mean he comes back with you. I know. That's always been the plan. Yours, anyway. Your Gary Powers. A gift to the Service. Another show trial. But I couldn't let you do that. Help you. That would be treason." He stopped. "I'm not you."

Frank's eyes narrowed, as if they were taking aim.

"Treason?" Jo said. Nobody listening.

"So we'll go through with the original plan. You go to DiAngelis. Tell him what he wants to know. A little payback. For everything."

Frank was still staring at him.

"What made you think I'd go along with this?"

"You have to. The only way to save yourself now is to go through with it. Defect."

"The Service knows all about—"

"Your plan? With the Estonians who aren't there? Except they're already there. Where you put them. They'll be sacrificed whatever happens, won't they? And now you pull in DiAngelis. A real Cracker Jack prize. Your plan. And they'd believe you. If you'd stuck to it. But you didn't. You ditched Boris. Took off in a car with UPI. To the border. A day ahead of plan. There's no other way to interpret that. Their worst nightmare."

"I was forced."

"By me? The naïve little brother? Who'd believe that?"

"The Service. I'm an officer."

"You think so? I don't. They'll eat you for breakfast. Just what they like. The double-dealing foreigner. Their favorite story. You're not going to talk yourself out of this."

"And you? What are you going to say? You don't actually think this can work, do you? You'll be—you'll be the Gary Powers. You don't want that. I didn't bring you here for that."

"No. Just to use me," Simon said, his voice suddenly bitter. "Play me like a harp. Use Joanna—'you have to save her.' Knowing I'd want to. Use Richie. Jesus Christ, Frank, a dead child. Making me feel sorry for you. And it's just part of the bait. Even use yourself. How's your health? I'll bet you're not even close to dying. I'll bet you're in the pink."

"No," Frank said, still looking at him. "That part's true. Maybe not as soon, that's all."

"What part?" Jo said. "What do you mean, dying?"

"Jimbo, stop. They'll put you in prison. Worse. I never meant—"

"What did you mean? You thought you'd get away with it. I'd be on the ferry, so that was all right. But there was Jo. That was a wrinkle. She had to stay. So send me back with Marzena and fly me out. And what do I say when I get there? To the Agency? I'm the one set it up in the first place."

"They'd know it was me."

"With me as your tool. I'd still be guilty. But so what? Just crack a few more eggs to make the omelet. You used us, Frank. All of us. All of us. Christ, for what? To make yourself look good to them? Who don't trust you anyway? You even used them. Kelleher? Finished anyway. Ian? Somebody had to do it. Gareth—"

"That's enough," Frank said, his voice gravelly. "You'll outsmart yourself."

"What about Gareth?" Jo said.

"But not you. I could never outsmart you."

"You think you have. Stop. Now."

"We can't stop now. It was too late the minute we left Boris behind."

"And when he catches up?"

"We're almost there," Hal said. "What do you want me to do?"

"There's a train station with a little park. In the center. Drive there first."

"I'm not getting on that boat," Frank said, his eyes hard, fixed. Simon felt the car closing around them, windows trapping them inside, unable to move, Frank at the other end. Finally afraid, recognizing the glass around them, the faint scratching, two scorpions.

"No," Simon said, keeping his voice steady. "But DiAngelis thinks you are."

"What does that mean?"

"What does any of it mean?" Jo said. She looked at Frank. "I won't go to the Agency."

"You'll be all right," Simon said. "You're part of the deal. When Frank made them think there was a deal. So now there is."

"I won't go to the Agency."

"You can't stay here. None of us can now. It's too late."

"None of us," Nancy said, pushing herself into her corner. "Oh, my God."

"I meant us," Simon said, "not you and Hal. You're not part of this."

"I'm driving," Hal said.

"Stop the car," Frank said, reaching over to him.

"Take your hands off him. I have a gun."

"What?" Turning, incredulous, a sharp intake of breath, the beginning of a laugh, then a stillness, seeing Simon's face. "There's only one way you could have got it. What did you promise him?"

"That you'd go through with the deal. And you will."

"Jimbo, a gun from the CIA? That's a death warrant. There's no diplomatic cover for that. Not if you have a gun. Let me have it."

Involuntarily Simon clutched at the coat in his lap, Frank glancing down.

"The idea was that you'd be at the other end of it. If there was any trouble."

"Get rid of it then. Toss it off the pier, junk it somewhere—just get rid of it."

"Later. When everything's okay."

"You'd never use it."

Simon stared at him.

"A gun," Nancy said.

"Why didn't you tell me?" Jo said to Frank.

"Because you were never going to go," Simon said, answering for him. "Nobody was. It was just a story he told to get them to come to him. You weren't part of it."

"But now I am? Thanks to you?"

"We'll get you out."

"Out."

"Don't make promises you can't keep," Frank said.

Simon looked at him. "Don't try to stop this. We all have to go now. We're on the same side. The Service just put us there."

"You put us there."

The outskirts of Vyborg were ugly, an industrial wasteland of chemical smoke and rusting pipes and chain-link fences, the old Finnish fishing port lost to one of the five-year plans. The center, with a cluster of historical buildings, was more attractive but just as dilapidated, everything sagging with neglect. Narrow streets, Simon noted. Traps.

"Go to the station, but don't stop. Just drive by and then around the park."

"What are we doing?"

"I want to see who's there. If there's a reception committee. I told DiAngelis the quay was a short walk from the station. So he'll think we're coming by train. If there's a leak, so will they. Frank, this ought to be easy for you. They'd be your people. You should be able to spot them right away."

"You're expecting me to help you?"

"It's your skin. You're the one trying to escape, not me."

"They won't believe that."

"Yes, they will. I can leave anytime. I don't have to make a run for the border. Now tell me what you see. Hal, slow, so we can get a good look."

The park on the map turned out to be another Soviet public space with a statue, some untended flower beds, and a swing set. No children playing. The station looked abandoned, a station without passengers or taxis. There were a few utility vehicles parked near the end, but otherwise the street in front was empty. Across, on the square, a few cars, all black, indistinguishable, the Volvo an exotic by comparison.

"The Leningrad train's due in about fifteen minutes," Simon said. "So they should be here. If they're here."

"How do you know? About the train?" Frank said.

"I checked."

"Checked how?" An almost professional curiosity.

"The concierge. Who will confirm that we took the train."

Frank raised his eyebrows, a kind of salute.

"What are we looking for?" Hal said.

"Two men sitting in a car," Simon said. "Your next gift to DiAngelis," he said to Frank. "Kelleher was the deposit. This will be something on account. Give your credentials a boost."

Frank looked at him, uncertain, still trying to work everything out.

"Too many people know about Tallinn. But nobody knows

about this, just me and DiAngelis. If there's a leak, all he has to do is make a list of who else he told. A short list this time. And he has him. Thanks to you."

"If there's a leak."

"I'm guessing there is. And if there is, we'd be sitting targets in a boat. So let's find out."

"They're empty," Hal said, looking at the parked cars. "Wait. There's somebody."

"One. There'd be two."

"He's in the station," Frank said.

Simon looked at him.

"One inside, one out. Service rules. Target covered front and back. When he hits the street, the grab. No scene in the station."

Simon nodded. "So now we know. What was that?" he said to Frank, sharp.

"What?"

"With the hand. Some kind of signal? I mean it, Frank—"

"Nervous?" Frank said, unable to resist.

"You still don't get it. If there's a leak, they know I arranged for another boat. For you. Otherwise, why not just wait for Tallinn? You don't want to try anything. They think you're running."

Frank said nothing, eyes still calculating, someone looking for an exit.

"This street goes to the port," Hal said.

"No, turn left, go around behind the park. We don't want to go near the boats. They've probably got another car there."

"What makes you think that?" Frank said. "If we're coming by train."

"You're a big catch. They wouldn't want you to slip away. How often do they get the chance in Vyborg? So what's another car?"

"And when we don't get off the train?"

"They wait for the next. Pull up over here," he said to Hal.

They were at the far end of the park, the station entrance still visible through a few scraggly trees.

"Now what?" Hal said.

"Now you and Nancy get out and take the train." He glanced at his watch. "Time enough to get tickets but not enough to sit around and have people wonder. You'll be in Helsinki in a few hours."

"But my story. You promised—"

"You've got plenty of story already and I'll give you more. But now it's not safe. We're going to have to drive. That means border crossings. I don't want you to have to risk that. Or Nancy. You're still okay on your own. With us—"

"More scruples, Simon?" Frank said. "I told you they'd trip you up."

"But this is the story," Hal said. "This is what I came for."

"But if it's risky," Nancy said.

"Trip me up how?" Simon said to Frank.

"The smart one," Frank said. "Take a look around. What do you see? Leningrad? How many American couples do you think just walk into that station and buy a ticket for Helsinki? I'd say none. Exit visa? I doubt they've even seen one. They'd have to check. With the authorities. And there goes the train. Your problem is that you don't know the Soviet Union. You're a stranger here. You don't know what's plausible."

"Oh, God," Nancy said.

"He's right," Hal said. "And what do I say about the car?"

"We stole it."

Hal shook his head. "To take it out of the country, the registration has to match the visa. It has to be me."

"Another detail," Frank said.

"Anyway," Hal said, "we've already taken the risk. We'd be accessories. We have to get you out now."

Simon was quiet, looking from Hal to Frank and back.

"The clock is ticking," Frank said.

"What's involved?" Simon said finally. "The drive. Checkpoints."

"We're about an hour from the border. Two checkpoints. First is the formal one—customs, search the car, all that. Then one military, just a pole barrier, like for a train. Then the Finns."

"Two checkpoints?"

"It's the Soviet Union."

"And the Finns have the same thing on the other side?"

Hal shook his head. "Nobody's going into Russia. Just trucks coming back. The road's okay. I've driven worse. About an hour. The big holdup's the first crossing. They like to go over the car. After that it's just woods. The soldiers get curious—there's nothing else to do—but a cigarette or two and they're all smiles. Assuming your papers are all right. You have visas?"

Simon nodded, patting the pocket of his raincoat.

"But no passports," Frank said. "Another detail. Passports to match the visas."

"I have those too. You look a little younger but it's still you."

"That's what you wanted them for?" Jo said, her voice accusatory. "For the book? No, for this. You were planning this even then? And the visas? Where did you get them?"

"Courtesy of the Agency, I would imagine," Frank said. "Let's hope they did a good job."

"That's when I knew," Simon said. "That you weren't planning to go. DiAngelis thought of them. You didn't."

"My passport expired," Jo said.

"I know," Simon said. "But you have to really look to see the date, do a little math. The border guards aren't going to be familiar with American passports. They just want the names and faces to match the visas. Which are in Cyrillic. Which they can read. The odds are good. If anybody does ask, just say it's a renewal date, a kind of reminder. And here's the visa, so it must still be good. All right," he said to Hal. "Can you get to the highway without passing the station again?"

"There is no highway. You take the street past the castle and that becomes the road. Two-lane. We can cut down toward the water, then back around. Should be all right."

"Unless they follow us."

"They won't leave the station," Frank said. "Not until somebody tells them to."

"Let's go."

Hal put the car in gear and began to pull away from the curb, then stopped. "Look."

A car coming fast, screeching to a stop in front of the station. The same road they'd taken. Boris jumped out, looked around, as if he were trying to pick up a scent, then crossed over to the stakeout car, asking questions, in a hurry. The man in the car climbed out, shaking his head. More questions. The man now pointing in the direction they'd gone, his arm making a sweep to the left, around the park. Boris looked up.

"He knows about the car," Frank said. "The Volvo."

"How? You didn't until this morning. Why not a hired car?"

"There would have been someone in St. Isaac's. Covering the hotel. See us leave. And in what." He looked at Simon. "It's the Service. This isn't going to work."

"Or maybe you signaled the guy at the station."

"I didn't. But either way, we've got Boris now. Call it off."

"Let's go," Simon said to Hal. "Quick."

Hal pulled out into the street and headed to the port, away from the park.

"He's coming," Nancy said, looking out the window. "He went back to his car."

"Alone?"

"The other man's still standing there. But he's driving fast, the new man. Around the park. He knows where we are."

"Call it off," Frank said. "I can still fix it."

"Listen to you."

They could see cranes and masts now, the port straight ahead. Hal went another block, then swerved left, then left again, a parallel street, backtracking.

"Is he behind?"

"No."

A major street ahead, big enough for trucks. Hal turned left again, shooting north, toward the castle. An island. A truck behind them, blocking them from view. They passed the road to the station.

"He's there," Simon said, head turned to the rear window.

"Hold on," Hal said, veering sharply, across the incoming traffic. A horn, loud. Back to the port. "We're supposed to be heading for a boat, right? Not the border. So we'd want to lose him somewhere down here."

"If we can," Frank said.

Port buildings, warehouses and repair shops, the streets a grid, oddly drowsy away from the noise of the port. On the quay itself people barely looked at the car, locked into themselves, as if they'd been deafened by the winches and clanging chains, dropped metal and hissing repair blowtorches. Hal weaved in and out, accessing the quay, then moving away from it. An alleyway. Hal glanced in the rearview mirror, nobody, and pulled in. Not an alley, a driveway, L-shaped, swooping around to a loading area, hidden from the street. A man in overalls came out, waving them away.

"We can't stay here. It's a dead end," Simon said.

"Give it a minute. Make him think he's lost us."

The man came over, a flood of Russian. Frank answered back.

"What's Frank saying?" Simon said to Hal.

"He's asking directions. Says we got lost. It's okay."

Now a laugh, Frank charming the watchman. Nobody else around.

Hal turned the car and swung back into the driveway. Nothing at the end. He nosed out into the empty street then headed quickly toward the port again. Another left onto a parallel street, the maneuver from before.

"He'll be looking for us on the quay," Hal said.

No one saw it coming, just some blurry motion from the side street, then Boris's car crashing into theirs, pushing the Volvo into the wall, a scrape of metal, wedged in. Boris flew out of the car, as if he were being carried by the momentum of the crash. He tore at the back door, flinging it open, a gun in his hand.

"Get out." Pulling Nancy out to get to Simon. "Get out. Bastard."

He grabbed Simon's arm, yanking him out, the raincoat flung aside on the backseat.

"CIA bastard. I knew. From the first." He slammed Simon against the car, face pushed down, an arrest. "You all right?" he said to Frank.

Frank nodded, getting out of the car.

"You think I didn't know?" Boris said, twisting Simon's arm up, immobilizing him. An involuntary grunt, the pain shooting through him. "At the Bolshoi. You think we didn't know who he was? Why such a meeting? What, what? On the train, so innocent. Me, worried about Tallinn. But not you. The Agency had a new plan. But we have ears, so now I know too. Bastard." He turned to face Frank. "I told you not to trust him. One step in that boat and they have you. And who puts you there?" he said, looking back at Simon, giving his arm another twist. Simon gasped, the words rushing by him, driven by their own logic, the story they'd want to believe. "I always knew. To send his brother. Who would believe it? Not even him." A nod to Frank. "But I knew. And you," he said to Hal through the front door, still open, Frank standing next to it, "another press cover. Another one. Don't they have new ideas? Another one to send home. But not this time. This time it's serious. To kidnap an officer of the Service. What should we do about that? What should be Soviet justice?"

"No," Nancy said from the car.

"Be quiet," Frank said.

Simon turned his head toward him, Frank not meeting his eye, blank, taking everything in. And now the pain in his arm spread through the rest of him, how everything would feel when they broke him, the bones of his face smashed, kidneys throbbing until he said what they wanted him to say. Everybody did, even the old Bolsheviks, confessing to anything. Just to have an end. A crowd in the Hall of Unions. Or maybe not. Maybe something simpler. He looked at Frank's blank face, his expressionless eyes. But why should he be any different? How many had Frank killed now? The hapless Latvians. How many hundreds of others, just by leaving something folded in a newspaper on a park bench. Collateral damage, nothing personal.

"Where are the others?" Frank said to Boris.

"Two down there," Boris said, nodding to the port. "Two back at the station."

"What about the boat?"

"Taken care of."

"The station, then. We can call from there. I'll drive. Hold him in the back."

Simon stared, his body beginning to shake. Don't pee. Really happening now, a louder scratching against the glass, Frank still expressionless, not savoring it, just business, saving himself.

"What about—?" Boris motioned toward the others.

"Oh, I think they'll stay right where they are. Won't you? Otherwise, you'd be resisting arrest. Shot trying to escape. For real. Keep an eye on them, Jo."

"Oh," Nancy said, a kind of yelp.

"Frank—" Simon started, cut off by Boris pushing him more tightly against the car.

"You should have thought about this before." Bloodless. "You have him?" he said to Boris. "I'll just get my coat." He bent down to reach into the backseat, gathering up the raincoat.

First the explosion, the air clapping over his ears, so loud that it seemed to go through him, his whole body knocked forward. Something sticky running down the side of his head, still pinned against the car, Boris slumping over him. No pain, the liquid coming faster now, hot. A groan, Boris's body lying on his, dead weight, and then sliding down, pulling Simon with him, falling back, a thud on the pavement. Another groan, still alive. Frank stepped over, the gun in his hand, Boris's eyes open wide, astonished, one last second and then the gun fired again and Boris's head split open, dark liquid oozing out.

Simon, weaving, tried to stand up, moving away from the car, feeling the side of his face, the streak of blood, not his. He looked up, eyes locked with Frank's. Nancy screamed, then covered her mouth, as if a scream might bring someone running, only the gunshots drowned out by the clanging noise on the quay. Joanna stepped out of the car in slow motion, dazed, staring at Frank.

"Jesus," Hal said, looking down at Boris, blood and something else pooling beneath his head.

"Now we have to leave," Frank said slowly. "Boris." Looking at him, then up at the others, in charge, trained for it. "Get him out of the street. Before anyone sees."

"They'll come looking for him," Simon said.

"But not right away. Help me get him into the car," he said, lifting the body from underneath the shoulders. "Get his feet."

Simon, still stunned, hesitated.

"Quick."

Simon grabbed the feet, lifting the body, almost buckling under the weight, then staggering with it toward Boris's car. Carrying Gareth out of the monastery grounds.

"We have to stash the car somewhere. That alley. You'd have to be really looking to spot it there."

"The caretaker—"

"Don't go as far as the loading area. He can't see the driveway."

A heavy thump as the body was dropped into the backseat.

"I'll take Boris's car," Frank said to Hal. "You follow. Wait at the end of the driveway."

Simon looked up, a flash of alarm. Frank, catching it, smiled a little. "Nobody's going anywhere," he said to Simon. "Not now. Come with me." He handed him the gun. "Better? Here." He took out a handkerchief. "Wipe your face. People notice blood. The eye goes right to it."

They got into Boris's car.

"Oh, my God, what are we going to do?" Nancy said.

"We're okay. Come on," Hal said, putting his arm around her.

"Have her ride up front with you," Frank called over. "The way you usually would."

A car appeared at the corner.

"Quick," Frank said to the others. "Get in. Before they see your clothes."

He backed the car away from the Volvo, but by now the other car had seen them and slowed down, the eternal fascination of an accident. Not the men from the station. Frank rolled down his window, speaking Russian. They hadn't seen each other coming and now who was going to pay for it? The other car knew someone who could fix the scraped fender. An address. All of it so interesting that no one noticed the dark splotch on the road.

They drove around the block, both quiet, as if the body in the back had silenced them, a hush, Simon still shaky.

"Thank you," he said finally.

Frank said nothing, leaning forward, checking the street at the corner.

"So you were wrong," Frank said, still not looking at him. "They would have believed me. The Service. I'm an officer."

"Boris would have, anyway."

Frank nodded. "Well, it doesn't matter now. I couldn't let them hang you. Pa would blame me."

"Is that what they do? Hang people? Still?"

Frank made a half shrug. "I don't know. Shoot them, probably. But it's what they do before. You don't think I'd let them do that to you, do you? You don't think that."

Simon looked over at him. "Are you really sick?"

"Yes. It wasn't a lie. None of it. Actual lies."

"But you were never going to go."

"No."

"Jesus, Frank. All this, for what?"

"I can't leave the Service. Everything I did was for them. They were—the best. I'd never seen anything like it, even in Spain where things were such a mess. They knew what they were doing. I wanted to be part of that. People who always knew what they were doing. The best." He turned to Simon. "And I was. I was valuable to them. I don't know how much time I have left, you can't trust the doctors, but I'll be damned if I'm going to spend it doing crosswords. I want to be buried at Kuntsevo. Full honors. An officer of the Service." He stopped. "But now— You can't argue with a corpse," he said, cocking his head toward Boris. "Not when there are witnesses. So, lucky DiAngelis."

Quiet again.

"You're going to lie to him, aren't you?"

"Let's see how good he is. Jimbo, I'm going. That's your pound of flesh. There isn't any more."

He turned into the alley. "Here we go. Let's hope they don't find him right away. Start calling the border. We need the head start. A little luck."

He stopped the car before the driveway forked left, not yet visible from the loading ramp. He got out, then stood for a second, looking into the backseat. "Boris," he said quietly. "You're supposed to suspect everybody. Even me. Service rules." He turned to Simon. "You realize they'll never stop now. Until they find me. It's bad enough, a defector, but to kill one of their—" He stopped, facing the end of the driveway. "Let's go. They're waiting."

They drove out of town, past the castle in the harbor, without seeing anyone tailing behind. How long would they have? The hour they needed? Less?

"I've never seen that before," Joanna said, between Frank and Simon but not really talking to either. "A man get killed."

"His head," Nancy said.

"We can't go back now, can we?" Jo said to Frank.

"No."

"So it's over. Now what happens to us?"

"We live somewhere. New names. The Agency protects us."

"New names. Like when we came here. Protection. So it's the same. It's always the same. I'm sorry," she said to Frank, touching his hand.

"But you'll be home," Simon said.

"Like prisoners." Moody, ready to snap.

"What were you here?"

"Yes, what? So it's the same. That's our choice." She picked up Frank's hand. "I'm sorry." Her voice intimate, something between them.

"No, no," Frank said.

"You should never have listened to me. I think about that all the time. What if we'd never started—"

"What if," Frank said. "But we did."

"And whose fault? Who said, yes, do it?"

"It's nobody's fault."

"If I had stopped you—"

"Stopped him?" Simon said. "He said you never knew."

"Where did he say that? In the book? That's all lies anyway. What else could it be? And you believe him?"

"Jo—" Frank said.

"What difference does it make now? He wanted to protect me. From what, I don't know. But now—are you listening, UPI? Such a scoop. The innocent wife talks." She turned to Simon. "Of course I knew. It was me. I said, do it. When he came back from Spain, he told me they had approached him. He thought I would be impressed. Since I was a Communist. And I said, you have to do it if they ask you. We all believed then. Oh, look at your face. Did you think there was nothing up here?" She pointed to her temple. "Just silly clubs? Dancing? Of course we believed it. And then—well, things changed."

"Changed how?"

"How can I explain it to you? Like alcoholics, maybe like that. We started drinking together. And then I stopped. But Frank couldn't. He couldn't stop. One more. One more. You know what's in the drink? Secrets. And he's the only one who knows. That's what he likes," she said, facing him, her voice sour, a look between them. "It doesn't matter what it is, the secret. As long as he knows it. And you don't. So he can smile while he does it—betray you. Then one more." She turned back. "He couldn't stop. So I started drinking something else."

"We can fix that. When we get home," Simon said.

"Fix it. You never understand anything. The knight to the rescue. I don't want to be rescued." She looked at Frank. "When I saw you shoot Boris, it all went through my head. What we are now."

Nancy had twisted in her seat to listen, her eyes wide and shiny, like mirrors, and suddenly, looking at her dismayed expression, Simon could see Frank and Jo in them, finally see because she saw it, what they had done to each other.

"And it's my fault," Jo said, skittish, her hands moving.

"It's nobody's fault," Frank said, calming her. Something they'd said before.

Simon found himself edging away from them on the seat, as if he needed more air. An inch, any distance.

"So there's a story for you," Jo said to Hal.

"We have to be careful with that," Simon said. "There's a big difference between knowing and doing. You've never been charged—"

"To the rescue again," Jo said, lifting her hand, a mock call to arms. "They're going to charge me? Where do they find me? That woman's gone. A new name. Only the Agency knows where I am. You think they'd tell? Not as long as Frank is talking. All those secrets. After that, who knows?" Fluttering her hand, her voice drifting, eyes following, somewhere inside now.

Frank looked over, a reassuring glance. "Give her a minute." Moving her hand down, a caretaker.

"She going to be all right? At the checkpoint?" Unpredictable, out of focus, guards peering at her.

She turned to him. "I was so happy when you came," she said, her voice still vague. "I never thought— So you're good at it too."

In the front seat, Nancy had begun to shake, a kind of crying without tears.

"Hey, it's okay," Hal said.

"I'm scared," she said.

"Not you. Come on."

"I keep seeing his head. Everything coming out—"

"*Shh.*" He glanced in the rearview mirror. "That's the same car for a while," he said to the back. "What do you think?"

Everyone turned to look, tense.

"Let him pass you. Then you'll know," Simon said.

Hal waited for an open stretch, then slowed the car. Almost

immediately, the car behind swung out and overtook them, leaving a stream of visible exhaust.

"They all look alike, that's the trouble," Hal said. "Not far now. We're making good time."

But in the car they seemed to be not moving at all, the flat landscape the same one they'd seen minutes ago. Frank had sat back, his mind somewhere else, but the others fidgeted, nervous. How long before the watchman checked the alleyway? But he'd call the police, not the men at the station, another delay. Unless they'd already started combing the streets for the Volvo and found Boris instead. Or nothing had happened, the winches clanging on the quay, the caretaker having a peaceful smoke.

"This is it," Hal said. "Where the trucks are."

Up ahead, a cluster of low buildings, with trucks parked at the edge of the road, waiting for inspection. As they got closer, they could see the barriers across the road, the tollbooth-like stations on either side, topped with red stars, customs sheds and huts for the guards in the winter, uniforms.

Simon reached into the raincoat pocket. "You'd better have these," he said, handing over the passports and visas.

"Give them all to Hal," Frank said. "Let him be group leader. How's your Russian?"

"Good enough for this."

"So that's what I looked like," Jo said, opening hers.

"You still do," Simon said. "You all right?"

"You keep asking that. And if I said no?"

"I'm thinking about the others." A nod to the front. "We have to do this right."

"Remember," Frank said. "They're not used to American passports. Americans fly in and out. They don't drive. So they'll be curious. It doesn't mean anything."

"Until it does," Jo said.

A guard waved the car over to the side. Hal rolled down the window and handed him the passports and visas in a stack. Some Russian that Simon couldn't follow.

"Honey, he needs the registration," Hal said, pointing to the glove compartment. "We have to get out. They want to go over the car."

Trunk. Under the hood. Seats, running their hands into the seams.

"What are they looking for?" Simon said to Frank.

"Nothing."

He turned his head slightly, away from the guard with the passports, peering now at their faces. As Simon had guessed, once he had matched the face to the picture, he moved on to the visas, in more comfortable Cyrillic. Frank's name apparently not recognized. Old news. A sharp question and an exchange in Russian with Hal.

"'Where are we going?' I told him shopping. In Helsinki. He wants to know why so many. People go to Helsinki, they want an empty car to bring the stuff back."

"Tell him we're picking up another car there," Frank said. "A new one." He glanced at the car. "A Saab."

"You tell him."

"No, be point man. The Russian speaker. Let him deal with you."

"He says you'll need papers to bring it in."

Frank nodded. "We know. The dealer's arranged it."

"Why no luggage?"

"Just pick up and back. We didn't want to take up room in the car. With all the stuff. He buying it?"

"I think so. It's why any foreigner comes through here, so he's not surprised. I can't tell if we should offer to pick up something for him. They all want stuff, but maybe he's—"

"No, keep it straight."

Simon looked around the post. Guns everywhere, a fence on either side of the road. Beyond the barrier a pine forest. What did they do at night?

The guard went back to examining the passports, the indecipherable English, any bureaucrat, making a show of being thorough. The others had finished with the car. Simon felt his leg jiggle, anxious, glancing back down the road. Why not just wave them through, everything plausible. The guard was handing Hal the passports, but now looked at Simon.

"He wants to see your raincoat. If there's anything—"

Simon looked up, alarmed. What if he wanted to pat him down? He felt the weight of the gun in his jacket pocket. A death warrant. But where else could he have put it? A body search at a border crossing? On an American passport? Led into one of the sheds, stripped. He handed over the raincoat, the guard jamming his hands into the pockets. Coming out with his notes.

"He wants to know what these are."

Looking at the pages, scribbles in English.

"Notes to myself. A diary."

"About Russia?"

"No, no. Personal."

A frown on the guard's forehead. Impossible to say the Service had already approved them. Impossible to say anything. Weeks of work.

"Offer to translate one," Frank said to Hal. "So he can see for himself. Make something up."

And then, as Hal was saying this, another guard came up.

"*Dobry den*," he said to Nancy, smiling. "*Kak dela?*" Then something to the first guard.

"He remembers us from the last trip," Hal said.

"Stockmann's," the guard said, rolling out the word, not really flirting, genial, showing he knew them, a connection to the larger world.

"Stockmann's," Nancy said, smiling back. "That's right."

Something with a laugh to the other guard, then some Russian to Hal.

"He wants to know what's on the list this time. They think it's something out of a dream, that you can just go and buy anything you want."

Nancy began to tick off a list on her fingers, playing along, Hal translating. "Sheets, pillowcases, summer dress, Band-Aids, toilet paper—"

The guard was shaking his head at the list, enjoying this. "Cigarettes? American?"

"No, only Russian," Hal said, taking out a pack.

The guard held up his hand. "We have." He motioned to the other guard to return the raincoat and waved his hand toward the car. "So. Stockmann's." Another nod and smile.

Simon watched the guard put the notes back in the coat pocket, almost an afterthought, and hand it to him. Get in the car. Hal and Nancy were saying good-bye, the first guard now one of the party too. Good wishes in both languages. Jo back in the car, Frank. They were going to get away with it. In the booth next to them, the telephone rang. Simon froze, hand on the door, still out of the car. The guard reached through the open window of the booth and picked up the receiver.

"*Allo*," he said, then shouted it again, a bad connection.

Simon craned his neck, not breathing, too far away to hear anything on the line, watching the guard's face instead. A quick exchange and then another "*allo*," evidently more static. The friendly guard came over and started waving them on. Simon stood, rooted.

"Get in the car," Frank said.

Finally the guard at the booth gave up, putting the receiver down, a disgruntled comment to the other guard, then a resigned shrug.

"Okay, okay," the friendly guard said, waving them on again.

Simon ducked into the backseat, head turned, anticipating another ring as Hal pulled the car out. The barrier rose. They were through. A straight stretch into the woods. Only a few miles now.

"How many phone calls do you think they get there?" Frank said, partly to himself. "Did you see how he jumped? What happens at the next crossing?" he said to Hal.

"Just a check. To see if your visa's been stamped. Then on your way. After that you're in Finland."

"Let's go a little faster if we can."

"What's the matter?" Simon said.

"Why would anyone call there?"

"Late for a shift. Maybe his wife. Headquarters. Well, they'd have a better connection."

"Unless the problem's on this end. I never looked at the wires. You?"

Simon shook his head, his face a question.

"If it's our friends, they'll call again, don't you think? Until they get through. There'd be some urgency."

"Okay," Hal said. "Let's make some time."

They were in the woods now, the border crossing lost behind a curve, the road shadowy with trees. No side roads or houses, nothing between the crossings, a forest no-man's-land. Simon sat up, alert, as if he were still listening for the phone.

"Lucky he remembered Stockmann's," Nancy said.

"He'd have taken the papers," Frank said to Simon. "Papers are always trouble. Especially these. If he could read them." Almost amused. "Shame after all that work. By the way. I never said. I want to dedicate it to Jo. I want it to read: For Joanna, who didn't know, but never stopped loving."

"Frank," she said quietly. "And people will believe that?"

"What do you think, Hal?" Asking something else.

Hal thought for a minute. "All right. I won't."

More trees, thicker, a Grimm setting. Still no one behind.

"We can't go back either, can we?" Nancy said to Hal.

"No. We can get Alex to pack up our stuff."

"I don't care," she said. "Leave it. God, no more Moscow. We can breathe again."

"Richie's room," Jo said to no one.

"It's here," Frank said, patting her forehead, then smoothing back her hair.

Hal slowed the car after the next curve.

"There they are."

A striped barrier pole across the road, a hut next to it. Two soldiers.

"No telephone wires," Frank said.

"But maybe they have a field phone."

"I doubt it. I haven't seen one of those since the war. Well, here goes. Hal, you're point man again."

They pulled up to the crossing. Both soldiers came over, curious about the car. Young, teenagers. The country where you could buy the car was only a few feet behind them. A hut to stay warm. No thought of running. They looked at the passports, checking the visa stamps. Simon held his breath. Then the passports were being handed back and one of the soldiers was at the barrier, cranking it up, like a railway crossing. Hal drove under the raised pole.

"Are we there?" Frank said. "No more crossings?"

"You're in Finland," Hal said. "Free as a bird."

"Okay, stop the car, then."

Hal slowed the car. "What—?"

"No, stop. I have to walk back. I just wanted to make sure you all got out."

"Frank," Jo said.

"*Shh,*" he said, touching her hair again. "It's going to be all right. Simon's going to take care of you, get you to a doctor. And I want you to go, promise? Promise?"

Jo looked at him, confused.

"Frank, for God's sake," Simon said.

"I can't do this," Frank said. "You know that. Betray the Service? Sing for old Pirie?" He shook his head. "I can't. I have to go back." He looked over at Simon. "It's where I live."

"They'll kill you."

"No, they'll believe me. I'm an officer.

"Believe you."

"They might. I'm good at it. It's worth a try. I can't do this."

"You killed Boris."

"No, you did. You don't mind, do you? You're out, they can't— It was your gun. I can make it work, the story. They think you're Agency anyway. Boris thought so and there's the proof. Dead in an alley. In fucking Vyborg. You're a tough guy." He turned to Jo again, touching the back of her head, kissing the side of her face. "My Jo. No good-byes. We know. Be happy. Do that for me." He moved back, looking straight at her. "It was never your fault. None of it. None of it."

Another minute and then he turned to Hal. "Thanks for the lift. Quite a story. Work with him on it." He pointed his finger to Simon. "He'll make you look good."

And then he was backing out of the door, Simon leaping out the other side.

"You're not going to do this," Simon said. "It's too late."

"Jimbo, I can't—"

"What, betray the Service? What about Kelleher? That was easy enough. You didn't think twice about him."

"He was already turned. We knew. They didn't know that we knew. So they ended up feeling twice as smart. Why do you think they moved so fast? They didn't even check the story out. They didn't have to."

"And Gareth?"

"Gareth got in the way. Mine, this time. But he'd been getting in the way for years. The Service never knew what to do with him. I think it was a relief, in a way."

"It won't be for Ian. And what about Perry?"

"What about him?"

Simon was silent for a minute. "You found the body."

"So you think I killed him?" He shook his head. "What a suspicious mind you have. You know what killed him? He stopped believing. He couldn't–adapt." He held up his hands. "Clean. This time, anyway. How about yours? Handing me over. Planning it. Who are you doing it for? Did you ask yourself? America? Pirie? Maybe just you. What did you think was going to happen to me? In the land of the free. Maybe not so clean either." He nodded toward Simon's hands.

Simon stared at him, a sound in the air, a faint scratching.

"But if it really bothers you about Ian, I can tell them it was you. After all, it was. I wouldn't. I think you'd be putting your head on a block, but it's your call. Do you want me to do that?"

Simon looked at him. "No."

"No." He moved behind the car to Simon's side. "Simon." His voice low, just the two of them. "I never said I was perfect. But I won't do this. Be Pirie's boy. I already changed sides. So say good-bye here. Wish me luck. I don't suppose we'll see each other again. Ever."

"Don't go back. You're going to run out of lies. Even you."

Frank took him by the shoulders. "Think of it this way. You'll get the house now. For sure. Everything. And the book."

"It's lies."

"Not all of it."

"Which parts do I believe?"

Frank smiled. "All of them. You'll sell it better." He moved closer, a quick hug, then dropped his hands. "I'm glad you came."

"Frank, for Christ's sake—"

"I know, not the way I expected it to go." He looked up, another smile. "You were too smart for me. But it was worth the try."

"And what would you have done with DiAngelis?"

Frank raised a finger, then wagged it. "Scruples." He turned to go.

"I could stop you. I still have the gun."

Frank stopped. "And I'd get rid of it soon if I were you. It's evidence."

"I could use it."

"But you won't."

"Why not?"

"Because it's me. And what would be the point? Much easier this way. I'll just serve out my time here." He looked to the other side of the car. "Jo."

"Where are you going?" she said, getting out.

Frank looked at Simon, a signal, and started walking away. Simon went over to her. "He told you, remember? He's going back to Moscow."

"He's leaving me?"

"No. He's just going back."

"How can he leave me?"

"He doesn't want to live in hiding." Making Frank's case, everything inside out again.

"Oh, look, they're coming to pick him up."

Simon turned. A black car heading for the crossing, the barrier pole still raised. The car from the station. Or any car. But coming fast, tearing down the road, running late, then screeching to a stop just before the barrier, some invisible line they couldn't cross, jumping out of the car, guns. The soldier guards pulled back, startled.

Frank was almost at the barrier now, holding his hands in the air, the universal sign.

"Comrades!"

Not one shot, two, then more, thudding into Frank, who stopped, knocked sideways by the bullets, then fell.

"No!" Joanna screamed.

Simon grabbed her, ducking, pushing her back into the car. "Stay down."

"What the hell—?" Hal said.

But the firing had stopped, the men just standing there, the soldiers still wide-eyed, everyone staring at the figure lying on the road. Still in Finland. Simon thought they would grab the body and drag it back, but no one moved. He ran to Frank, rolling him over. Still alive, a flicker of the eye, then a wince.

"Help me!" Simon yelled, but they stayed in place. Footsteps behind him, Hal, the women holding each other back at the car.

"Frank. Can you hear me?"

"They never tell you how much it hurts," he said, the words jerky, coming in gasps. "Getting shot."

"We'll get you some help."

He shook his head slowly, some blood now at his mouth, and grabbed Simon's hand. Simon looked down. Frank's stomach was welling with blood.

"Jimbo, don't be mad. It's me," he said, clutching him, and suddenly Simon's eyes were filled, as if they were welling blood too, everything blurry. And then, out of nowhere, in his mind's eye, he saw the train between their old rooms, connecting them.

"Don't talk. You're hurt."

"I know. So—" Opening his eyes, trying to focus. "Tell Pa I'm sorry. I—" Gripping him tighter. "I thought it was the right thing to do."

Simon looked up, frantic. "Call a doctor."

The men from the car stood there, not sure what to do. Service suits. Probably racing since Vyborg, afraid of losing them, even firing over the border, against Service rules. Or was it? What rules? Why not just snatch Simon? All of them? But nobody moved. And when he looked down again, it didn't matter, Frank had gone. He kept his hand for another second, then released it, prying the fingers away. He stood up, blood rushing to his head, dizzy for a moment, swaying.

Jo rushed from the car, her face wild, chest heaving. "Oh my God."

"We have to move him," Simon said. "Hal, take her back to the car. Wait. I need you to speak Russian."

"I speak English," one of the men said.

Simon nodded. "Then help me move him. He was coming back. He was walking back to Russia. You made a mistake."

The men looked at each other, paralyzed.

"He's a hero of the Soviet Union. A famous man. You made a mistake. Call Moscow. The Lubyanka. Everyone knows him. He didn't want to be in Finland. He was forced. I forced him. He's an officer of the Service," he said, his voice breaking a little. "A colonel. He wanted to be buried at Kuntsevo. Full honors. Do you understand? Full honors. Now help me carry him. He wants to be in Russia."

No one moved, staring at the border as if there were an actual line, some primitive arrangement of stones, a taboo.

"Okay," Simon said, moving around and lifting Frank under the shoulders. Carrying Boris, carrying Gareth, now doing it alone, having to drag him, shoes scraping against the road. Not far. Where would the line be? Where the pole was raised. The soldiers still stared at him. He stopped. Another foot and he'd be in Russia. He twisted slightly, heaving Frank onto the dividing line, careful not to cross it himself, then let the body fall out of his hands. Only the feet now in the West. He picked them up and pushed them across, following the rest of the body. Now theirs.

"Have him buried in Kuntsevo." No one said anything. He turned to go, then half-turned back. "He made a mistake too. He thought you were worth it."

And now he did turn, walking back, head high, almost daring them to come after him. As he walked he wondered what he was going to tell them, Jo, Hal, DiAngelis, what story would work, what Frank would want them to hear. But when he got back to the car he didn't say anything at all.

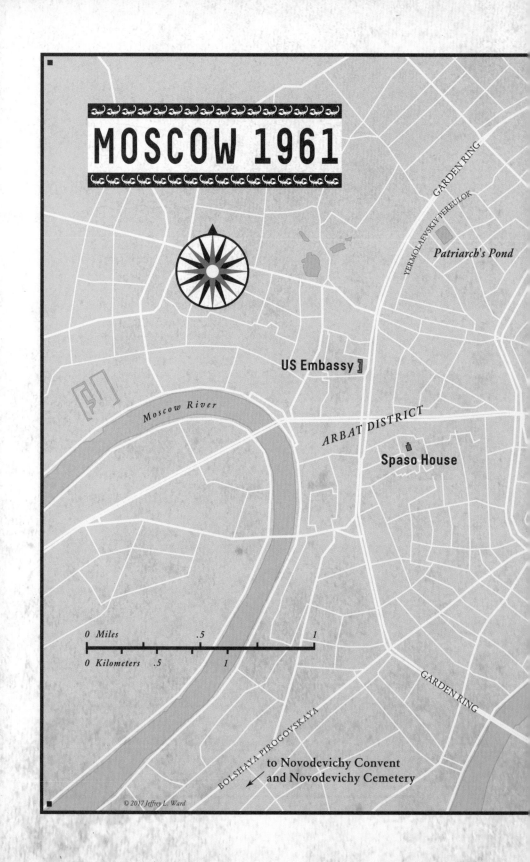

MOSCOW 1961

Patriarch's Pond

GARDEN RING

YERMOLAEVSKIY PEREULOK

US Embassy

Moscow River

ARBAT DISTRICT

Spaso House

GARDEN RING

0 Miles .5 1

0 Kilometers .5 1

BOLSHAYA PIROGOVSKAYA

to Novodevichy Convent
and Novodevichy Cemetery

© 2017 Jeffrey L. Ward